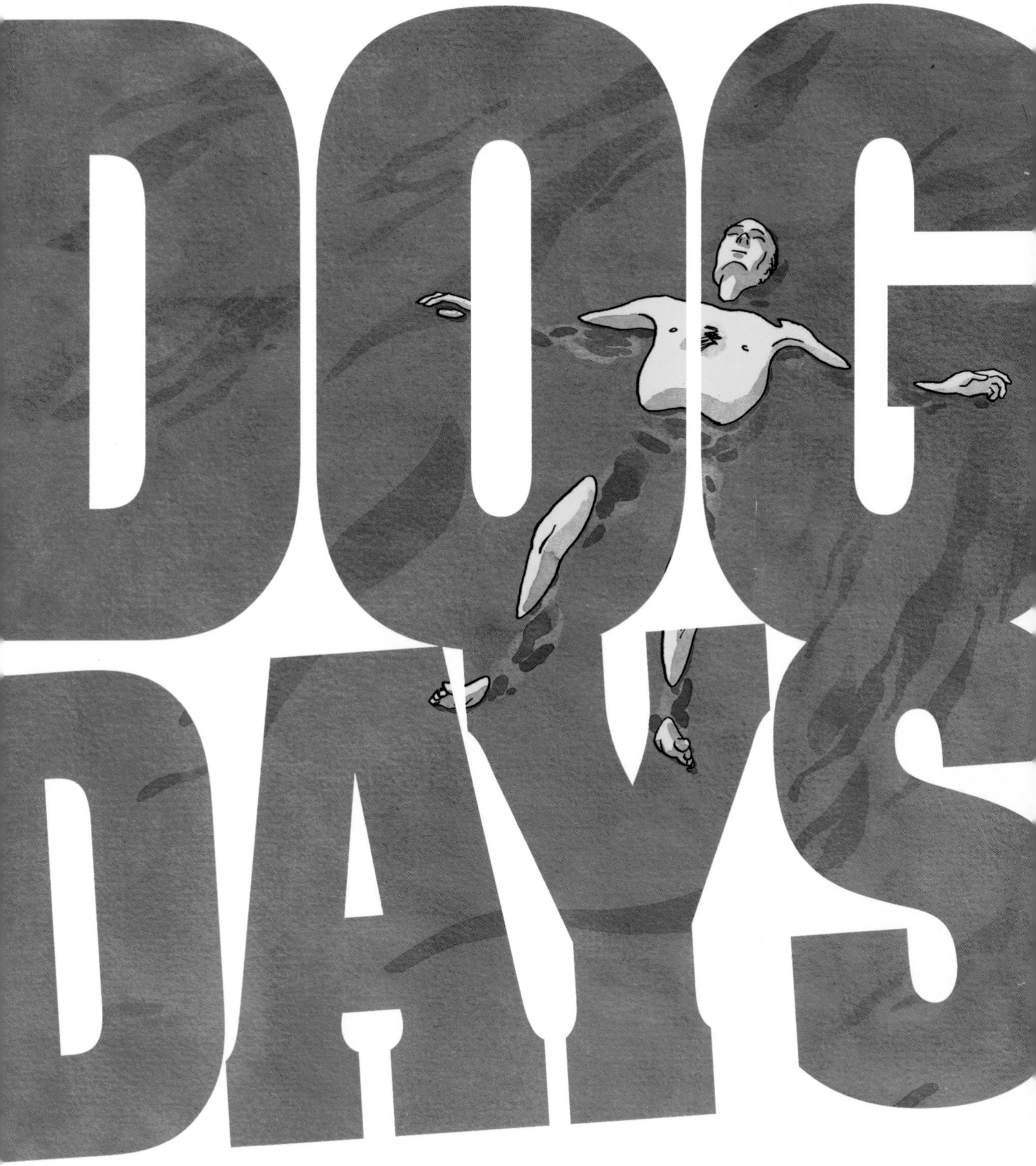
DOG
DAYS

CYPRIEN MATHIEU • REMY BENJAMIN • OLIVIER PERRET

DOG DAYS

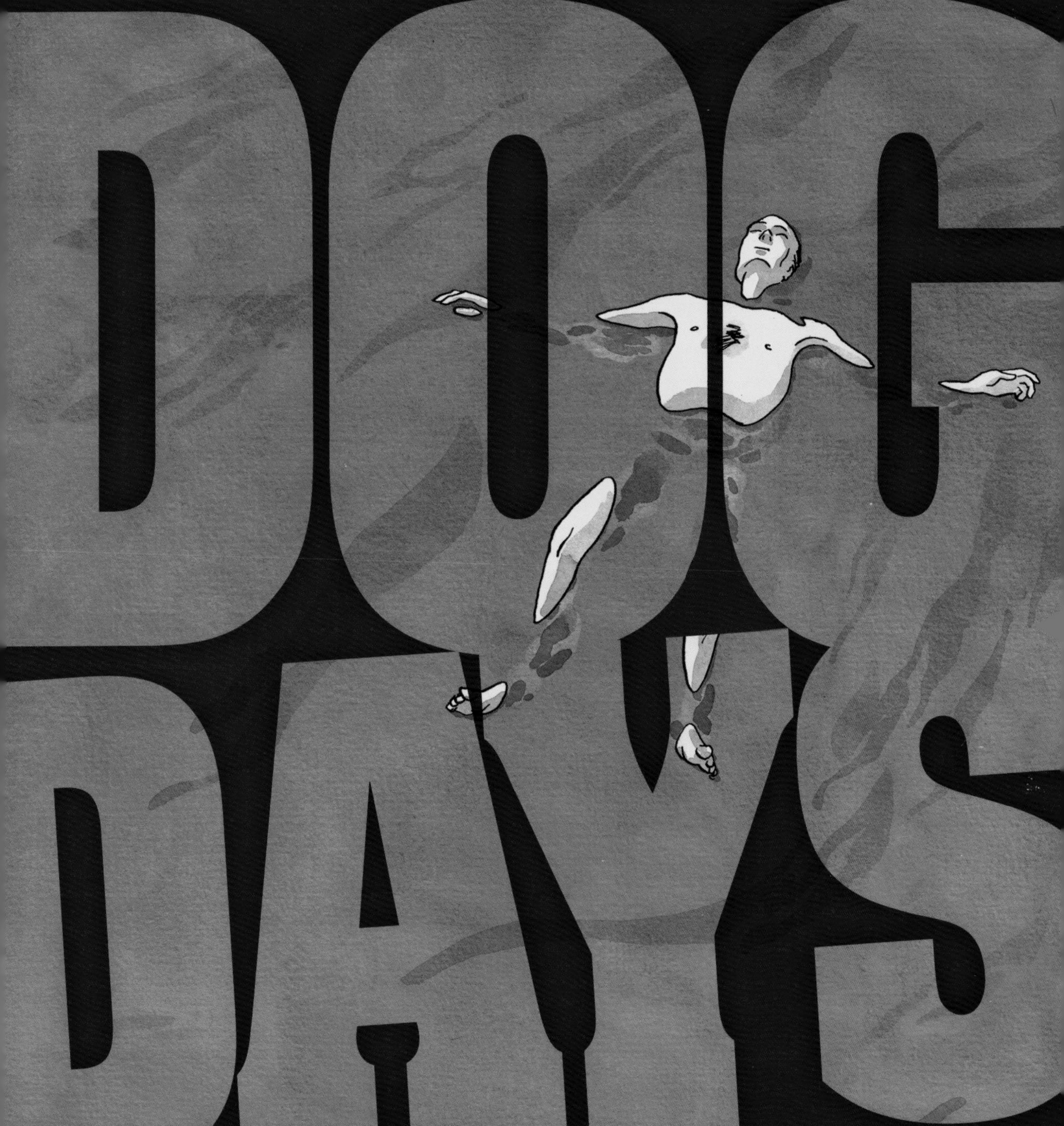

Life Drawn

CYPRIEN MATHIEU
REMY BENJAMIN
Writers

OLIVIER PERRET
Artist

REMY BENJAMIN
Color Artist

•

BENJAMIN CROZE
Translator

•

AMANDA LUCIDO
FABRICE SAPOLSKY
US Edition Editors

VINCENT HENRY
Original Edition Editor

JERRY FRISSEN
Senior Art Director

FABRICE GIGER
Publisher

Rights and Licensing - licensing@humanoids.com
Press and Social Media - pr@humanoids.com

DOG DAYS
This title is a publication of Humanoids, Inc. 8033 Sunset Blvd. #628, Los Angeles, CA 90046.
Copyright © 2020 Humanoids, Inc., Los Angeles (USA). All rights reserved.
Humanoids and its logos are ® and © 2020 Humanoids, Inc.
Library of Congress Control Number: 2020900414

Life Drawn is an imprint of Humanoids, Inc.

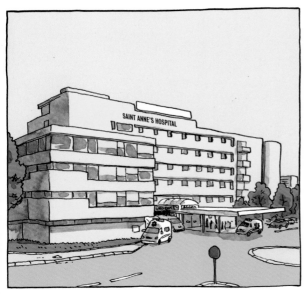

SAINT ANNE'S HOSPITAL

SOCCER: OM in Full Force!

THE PRO

The Case of the Missing Dogs Solved!

Just a minute, please...

EMERGENCY ROOM   ADMISSI

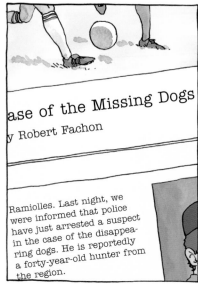

ase of the Missing Dogs

y Robert Fachon

Ramiolles. Last night, we were informed that police have just arrested a suspect in the case of the disappearing dogs. He is reportedly a forty-year-old hunter from the region.

Upon searching his home, the police found a large supply of carbofuran, the product used in the now infamous "blue meatballs"...

Investigators believe the man sought revenge after a dispute between hunters over hunting grounds. This new turn of events seems to dismiss the tourist lead, which had been privileged up until now...

Sigh.

Fucking hunters!

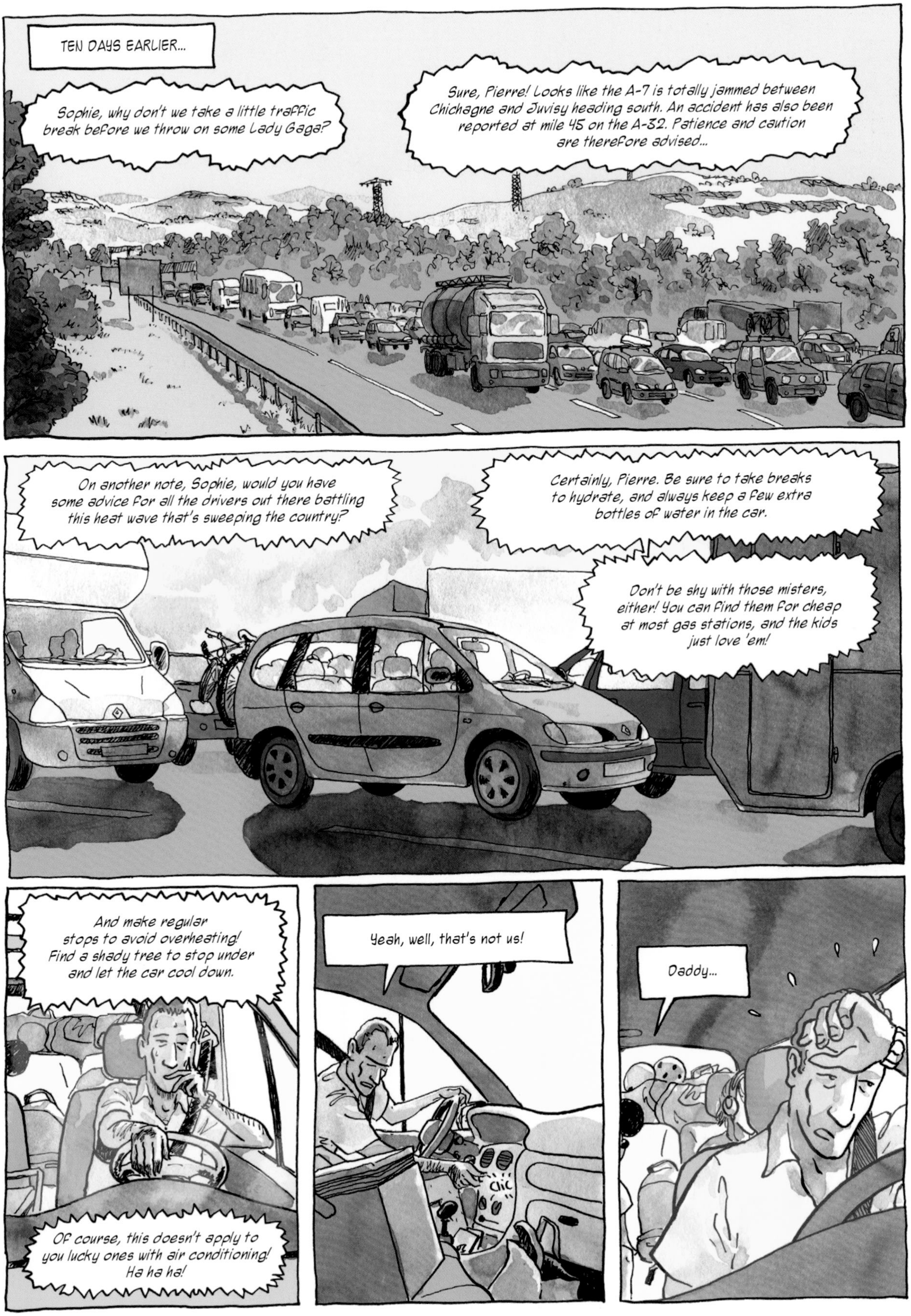
TEN DAYS EARLIER...
Sophie, why don't we take a little traffic break before we throw on some Lady Gaga?
Sure, Pierre! Looks like the A-7 is totally jammed between Chichagne and Juvisy heading south. An accident has also been reported at mile 45 on the A-32. Patience and caution are therefore advised...
On another note, Sophie, would you have some advice for all the drivers out there battling this heat wave that's sweeping the country?
Certainly, Pierre. Be sure to take breaks to hydrate, and always keep a few extra bottles of water in the car.
Don't be shy with those misters, either! You can find them for cheap at most gas stations, and the kids just love 'em!
And make regular stops to avoid overheating! Find a shady tree to stop under and let the car cool down.
Of course, this doesn't apply to you lucky ones with air conditioning! Ha ha ha!
Yeah, well, that's not us!
CLIC
Daddy...

Daddy, I'm hot...

Why is it so hot?

Me and Hermione are hot...

Kevin, give your brother some water.

What about Hermione, Daddy?

Right, well, she'll have to drink later, when we can pull over...

But, we're stopped right now, Daddy...

Kevin, give your brother some water!

Stop busting my balls, we're out of water!

Oh, For God's sake. *Kevin!*

Riiiiiing! Riiiiiing! Riiiiing!

Riiiiiing! Riiiiiing! Riiiiing!

Daddy, phone!

Riiiiiing! Riiiiiing! Riiiiing!

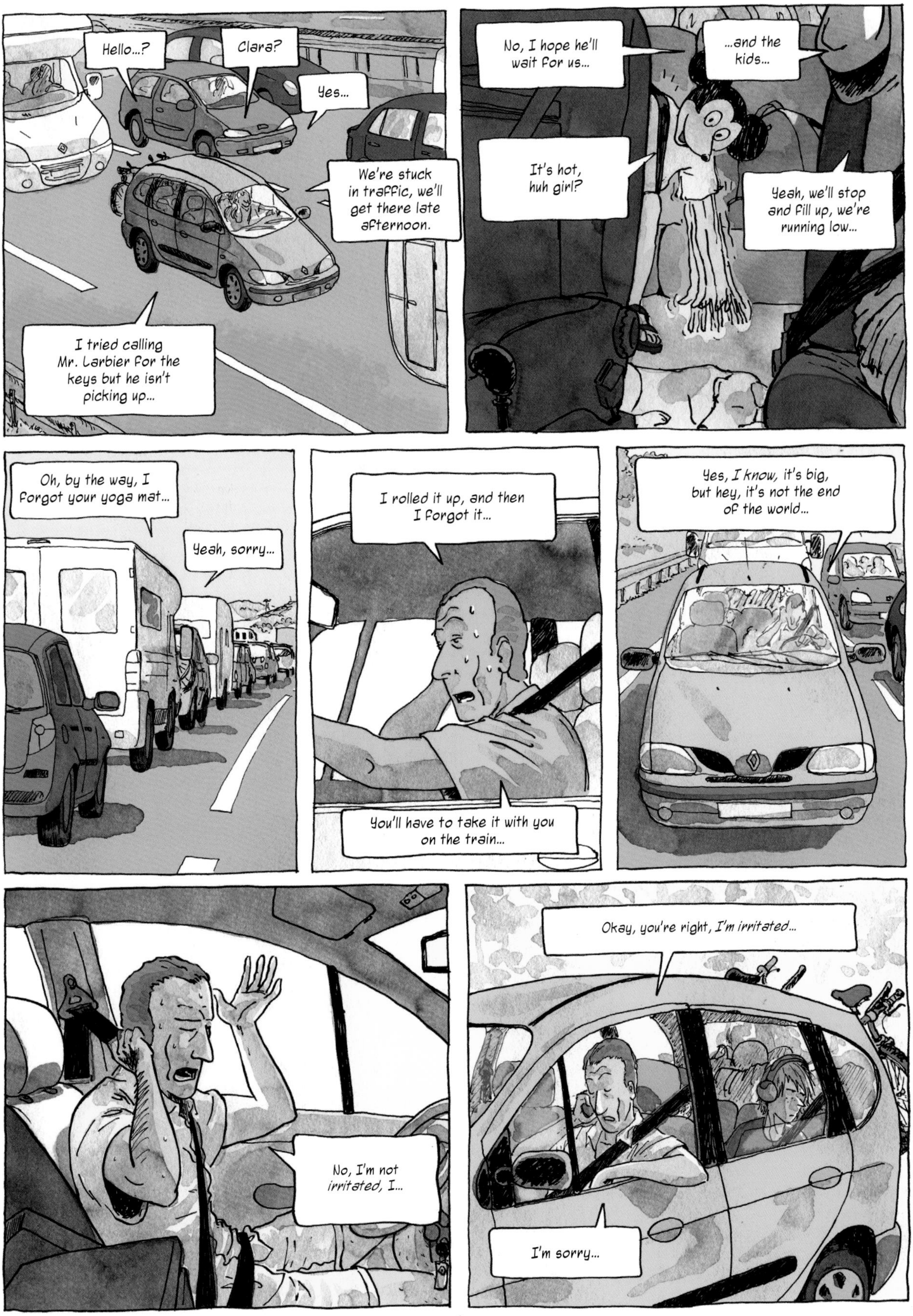
Hello...?
Clara?
Yes...
We're stuck in traffic, we'll get there late afternoon.
I tried calling Mr. Larbier for the keys but he isn't picking up...
No, I hope he'll wait for us...
...and the kids...
It's hot, huh girl?
Yeah, we'll stop and fill up, we're running low...
Oh, by the way, I forgot your yoga mat...
Yeah, sorry...
I rolled it up, and then I forgot it...
You'll have to take it with you on the train...
Yes, *I know*, it's big, but hey, it's not the end of the world...
No, I'm not *irritated*, I...
Okay, you're right, *I'm irritated*...
I'm sorry...

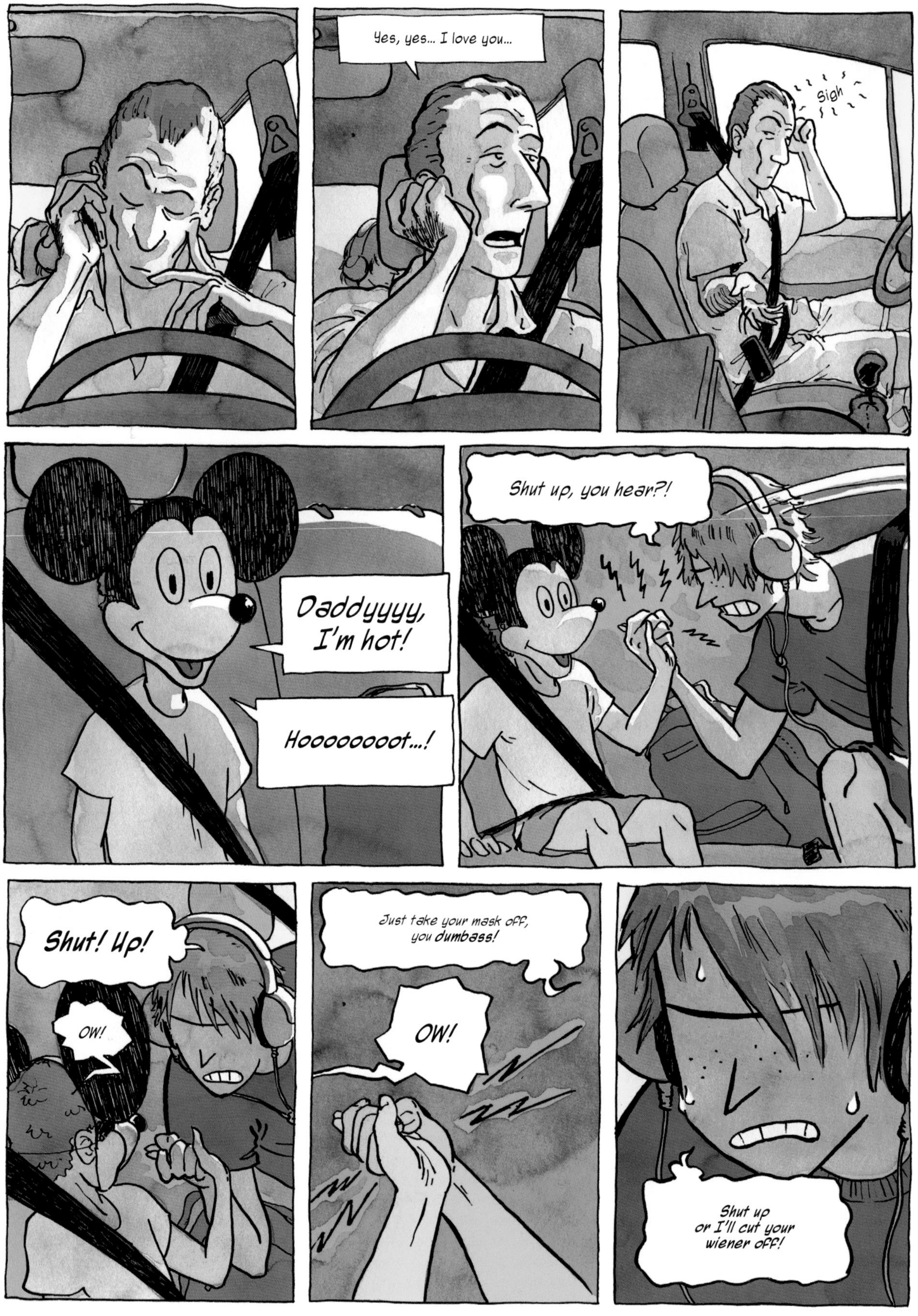
Yes, yes... I love you...
Sigh
Daddyyyy, I'm hot!
Hoooooooot...!
Shut up, you hear?!
Shut! Up!
OW!
Just take your mask off, you dumbass!
OW!
Shut up or I'll cut your wiener off!

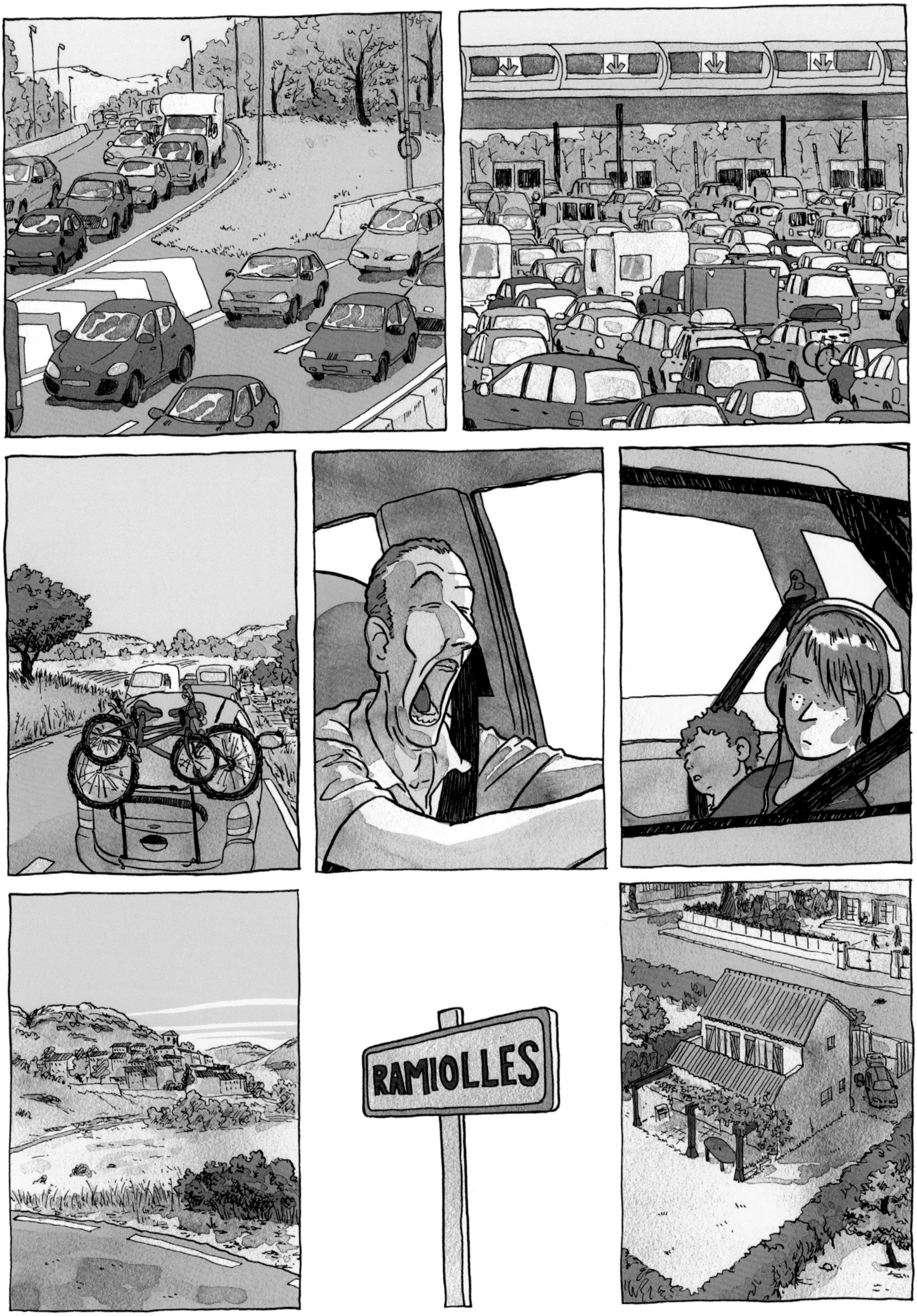
RAMIOLLES

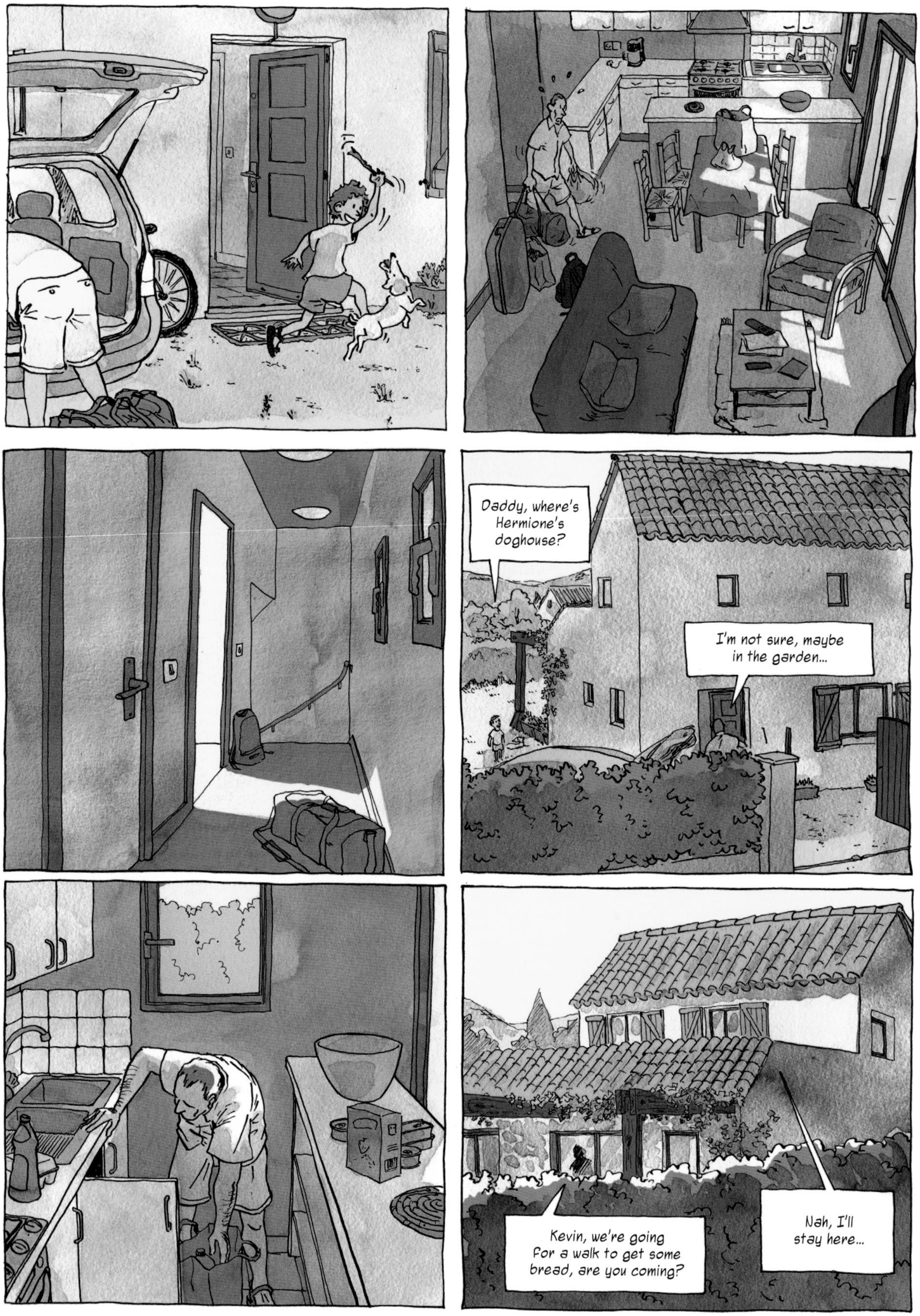
Daddy, where's Hermione's doghouse?
I'm not sure, maybe in the garden...
Kevin, we're going for a walk to get some bread, are you coming?
Nah, I'll stay here...

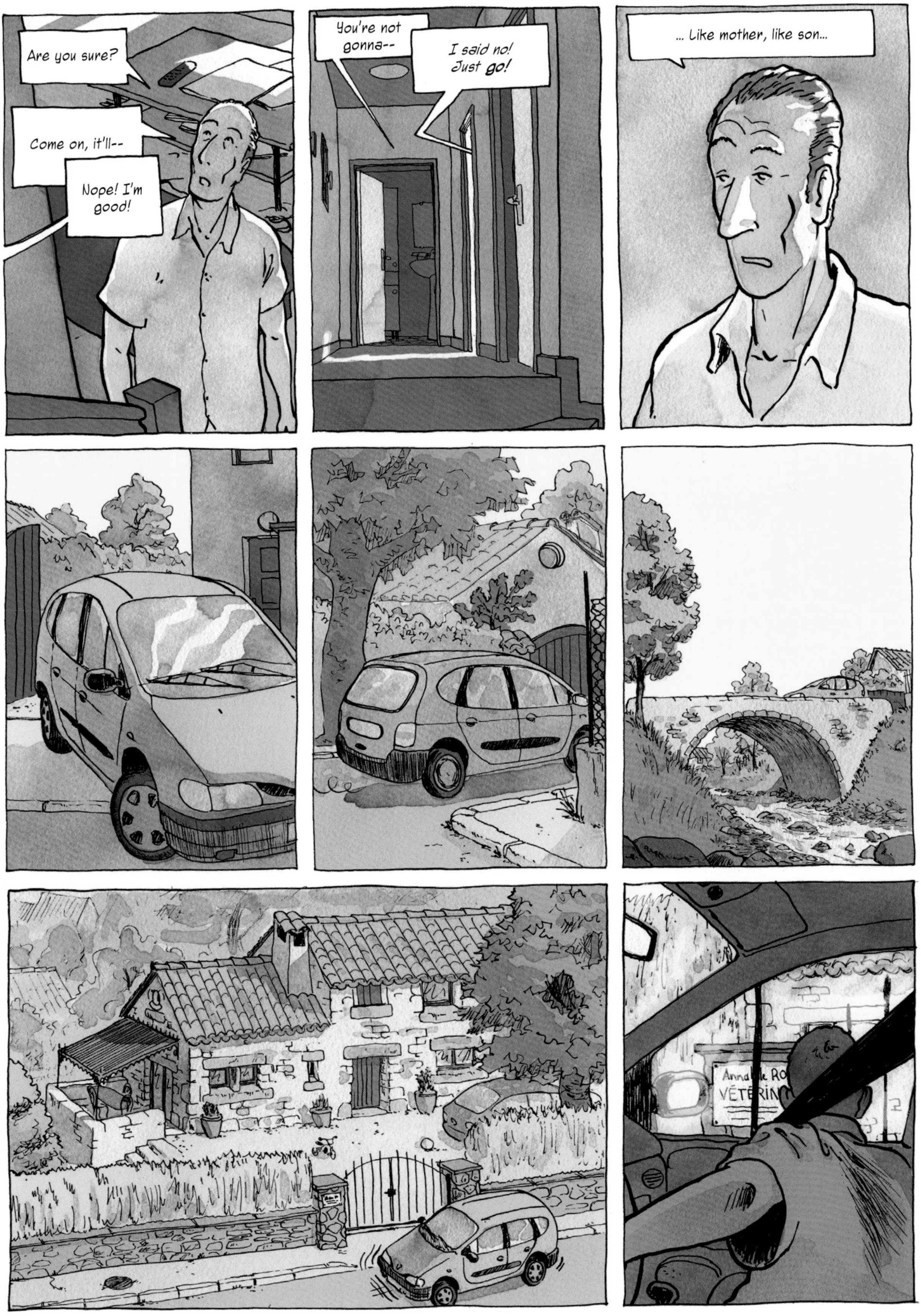
Are you sure?
Come on, it'll--
Nope! I'm good!
You're not gonna--
I said no! Just go!
... Like mother, like son...

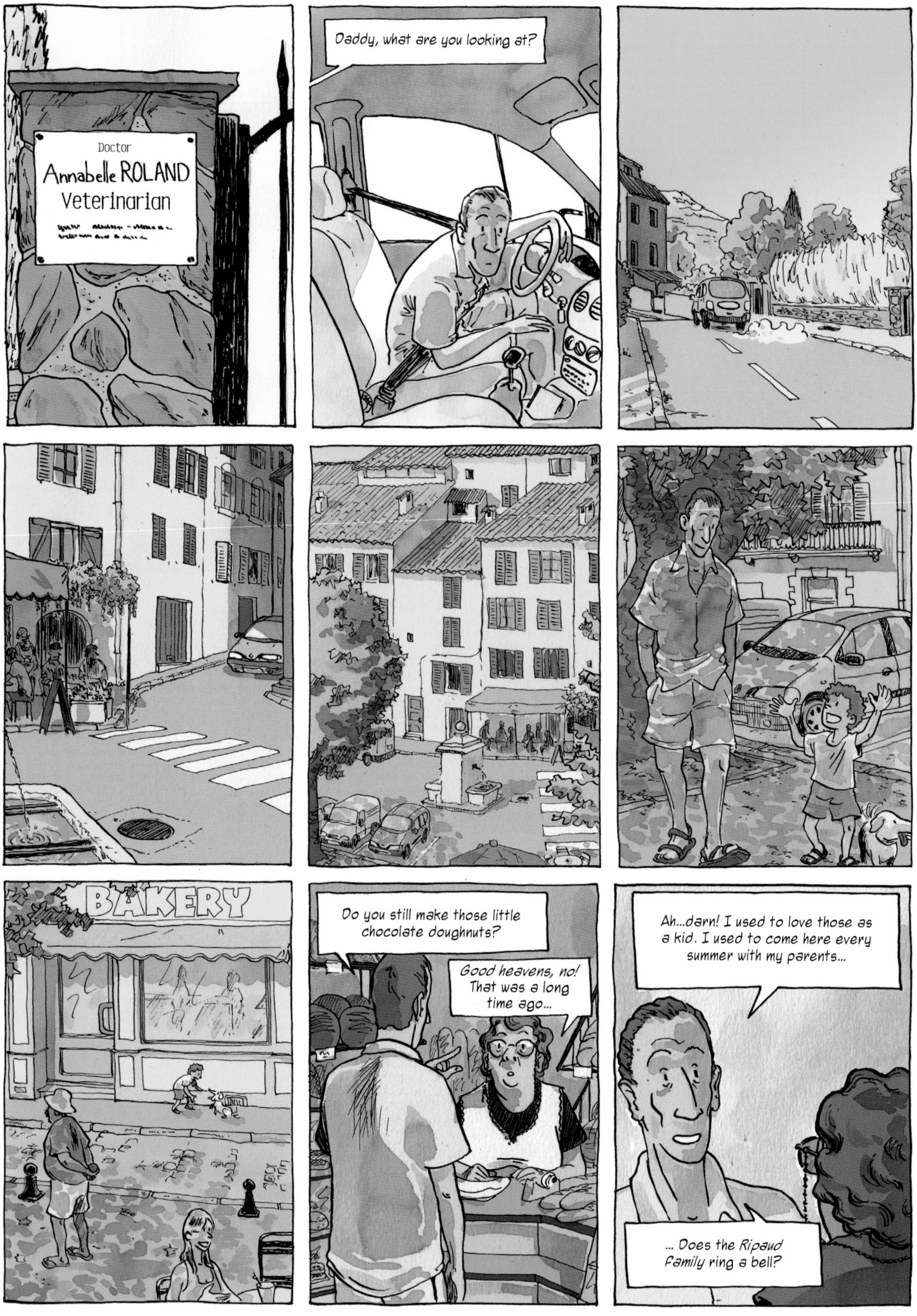
Doctor
Annabelle ROLAND
Veterinarian
Daddy, what are you looking at?
BAKERY
Do you still make those little chocolate doughnuts?
Good heavens, no! That was a long time ago...
Ah...darn! I used to love those as a kid. I used to come here every summer with my parents...
... Does the *Ripaud Family* ring a bell?

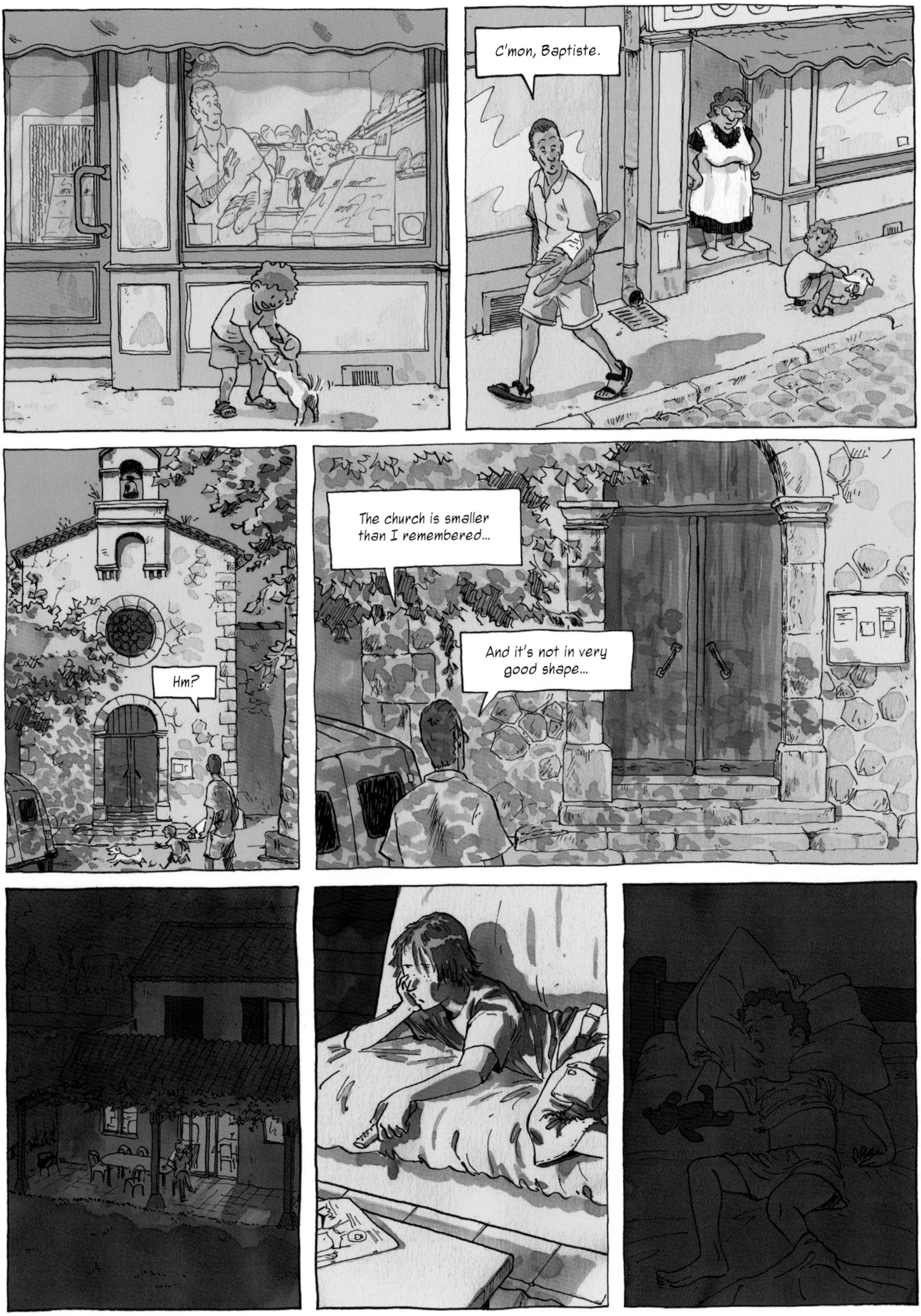
C'mon, Baptiste.
Hm?
The church is smaller than I remembered...
And it's not in very good shape...

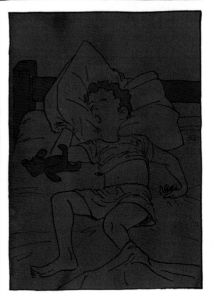

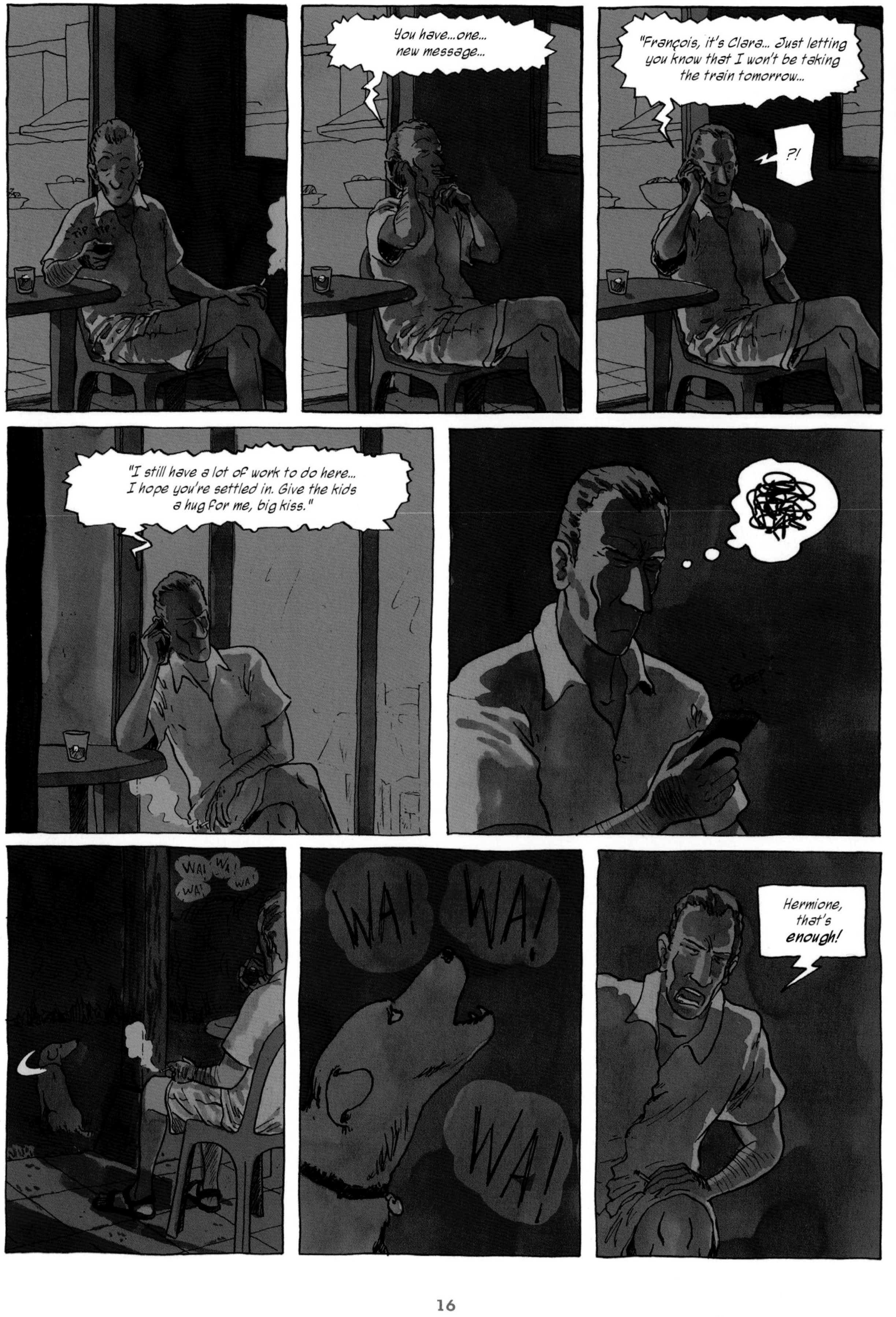
TIP TIP
You have...one... new message...
"François, it's Clara... Just letting you know that I won't be taking the train tomorrow...
?!
"I still have a lot of work to do here... I hope you're settled in. Give the kids a hug for me, big kiss."
WA! WA! WA! WA!
WA! WA! WA!
Hermione, that's **enough!**

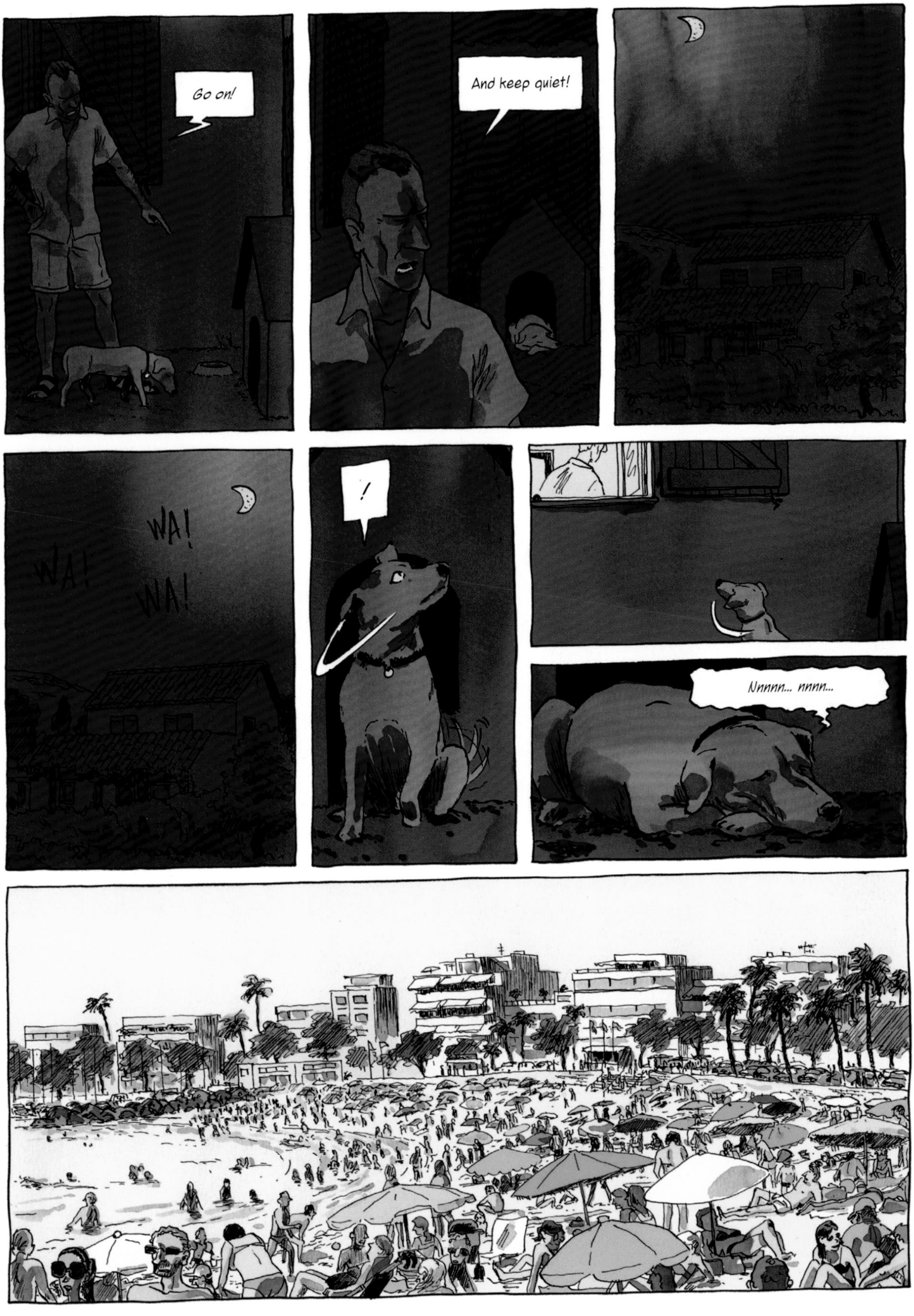
Go on!
And keep quiet!
WA!
WA!
WA!
!
Nnnnn... nnnn...

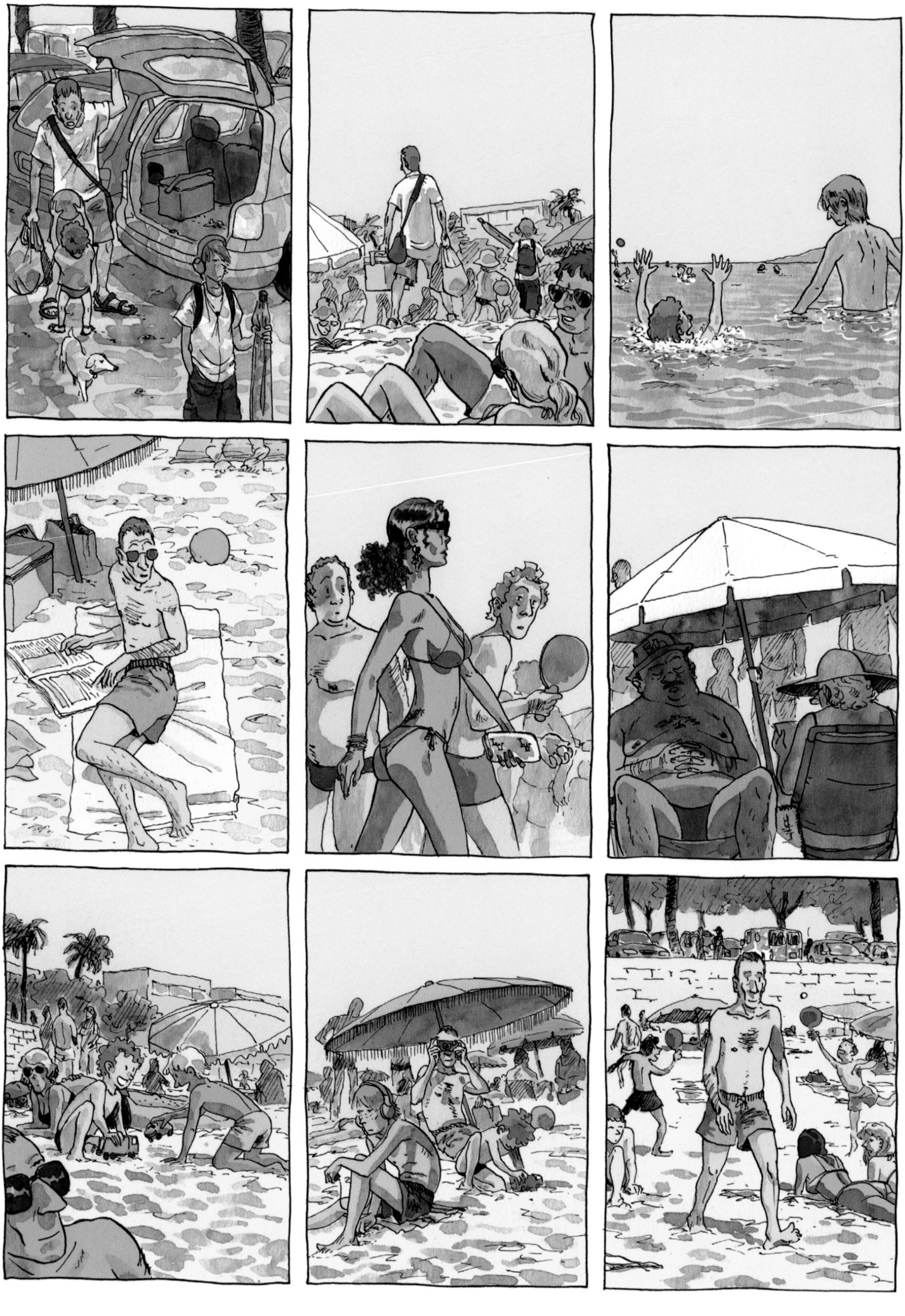

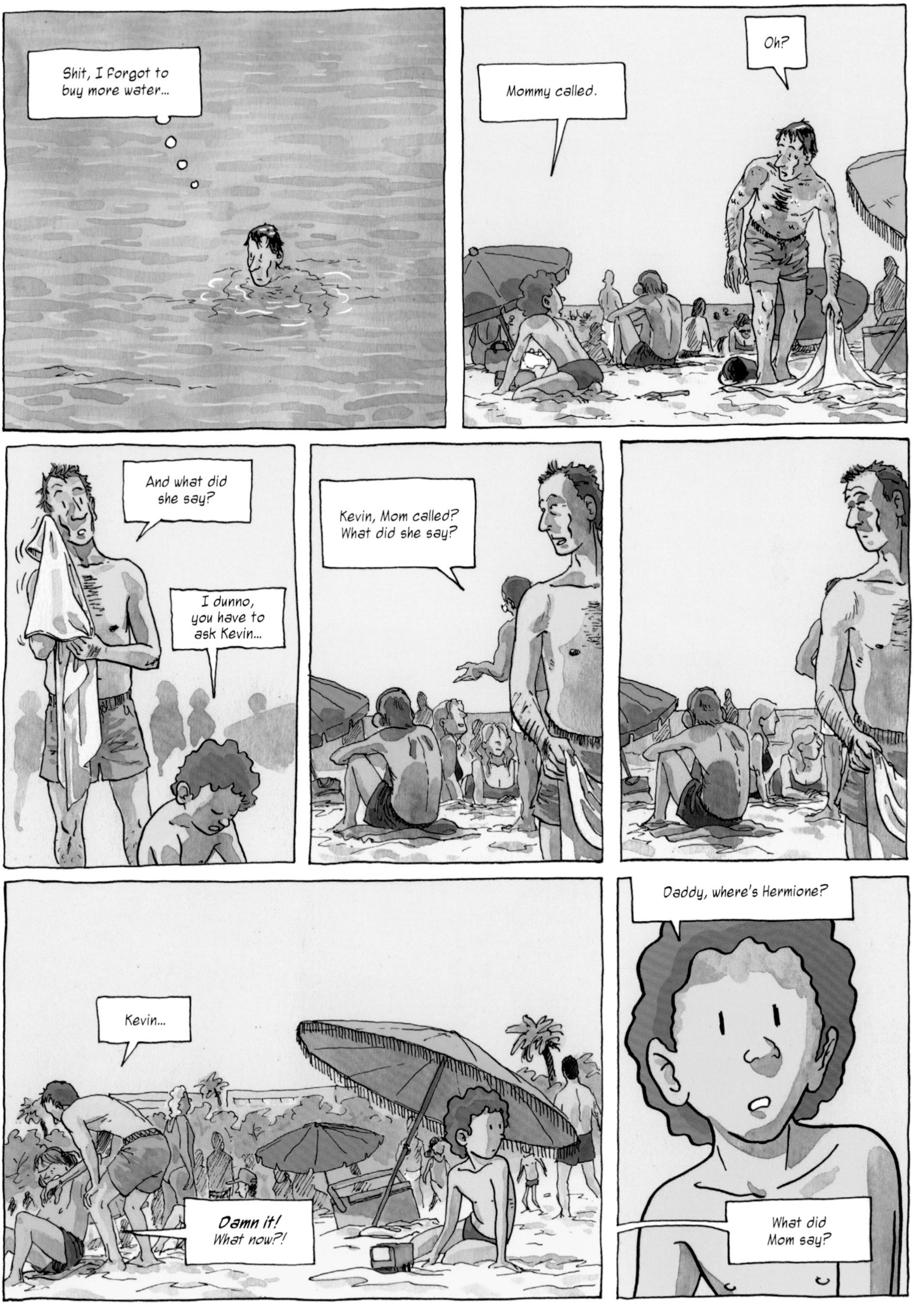
Shit, I forgot to buy more water...
Mommy called.
Oh?
And what did she say?
I dunno, you have to ask Kevin...
Kevin, Mom called? What did she say?
Kevin...
Damn it! What now?!
Daddy, where's Hermione?
What did Mom say?

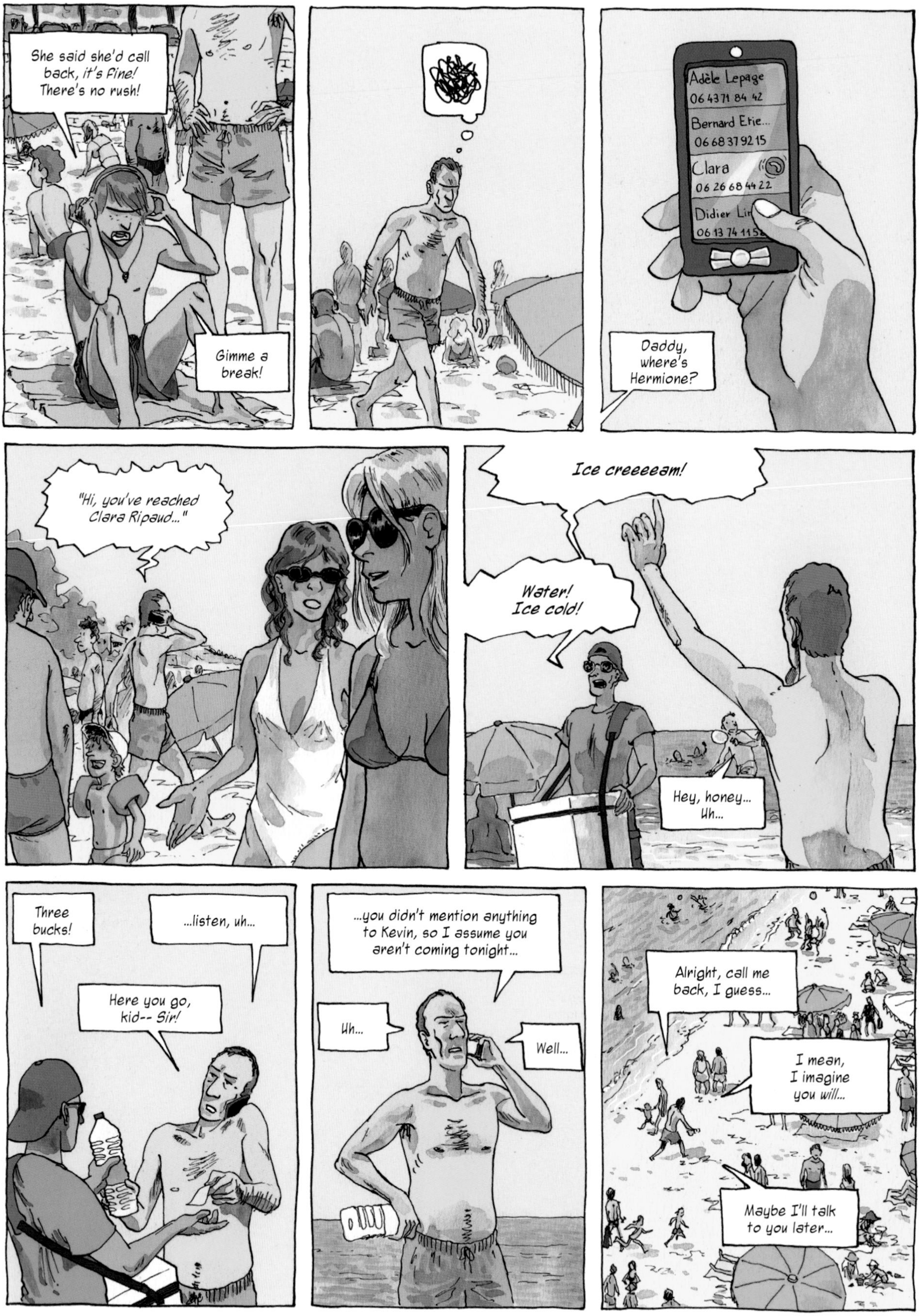
She said she'd call back, *it's fine!* There's no rush!
Gimme a break!
Adèle Lepage
06 43 71 84 42
Bernard Etie...
06 68 37 92 15
Clara
06 26 68 44 22
Daddy, where's Hermione?
"Hi, you've reached Clara Ripaud..."
Ice creeeeam!
Water! Ice cold!
Hey, honey... Uh...
Three bucks!
...listen, uh...
Here you go, kid-- *Sir!*
...you didn't mention anything to Kevin, so I assume you aren't coming tonight...
Uh...
Well...
Alright, call me back, I guess...
I mean, I imagine you will...
Maybe I'll talk to you later...

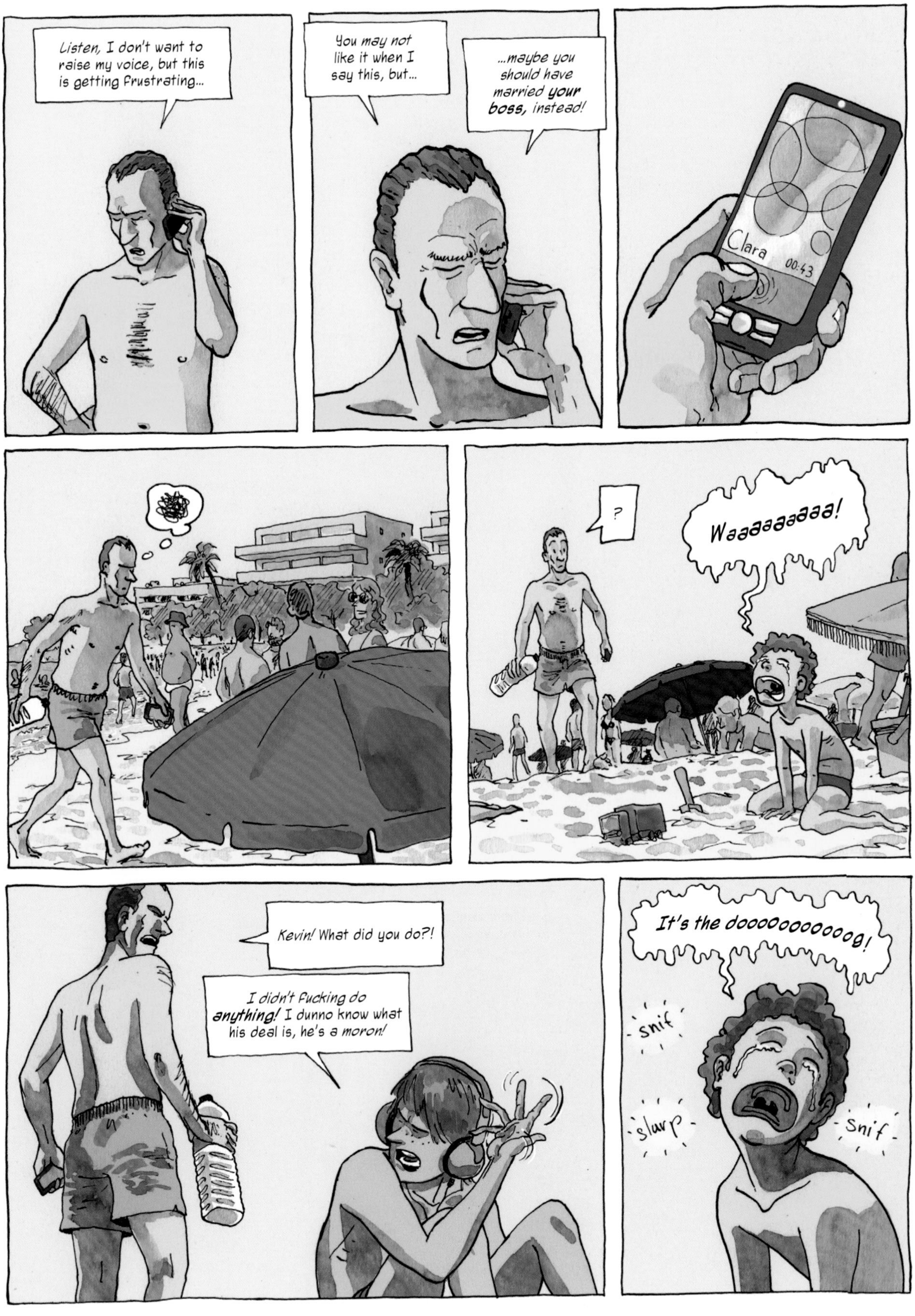
Listen, I don't want to raise my voice, but this is getting frustrating...
You may not like it when I say this, but...
...maybe you should have married **your boss,** instead!
Clara
00:43
?
Waaaaaaaaa!
Kevin! What did you do?!
I didn't fucking do **anything!** I dunno know what his deal is, he's a *moron!*
It's the doooooooooog!
snif
slurp
snif

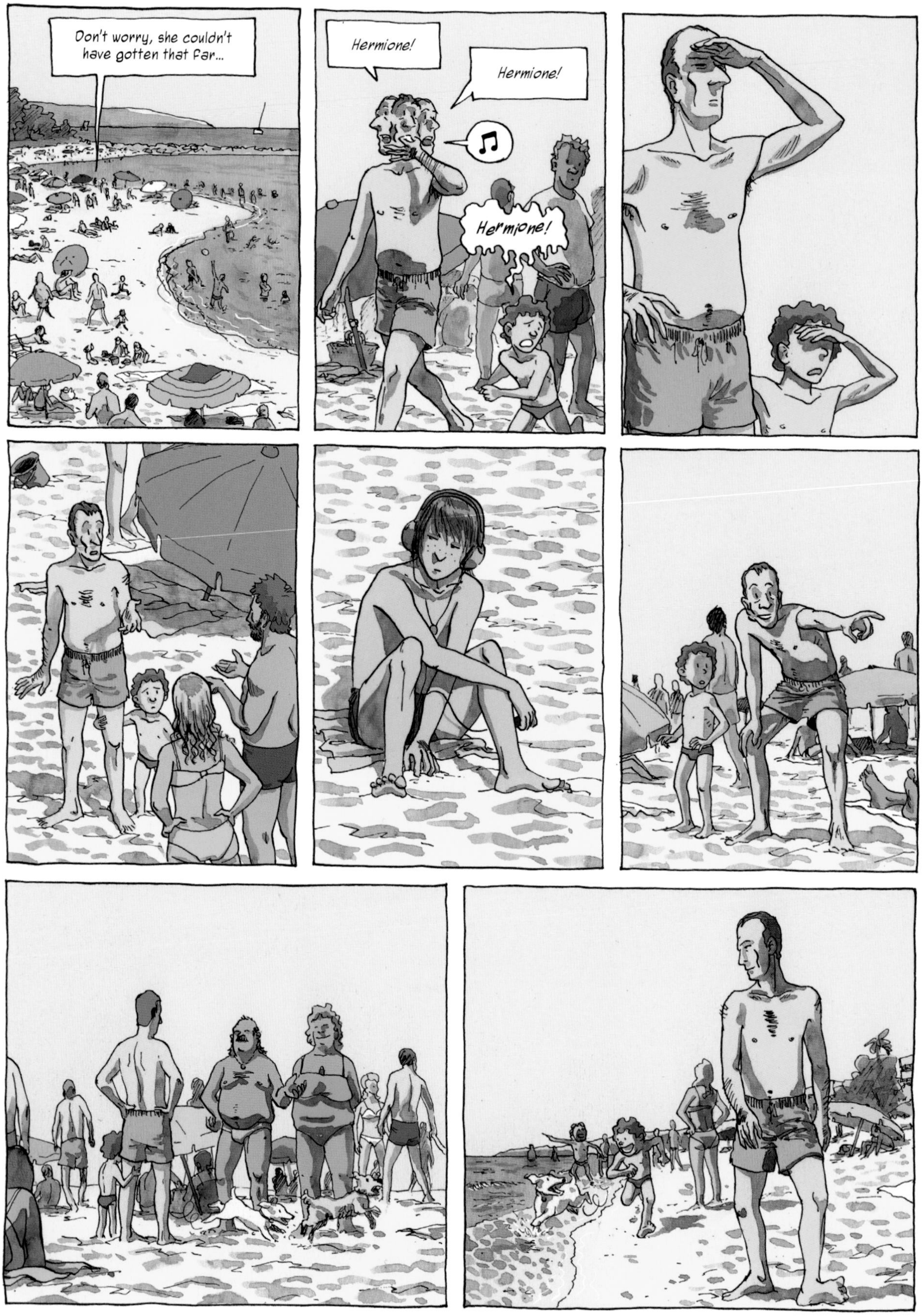

Don't worry, she couldn't have gotten that far...
Hermione!
Hermione!
♫
Hermione!

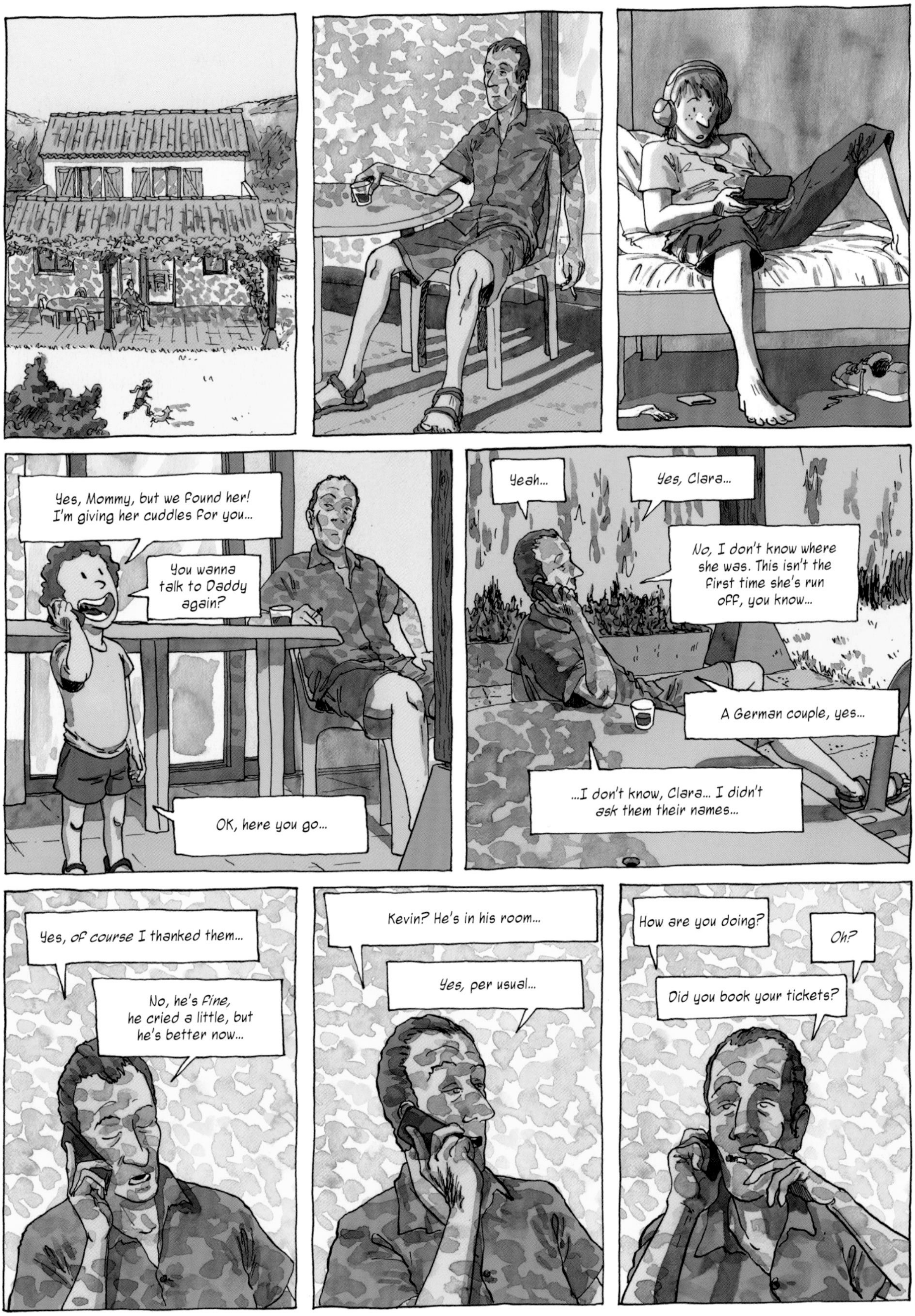
Yes, Mommy, but we found her! I'm giving her cuddles for you...
You wanna talk to Daddy again?
OK, here you go...
Yeah...
Yes, Clara...
No, I don't know where she was. This isn't the first time she's run off, you know...
A German couple, yes...
...I don't know, Clara... I didn't ask them their names...
Yes, of course I thanked them...
No, he's fine, he cried a little, but he's better now...
Kevin? He's in his room...
Yes, per usual...
How are you doing?
Oh?
Did you book your tickets?

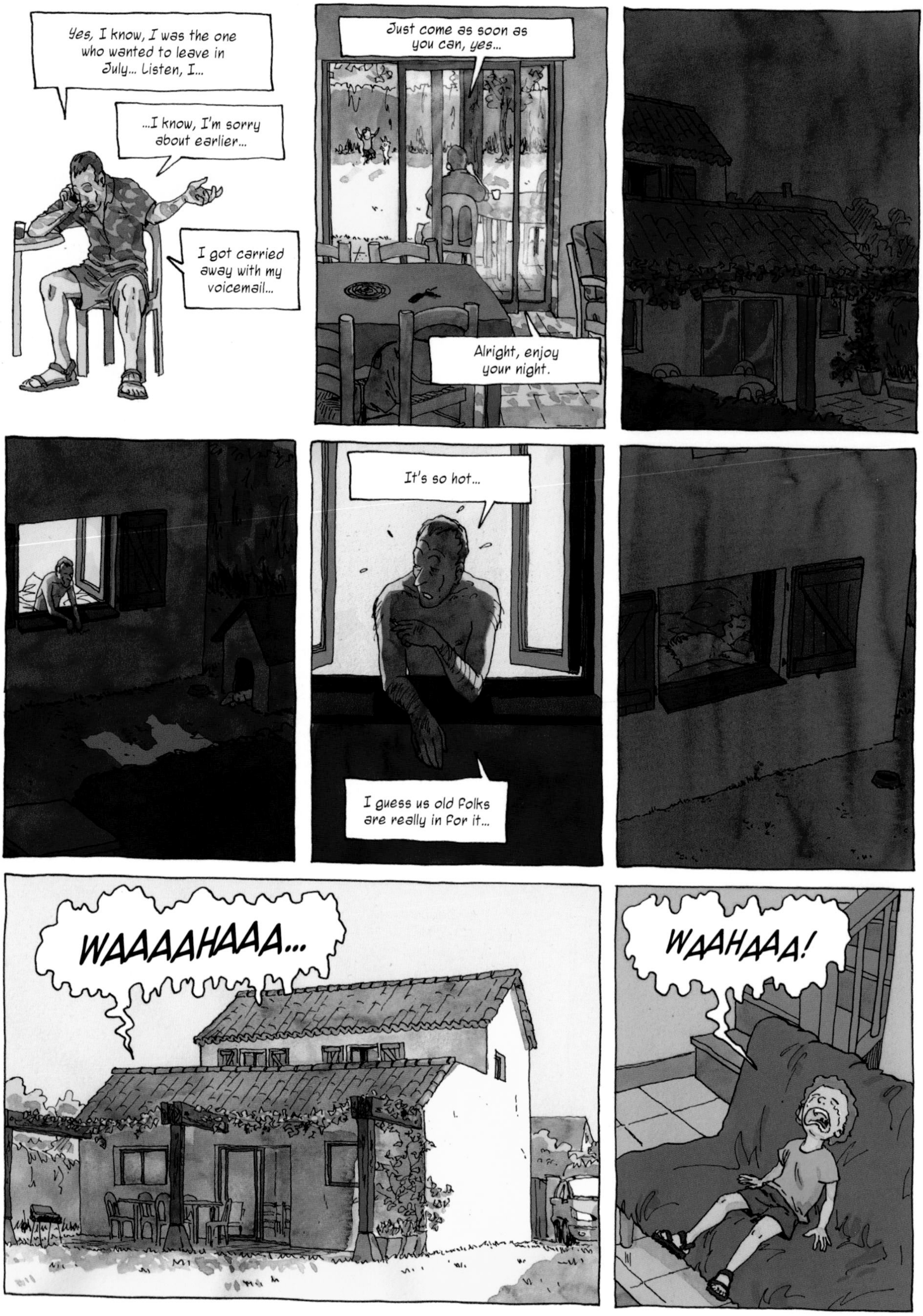

Yes, I know, I was the one who wanted to leave in July... Listen, I...
...I know, I'm sorry about earlier...
I got carried away with my voicemail...
Just come as soon as you can, yes...
Alright, enjoy your night.
It's so hot...
I guess us old folks are really in for it...
WAAAAHAAA...
WAAHAAA!

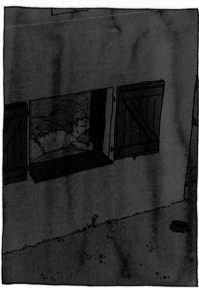

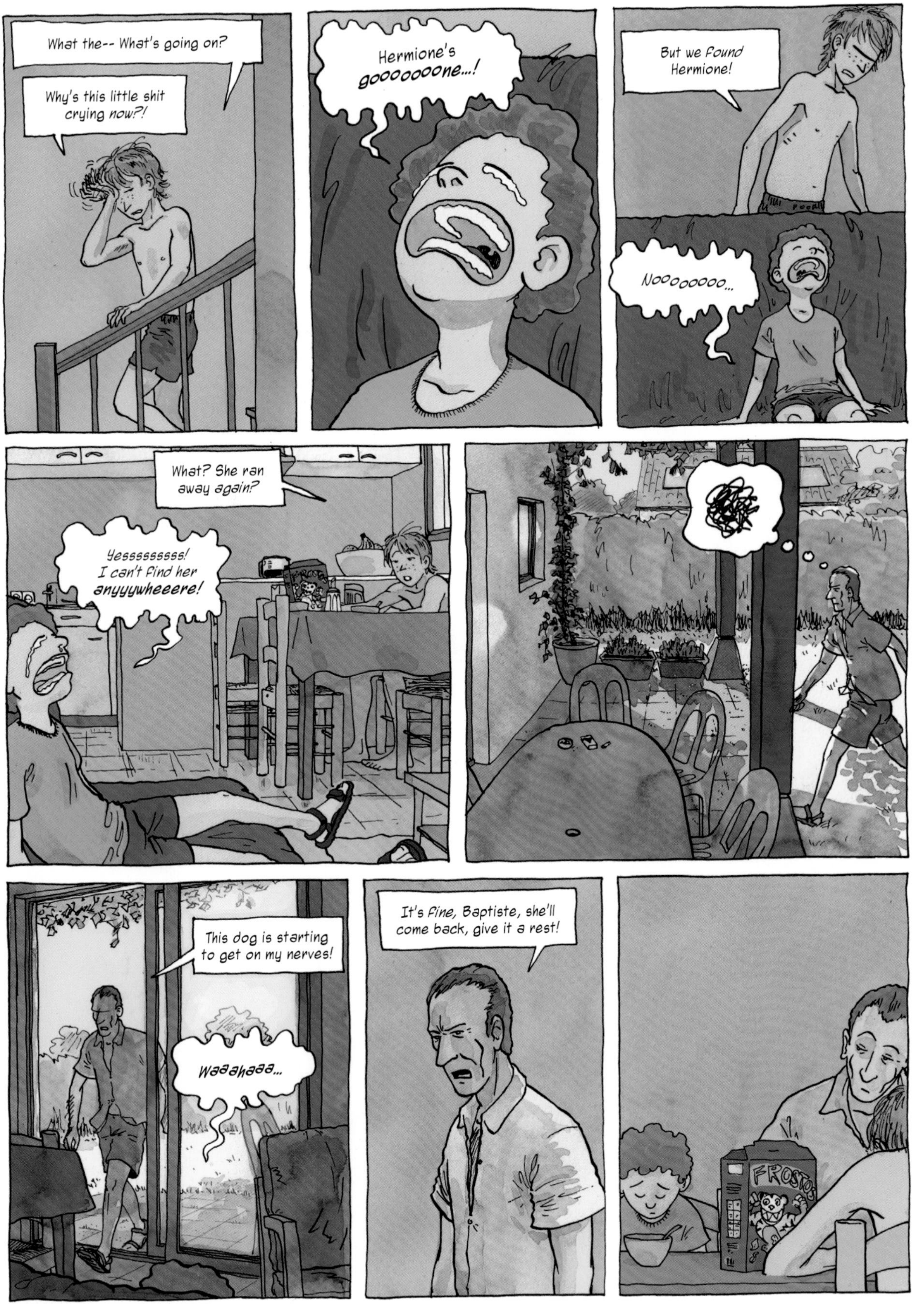
What the-- What's going on?
Why's this little shit crying now?!
Hermione's goooooone...!
But we found Hermione!
Nooooooo...
What? She ran away again?
Yesssssssss! I can't find her anyyywheeere!
This dog is starting to get on my nerves!
Waaahaaa...
It's fine, Baptiste, she'll come back, give it a rest!
FROSTIES

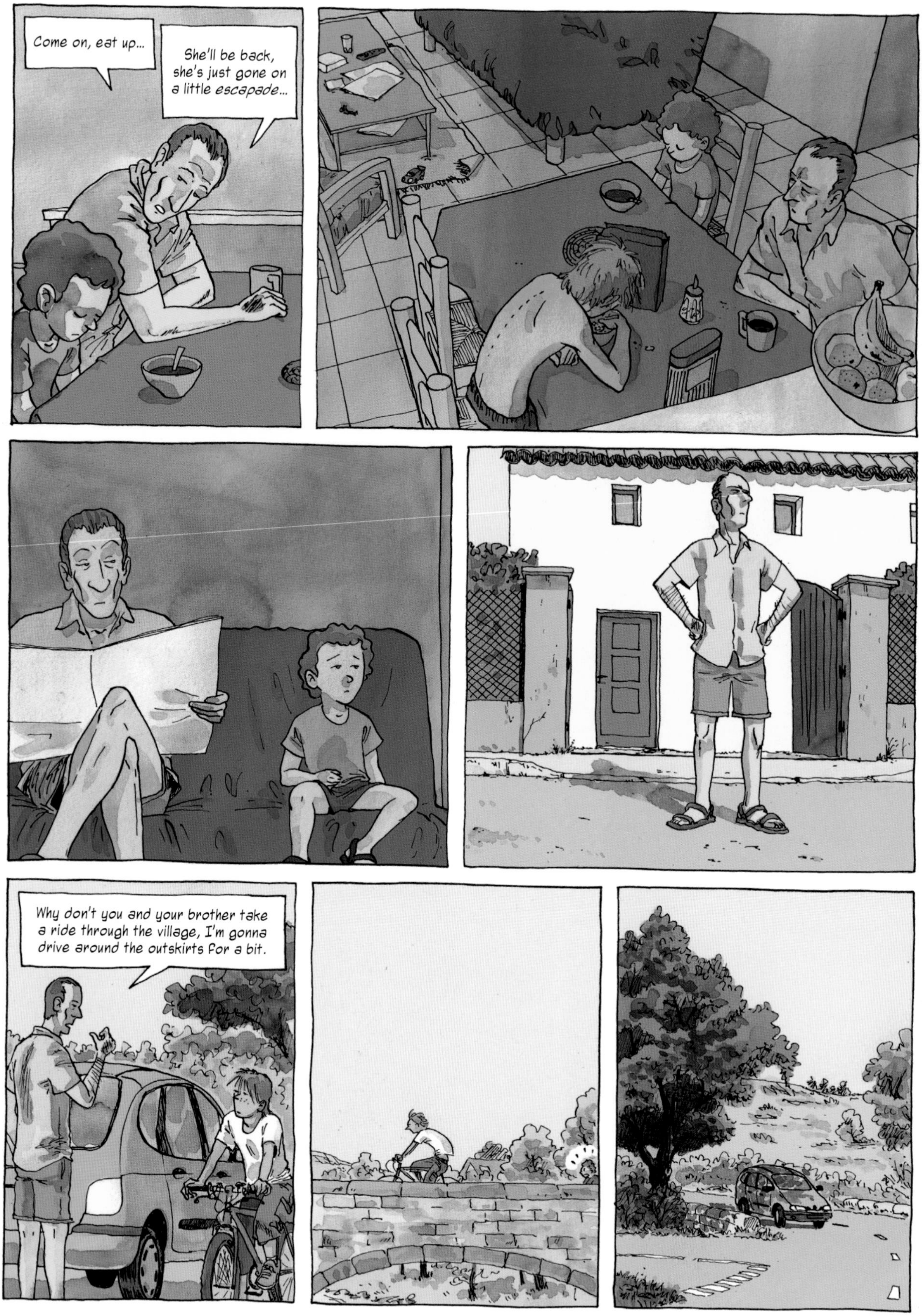
Come on, eat up...
She'll be back, she's just gone on a little *escapade*...
Why don't you and your brother take a ride through the village, I'm gonna drive around the outskirts for a bit.

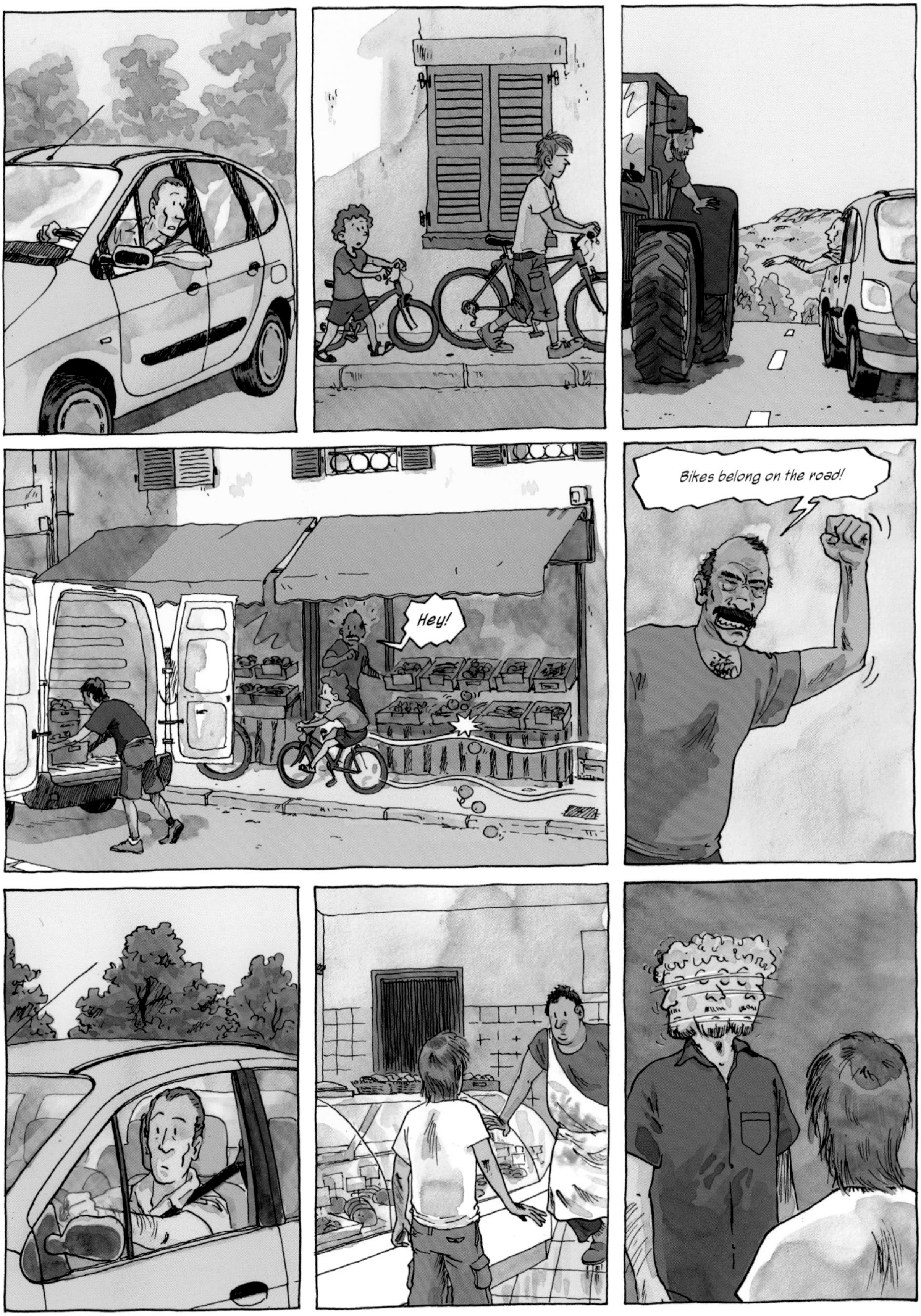
Hey!
Bikes belong on the road!

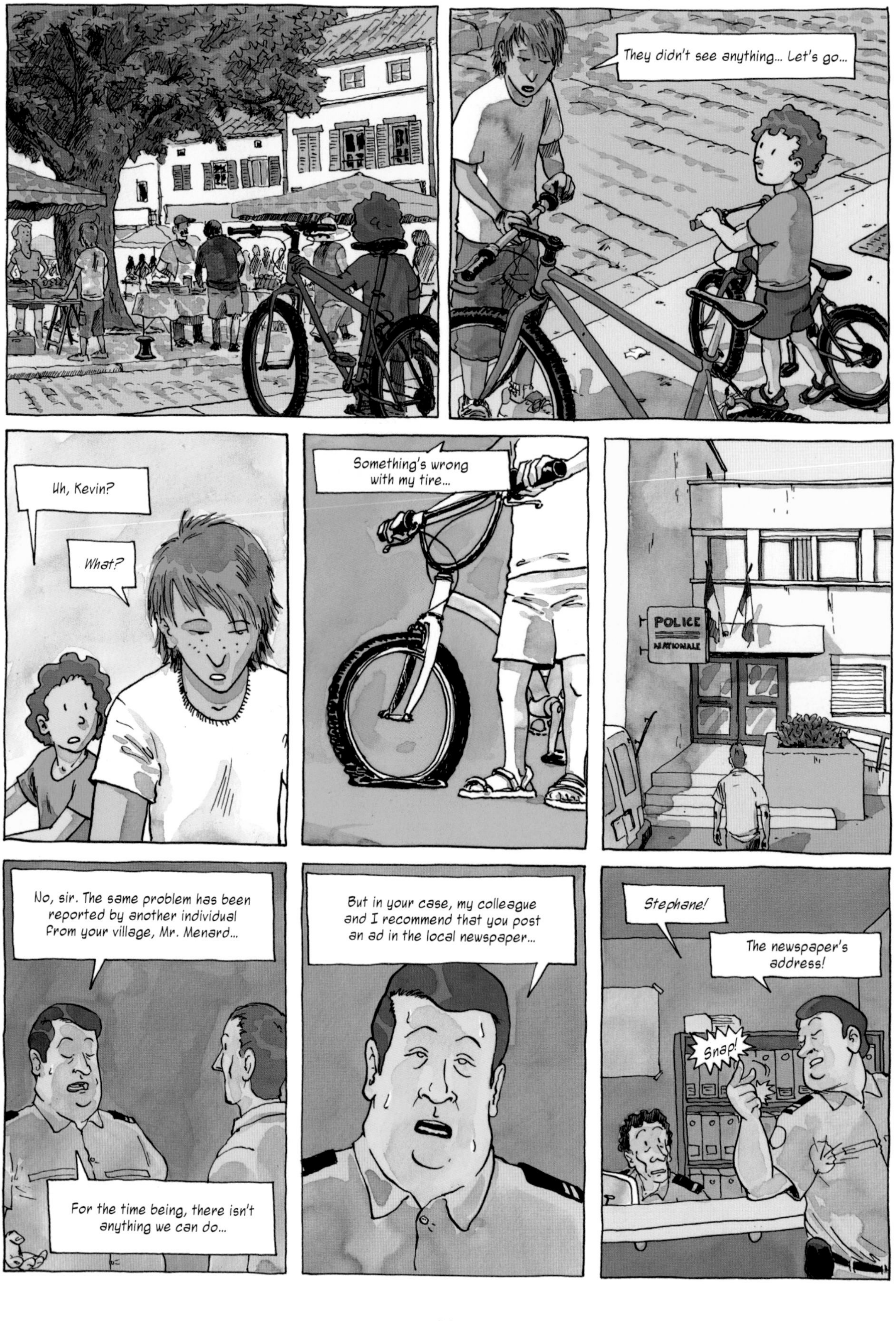
They didn't see anything... Let's go...
Uh, Kevin?
What?
Something's wrong with my tire...
POLICE NATIONALE
No, sir. The same problem has been reported by another individual from your village, Mr. Menard...
For the time being, there isn't anything we can do...
But in your case, my colleague and I recommend that you post an ad in the local newspaper...
Stephane!
The newspaper's address!
Snap!

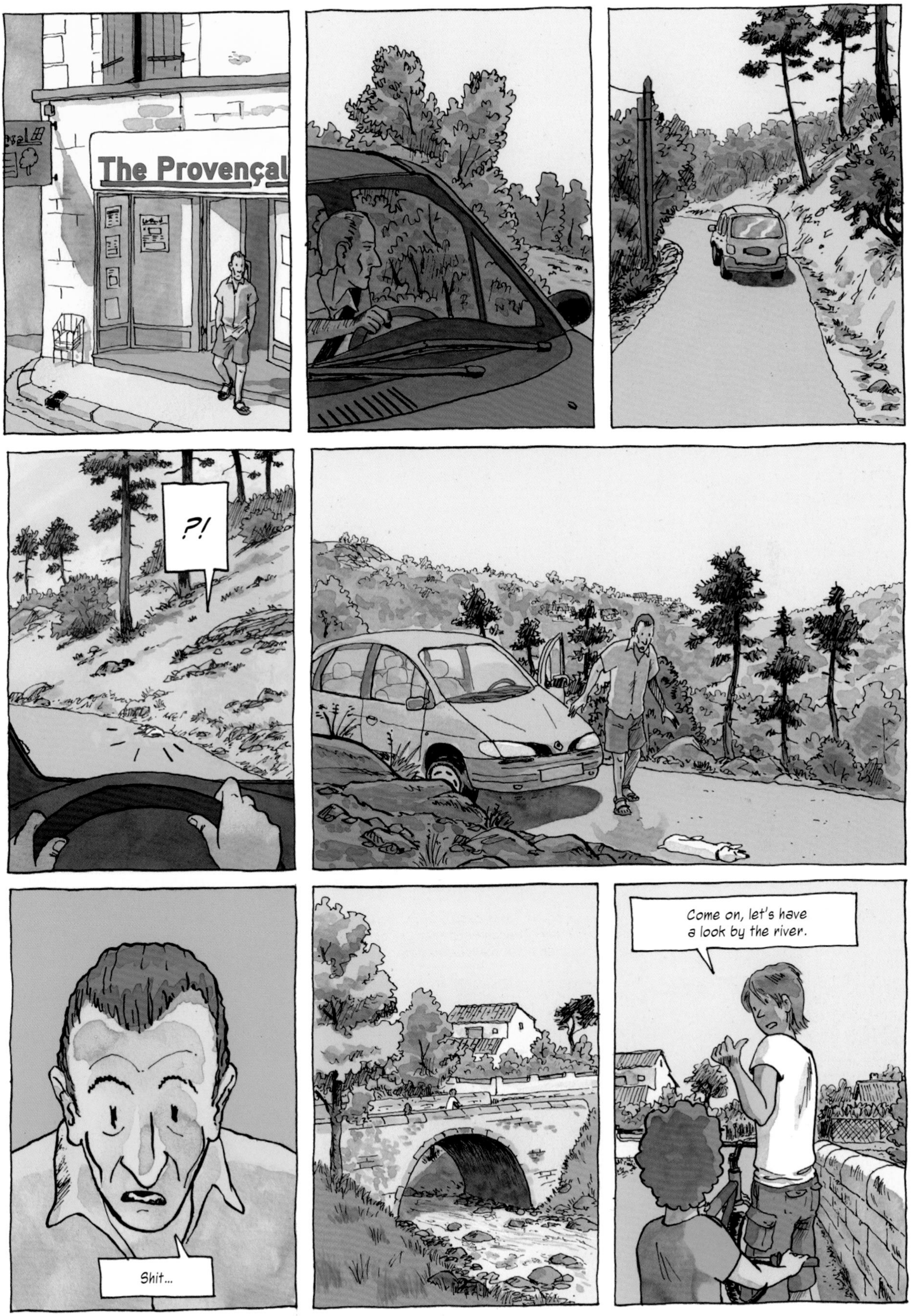
The Provençal
?!
Shit...
Come on, let's have a look by the river.

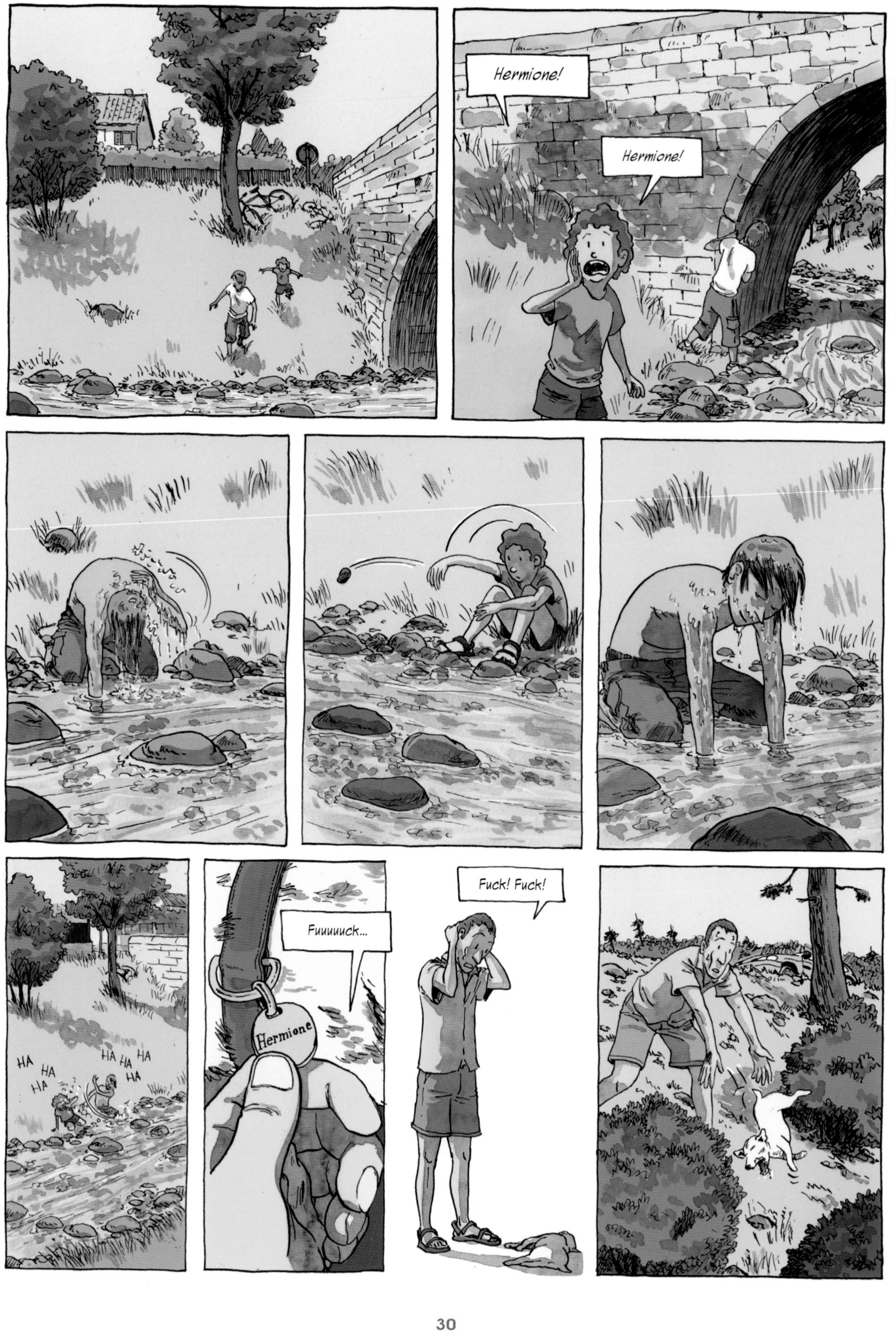
Hermione!
Hermione!
HA HA HA
HA HA HA HA
Hermione
Fuuuuuck...
Fuck! Fuck!

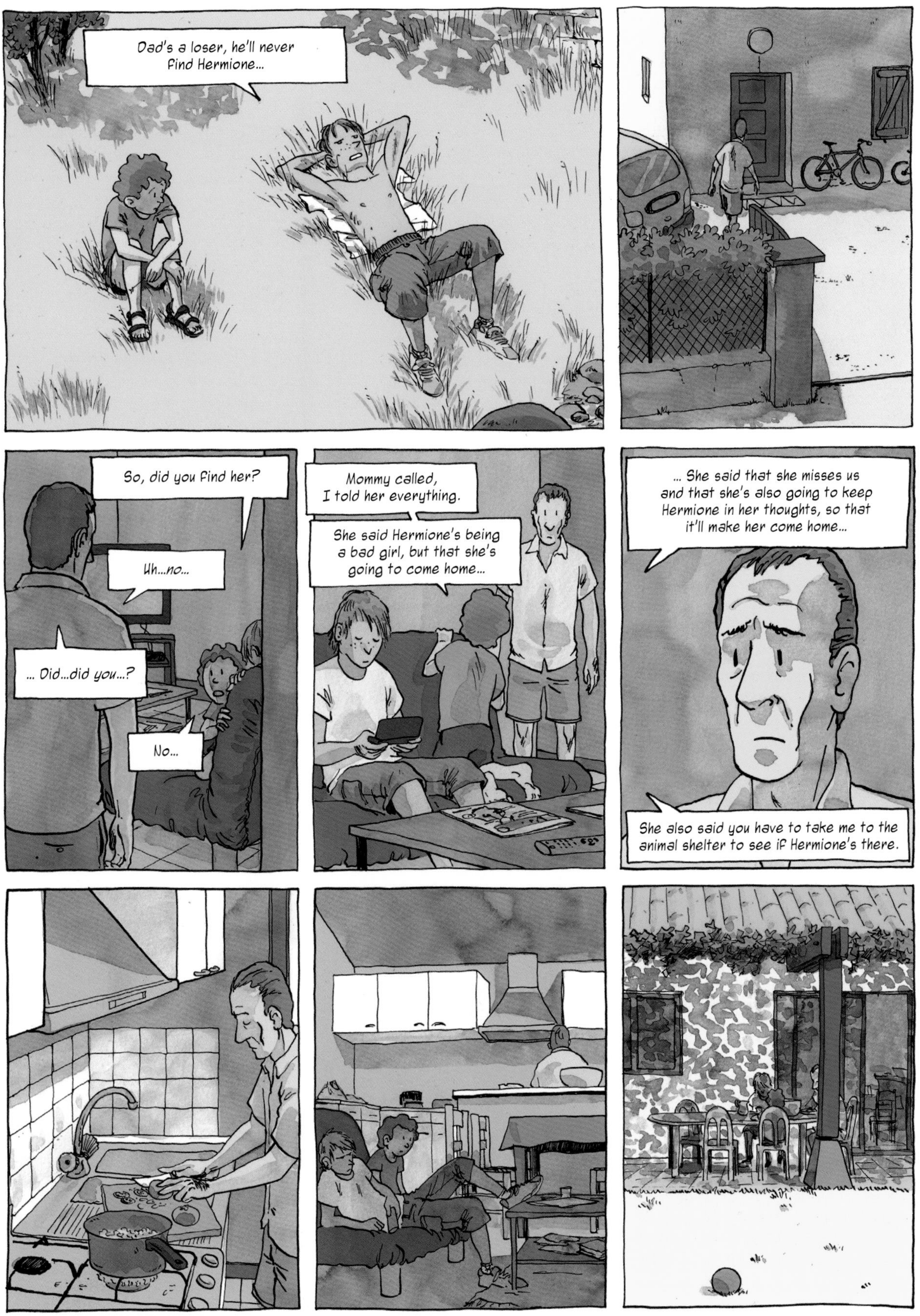
Dad's a loser, he'll never find Hermione...
So, did you find her?
Uh...no...
... Did...did you...?
No...
Mommy called, I told her everything.
She said Hermione's being a bad girl, but that she's going to come home...
... She said that she misses us and that she's also going to keep Hermione in her thoughts, so that it'll make her come home...
She also said you have to take me to the animal shelter to see if Hermione's there.

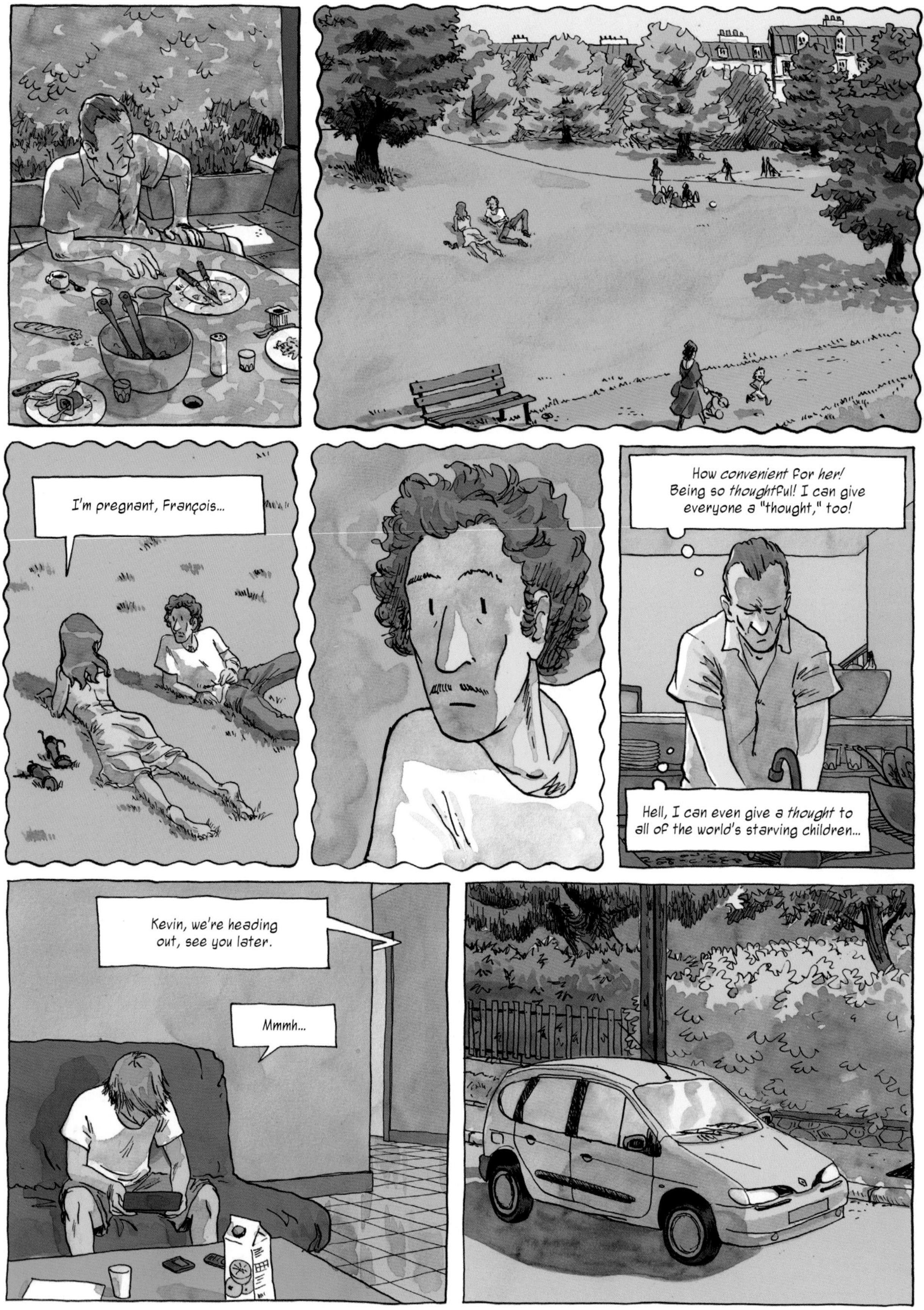
I'm pregnant, François...
How *convenient* for *her!* Being so *thoughtful!* I can give everyone a "thought," too!
Hell, I can even give a *thought* to all of the world's starving children...
Kevin, we're heading out, see you later.
Mmmh...

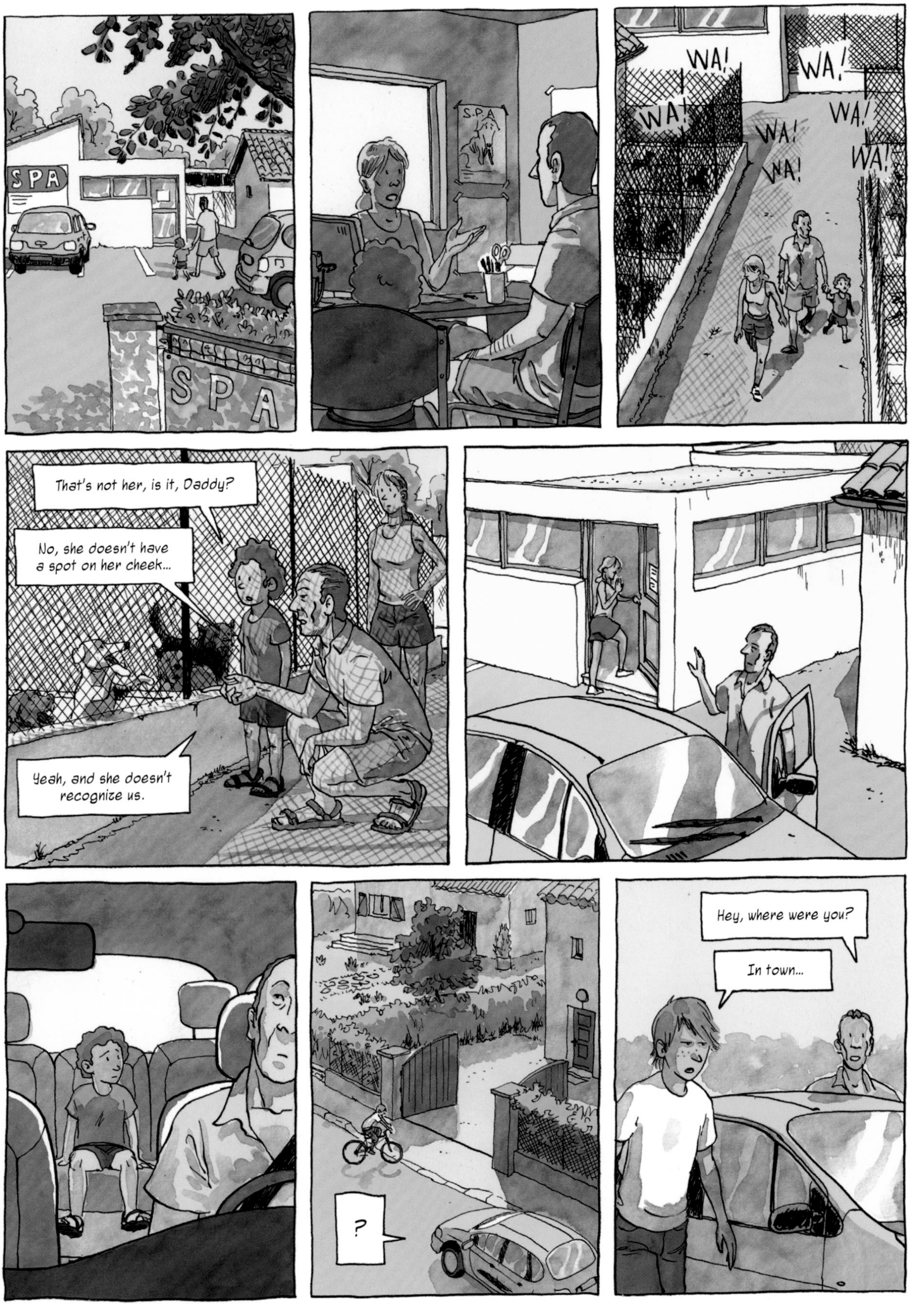
SPA
S.P.A
SPA
WA!
WA!
WA!
WA!
WA!
WA!
WA!
That's not her, is it, Daddy?
No, she doesn't have a spot on her cheek...
Yeah, and she doesn't recognize us.
?
Hey, where were you?
In town...

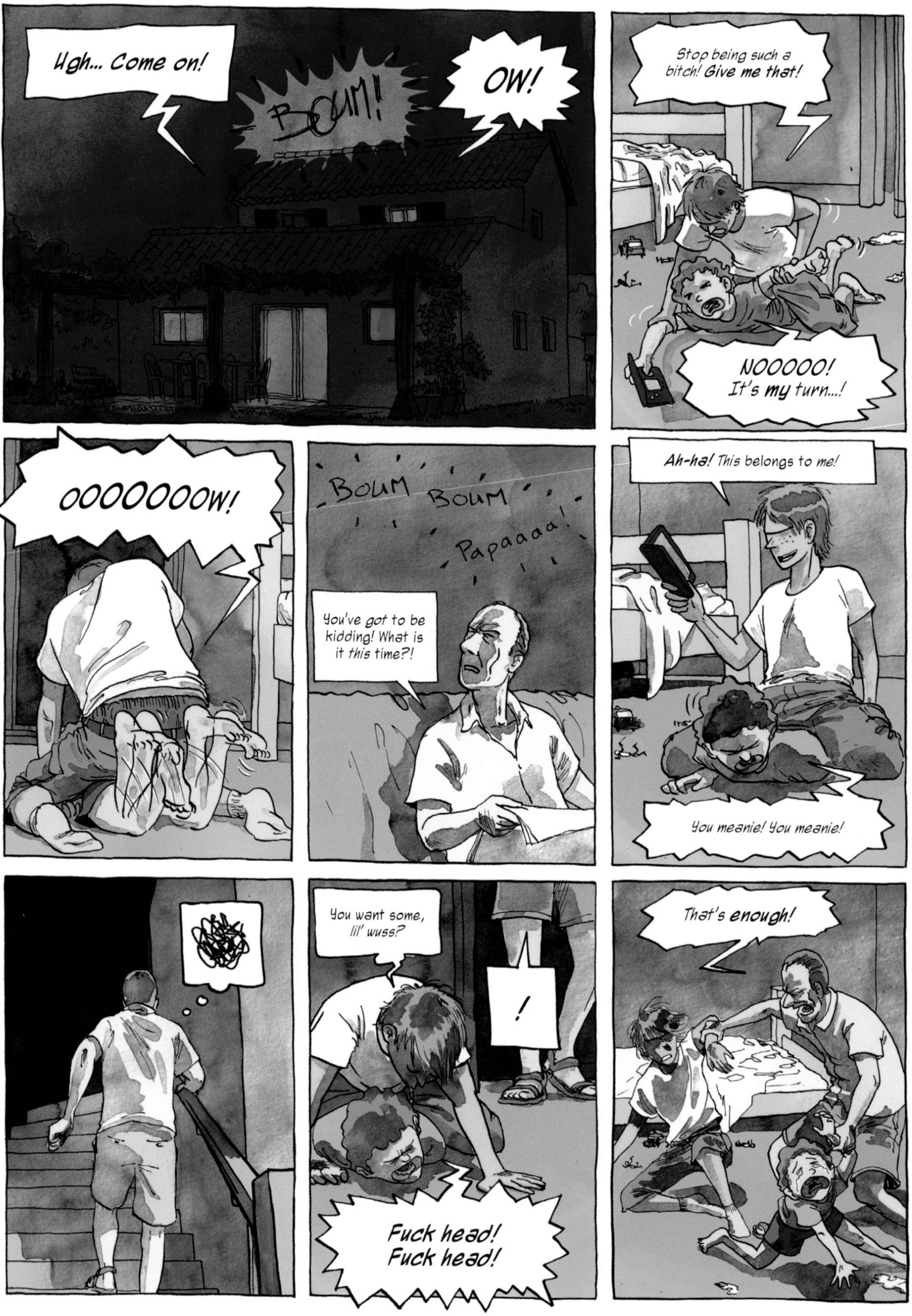
Ugh... Come on!
BOUM!
OW!
Stop being such a bitch! Give me that!
NOOOOO! It's my turn...!
OOOOOOOW!
BOUM BOUM
Papaaaa!
You've got to be kidding! What is it this time?!
Ah-ha! This belongs to me!
You meanie! You meanie!
You want some, lil' wuss?
!
Fuck head! Fuck head!
That's enough!

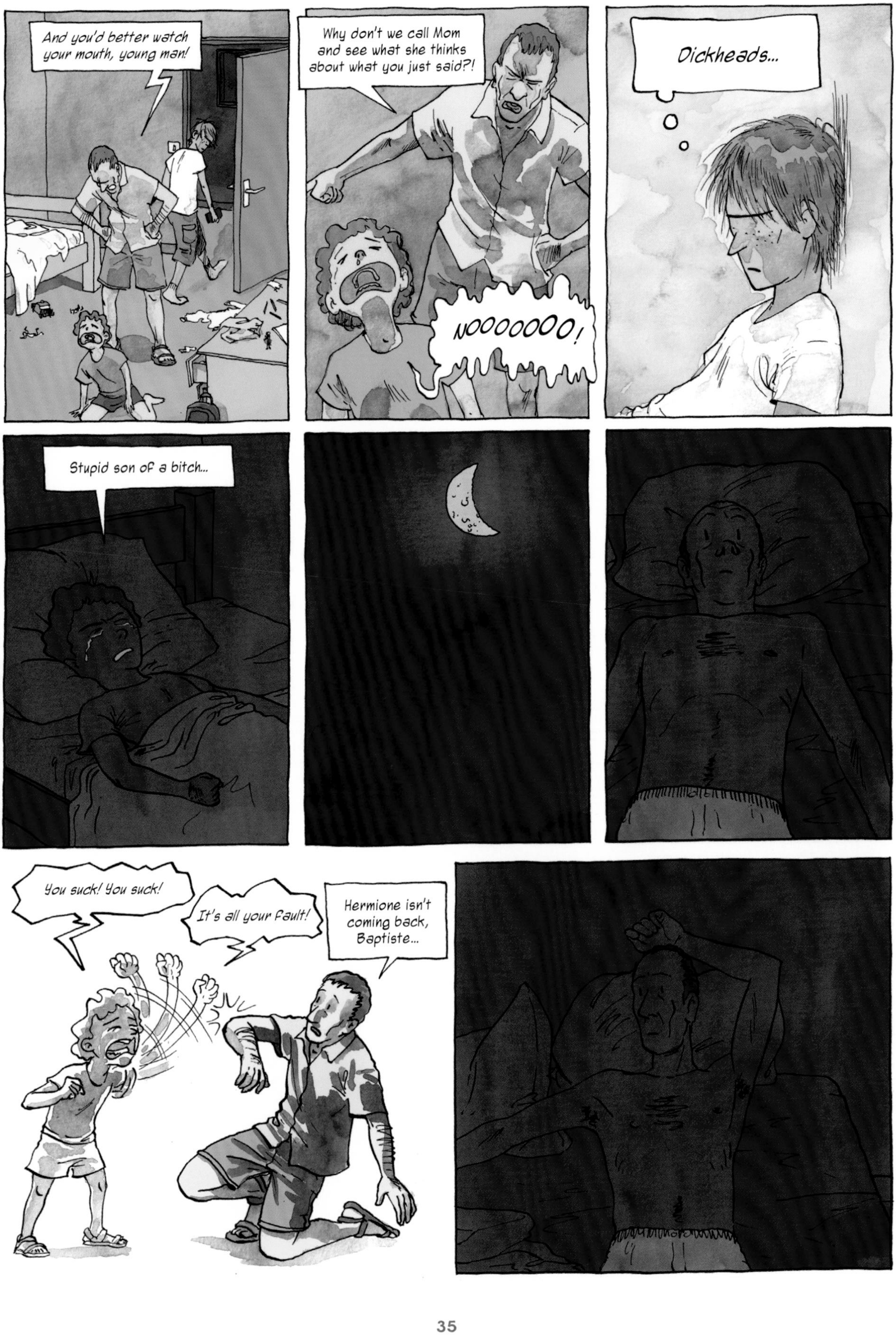
And you'd better watch your mouth, young man!
Why don't we call Mom and see what she thinks about what you just said?!
NOOOOOOO!
Dickheads...
Stupid son of a bitch...
You suck! You suck!
It's all your fault!
Hermione isn't coming back, Baptiste...

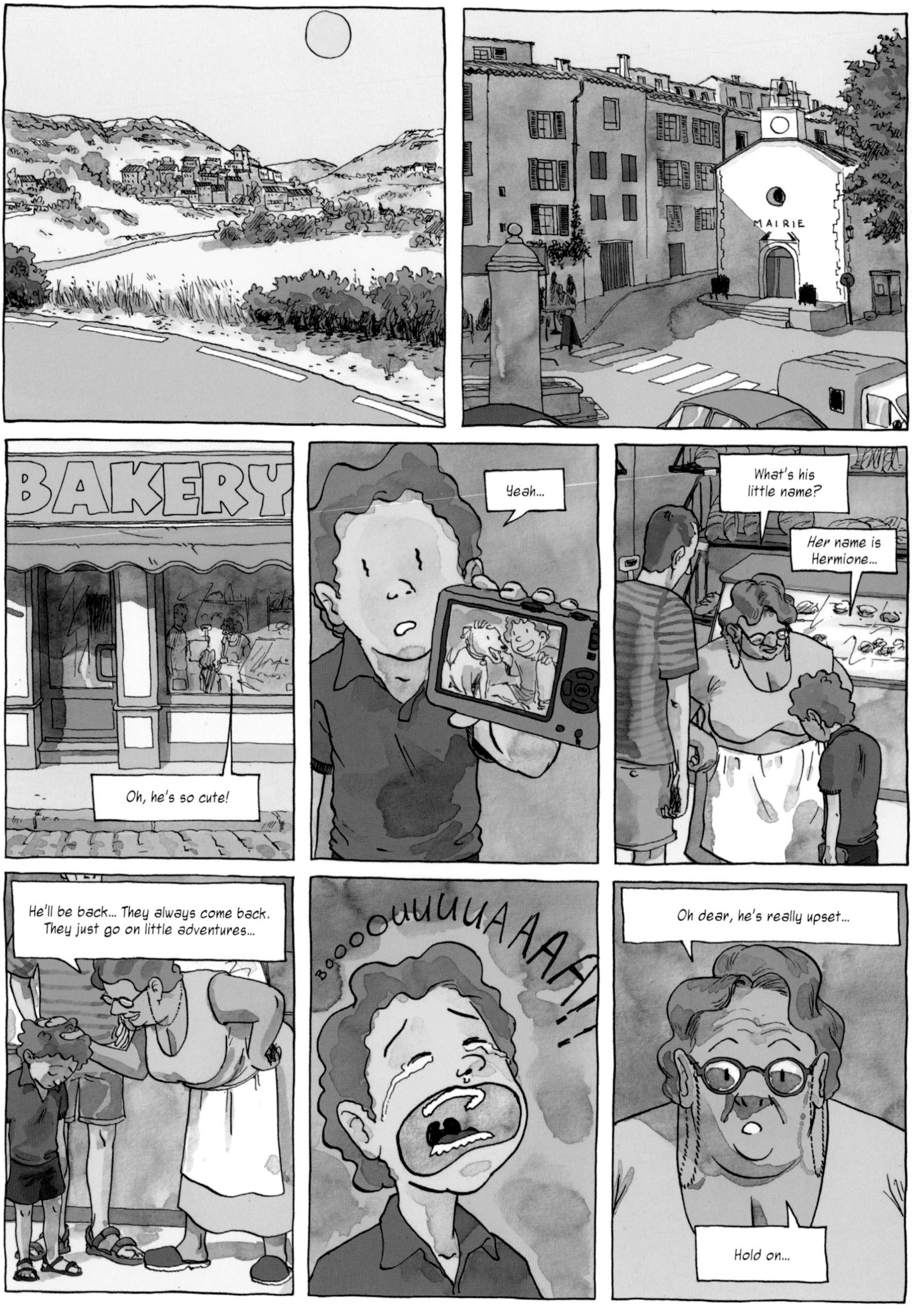
MAIRIE
BAKERY
Oh, he's so cute!
Yeah...
What's his little name?
Her name is Hermione...
He'll be back... They always come back. They just go on little adventures...
BOOOOOUUUUUAAAAH!!!
Oh dear, he's really upset...
Hold on...

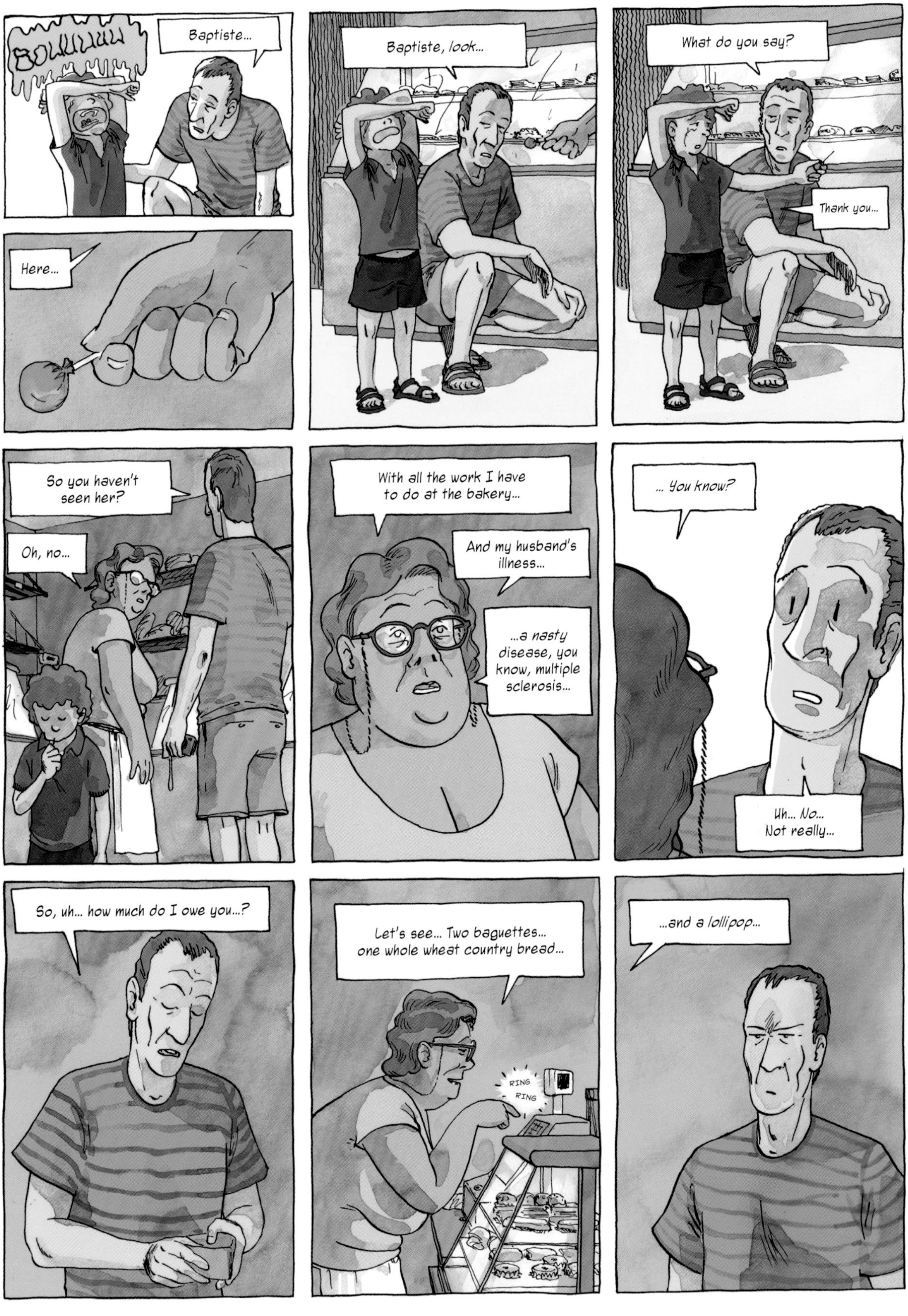
Baptiste...
Here...
Baptiste, look...
What do you say?
Thank you...
So you haven't seen her?
Oh, no...
With all the work I have to do at the bakery...
And my husband's illness...
...a nasty disease, you know, multiple sclerosis...
... You know?
Uh... No... Not really...
So, uh... how much do I owe you...?
Let's see... Two baguettes... one whole wheat country bread...
RING RING
...and a lollipop...

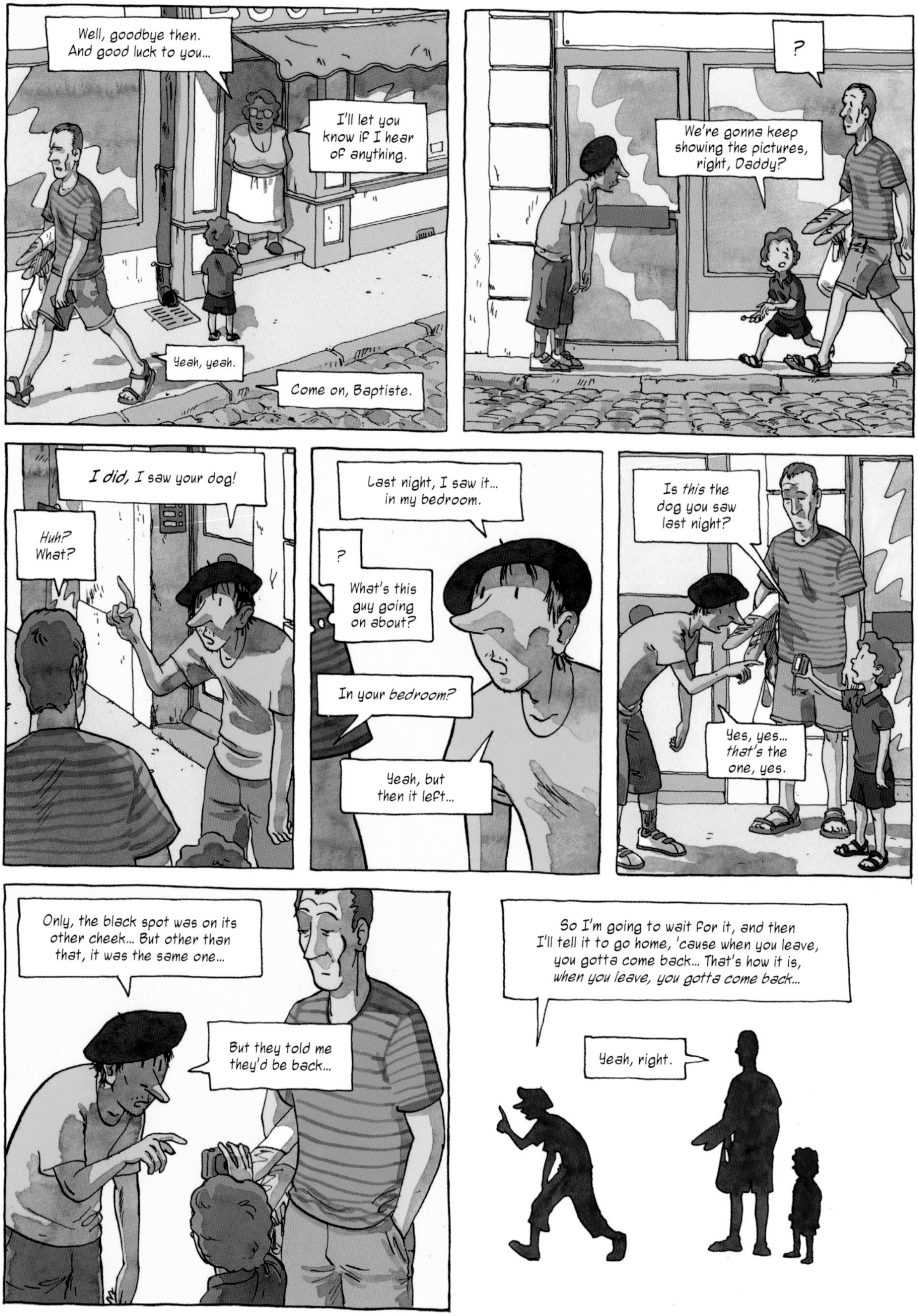
Well, goodbye then. And good luck to you...
I'll let you know if I hear of anything.
Yeah, yeah.
Come on, Baptiste.
?
We're gonna keep showing the pictures, right, Daddy?
I did, I saw your dog!
Huh? What?
Last night, I saw it... in my bedroom.
?
What's this guy going on about?
In your bedroom?
Yeah, but then it left...
Is this the dog you saw last night?
Yes, yes... that's the one, yes.
Only, the black spot was on its other cheek... But other than that, it was the same one...
But they told me they'd be back...
So I'm going to wait for it, and then I'll tell it to go home, 'cause when you leave, you gotta come back... That's how it is, when you leave, you gotta come back...
Yeah, right.

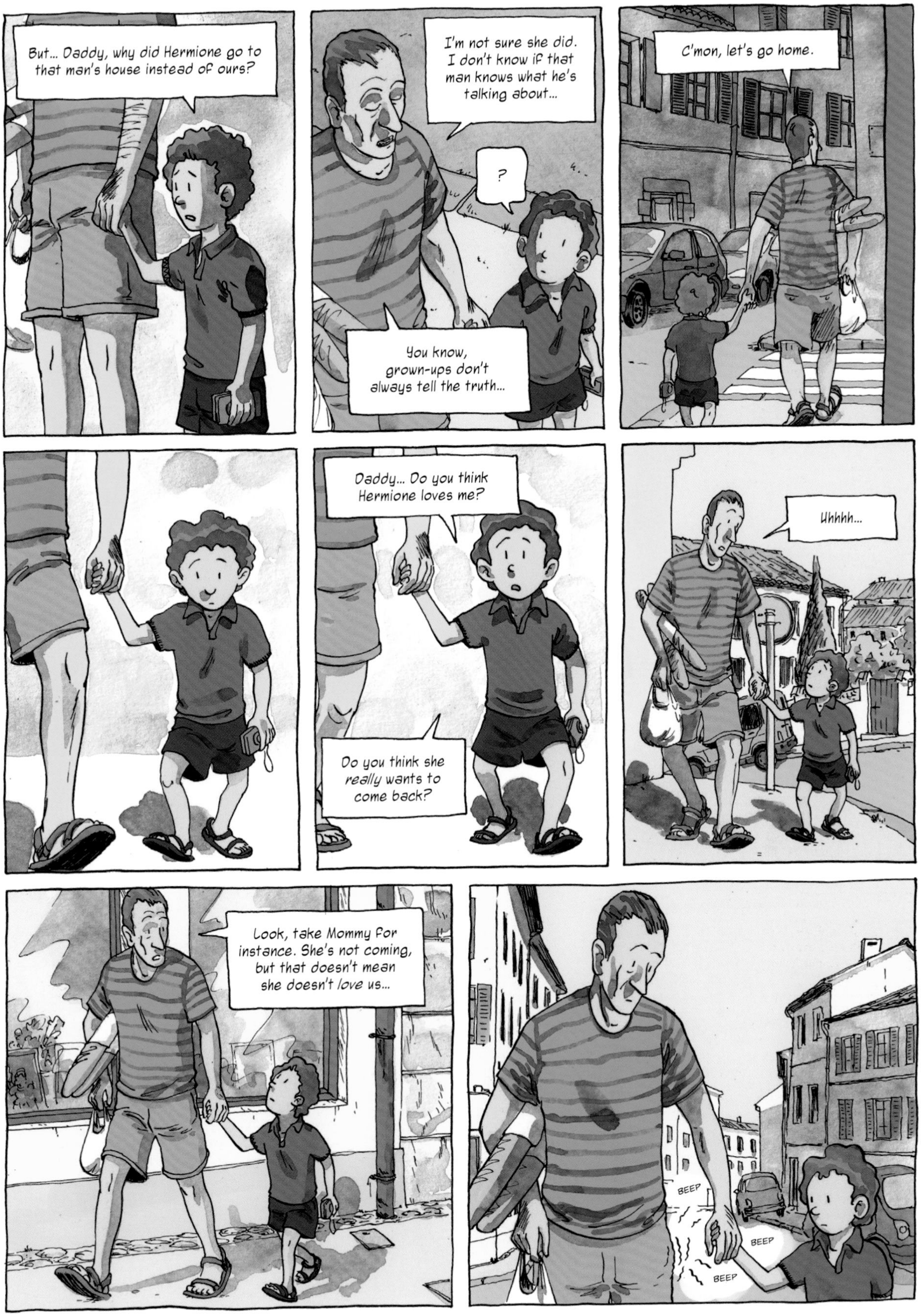
But... Daddy, why did Hermione go to that man's house instead of ours?
I'm not sure she did. I don't know if that man knows what he's talking about...
?
You know, grown-ups don't always tell the truth...
C'mon, let's go home.
Daddy... Do you think Hermione loves me?
Do you think she *really* wants to come back?
Uhhhh...
Look, take Mommy for instance. She's not coming, but that doesn't mean she doesn't *love* us...
BEEP
BEEP
BEEP

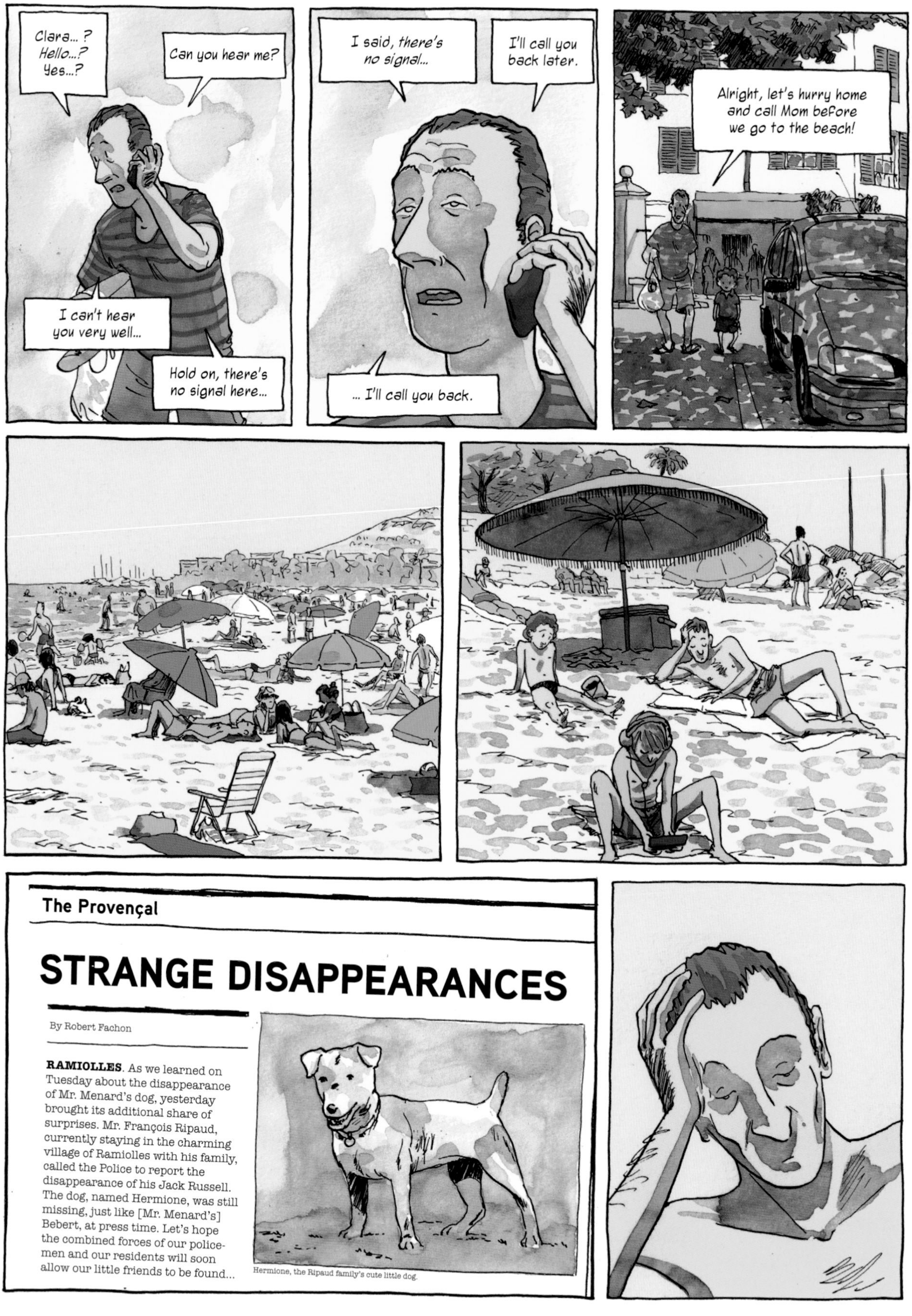
Clara... ? Hello...? Yes...?
Can you hear me?
I can't hear you very well...
Hold on, there's no signal here...
I said, there's no signal...
I'll call you back later.
... I'll call you back.
Alright, let's hurry home and call Mom before we go to the beach!
The Provençal
STRANGE DISAPPEARANCES
By Robert Fachon
RAMIOLLES. As we learned on Tuesday about the disappearance of Mr. Menard's dog, yesterday brought its additional share of surprises. Mr. François Ripaud, currently staying in the charming village of Ramiolles with his family, called the Police to report the disappearance of his Jack Russell. The dog, named Hermione, was still missing, just like [Mr. Menard's] Bebert, at press time. Let's hope the combined forces of our policemen and our residents will soon allow our little friends to be found...
Hermione, the Ripaud family's cute little dog.

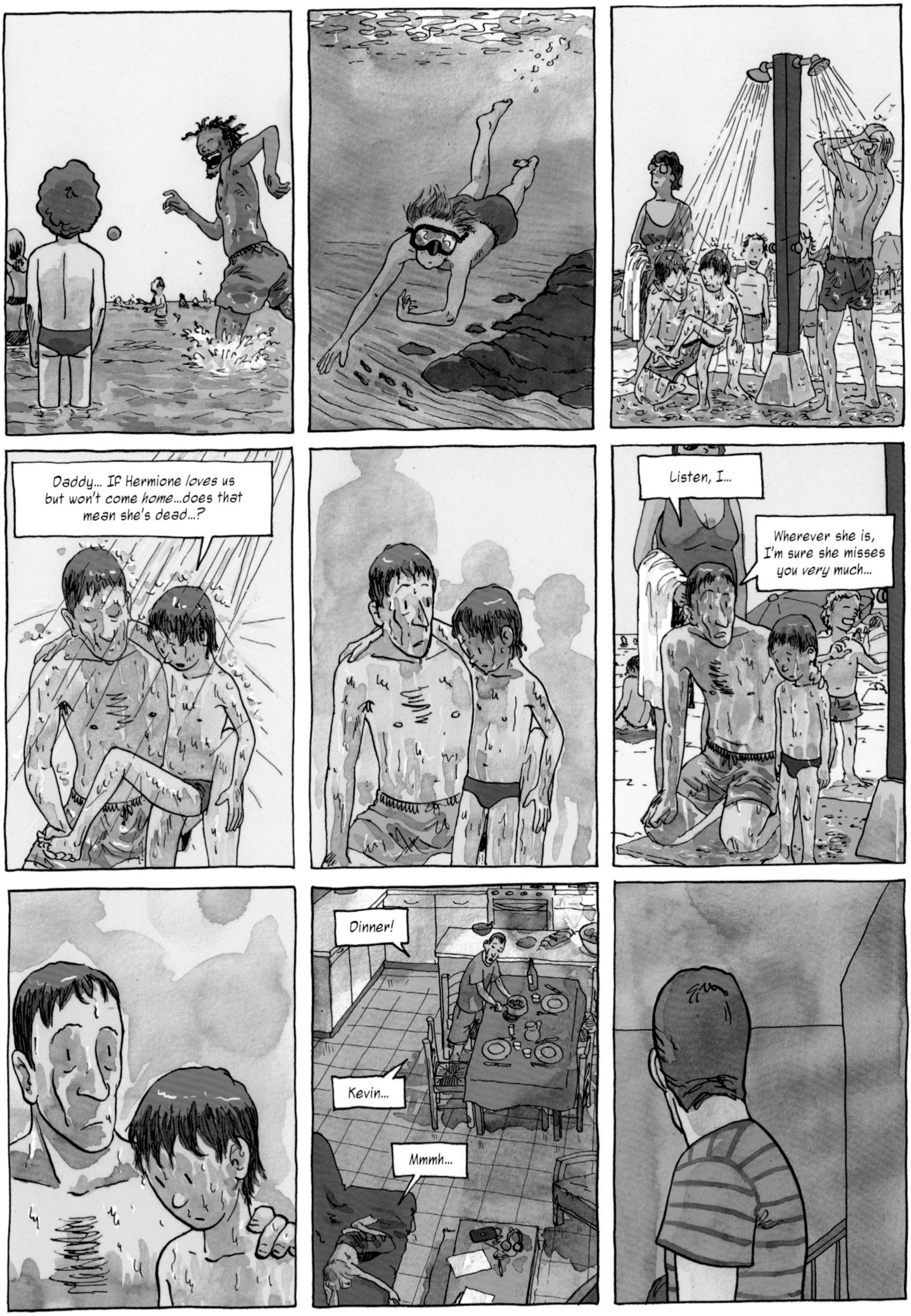
Daddy... If Hermione *loves* us but won't come *home*...does that mean she's dead...?
Listen, I...
Wherever she is, I'm sure she misses you *very* much...
Dinner!
Kevin...
Mmmh...

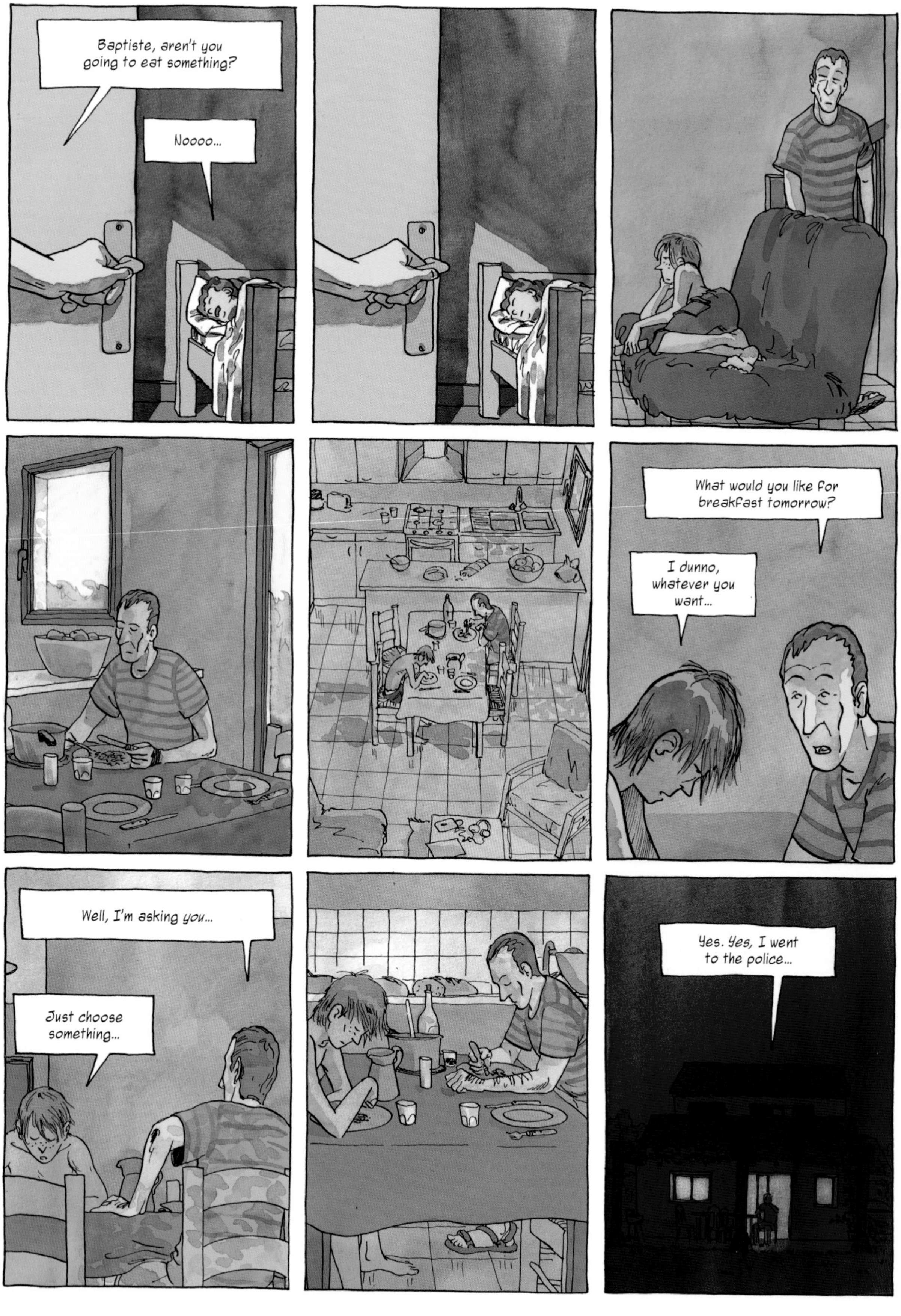
Baptiste, aren't you going to eat something?
Noooo...
What would you like for breakfast tomorrow?
I dunno, whatever you want...
Well, I'm asking you...
Just choose something...
Yes. Yes, I went to the police...

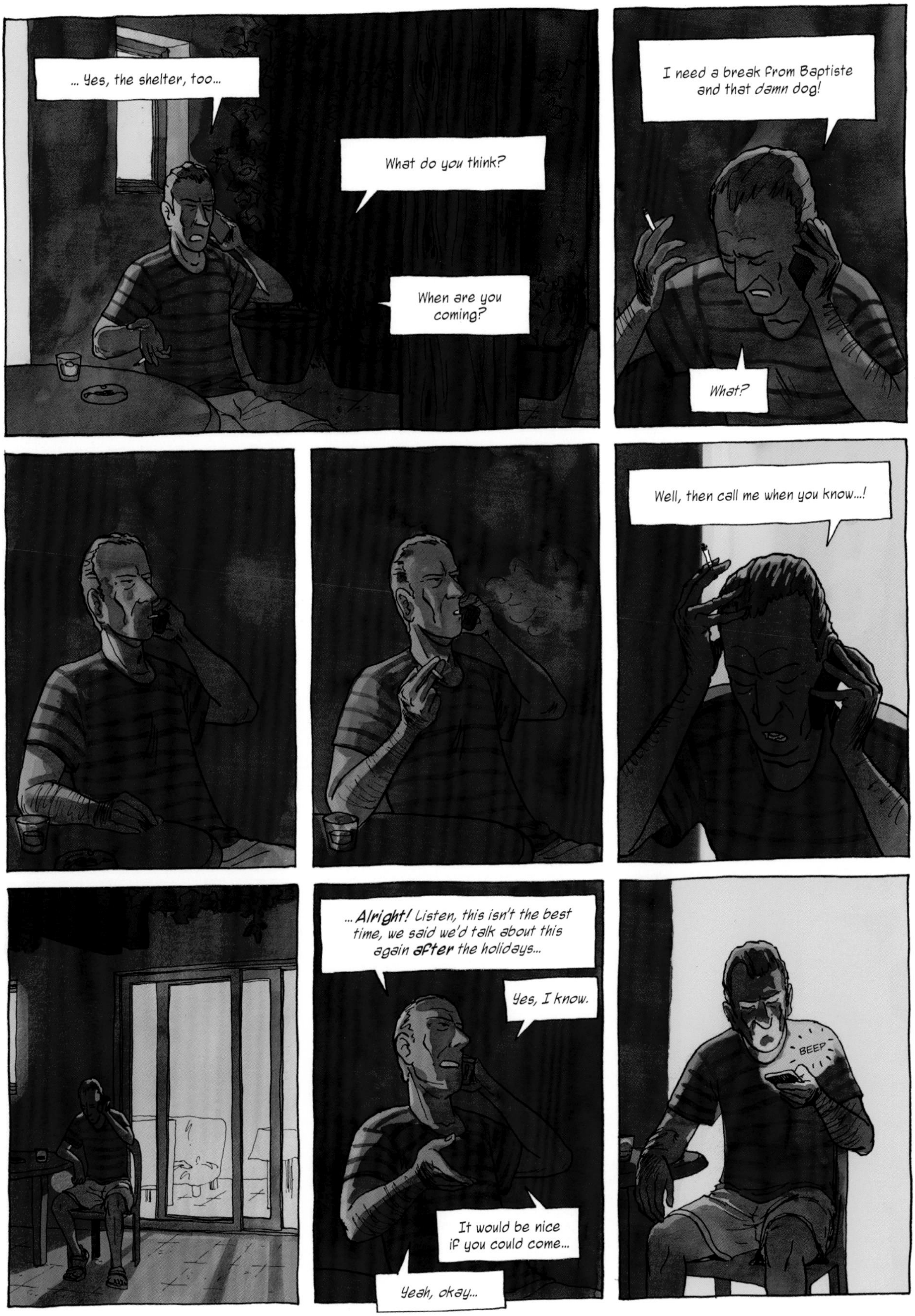

... Yes, the shelter, too...
What do you think?
When are you coming?
I need a break from Baptiste and that *damn* dog!
What?
Well, then call me when you know...!
... **Alright!** Listen, this isn't the best time, we said we'd talk about this again **after** the holidays...
Yes, I know.
It would be nice if you could come...
Yeah, okay...
BEEP

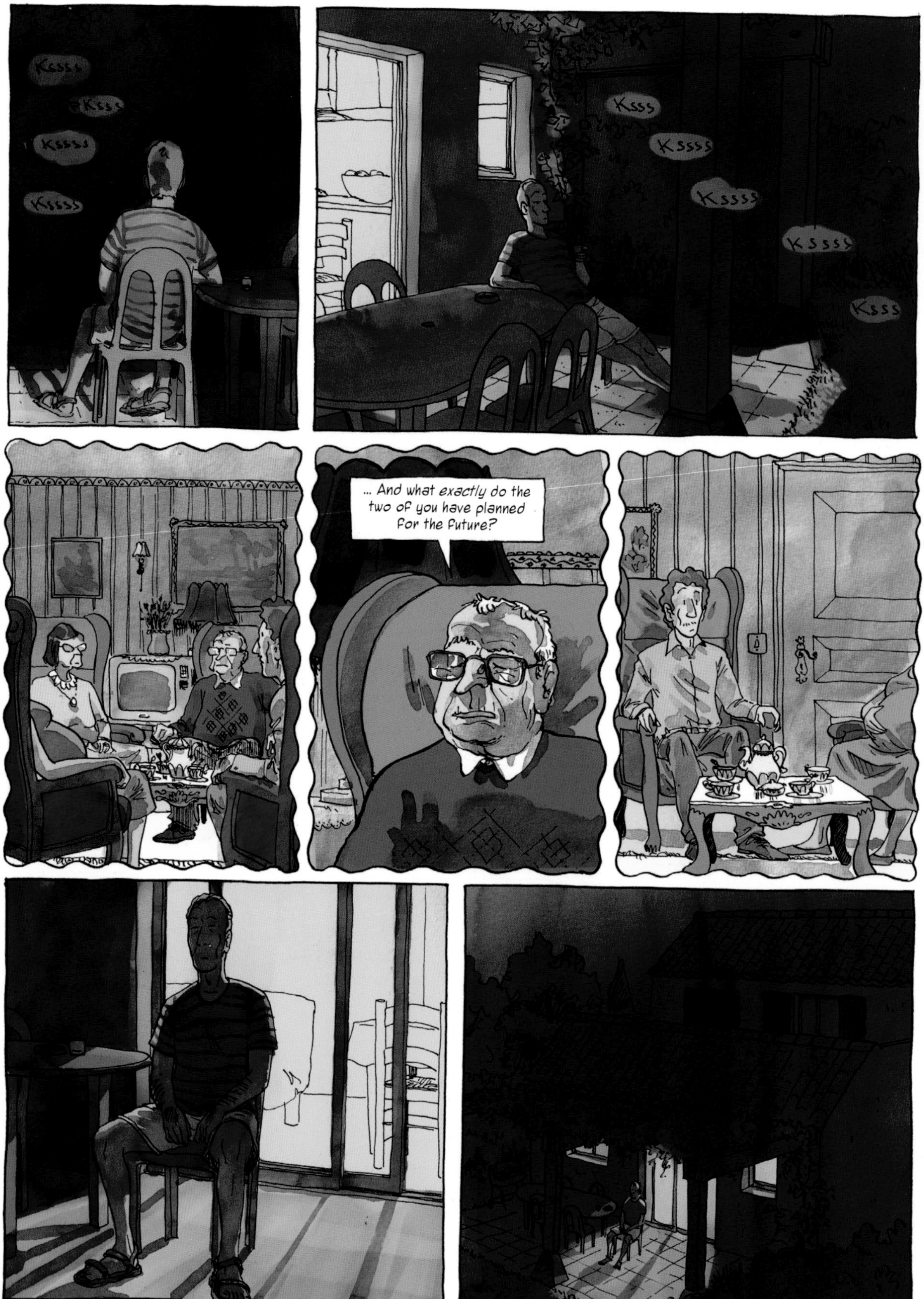
Kssss
Ksss
Kssss
Kssss
Ksss
Kssss
Kssss
Kssss
Ksss
... And what *exactly* do the two of you have planned for the future?

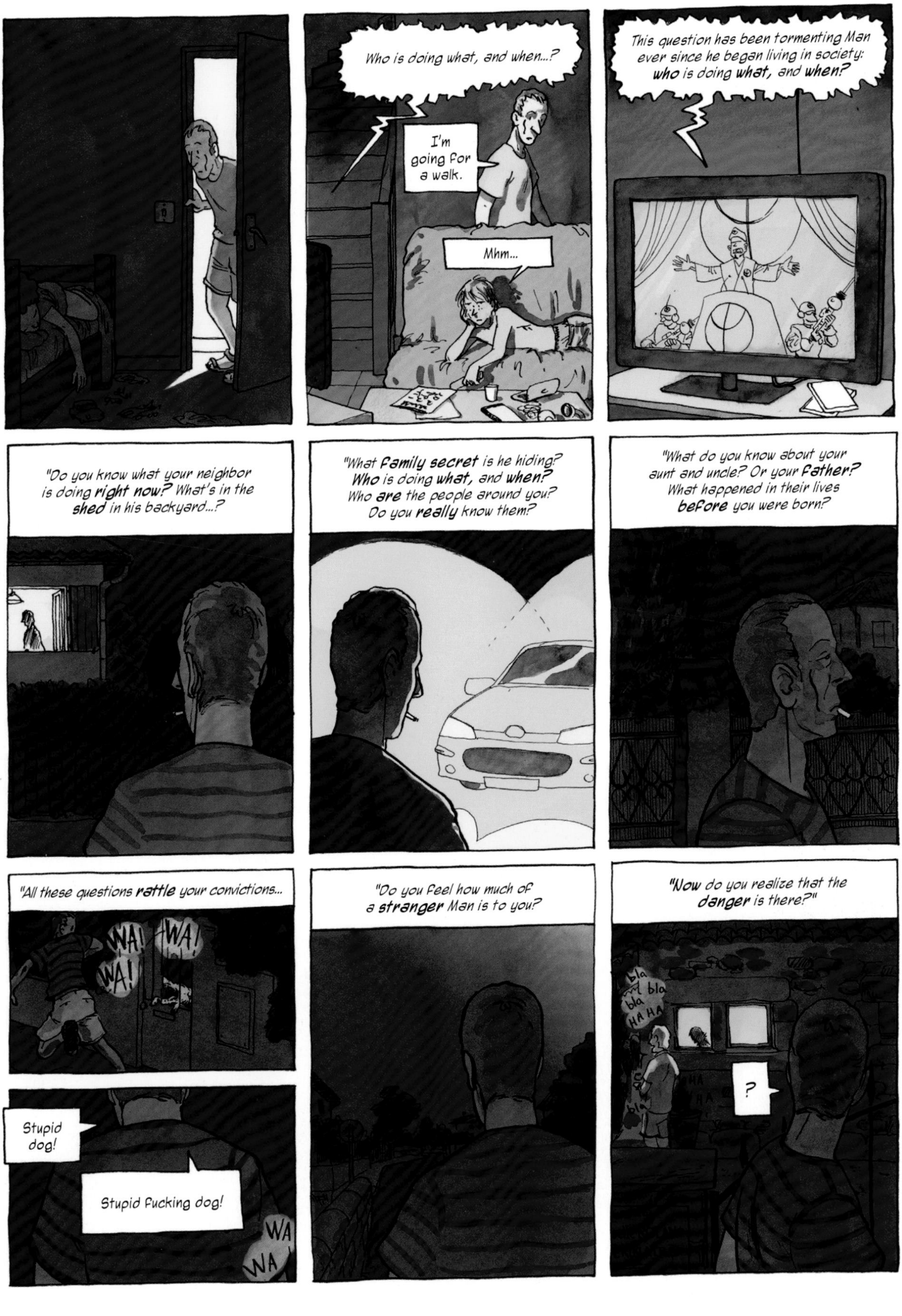
Who is doing what, and when...?
I'm going for a walk.
Mhm...
This question has been tormenting Man ever since he began living in society: who is doing what, and when?
"Do you know what your neighbor is doing right now? What's in the shed in his backyard...?
"What family secret is he hiding? Who is doing what, and when? Who are the people around you? Do you really know them?
"What do you know about your aunt and uncle? Or your father? What happened in their lives before you were born?
"All these questions rattle your convictions...
WA! WA! WA!
Stupid dog!
Stupid fucking dog!
WA WA
"Do you feel how much of a stranger Man is to you?
"Now do you realize that the danger is there?"
bla bla bla HA HA
?

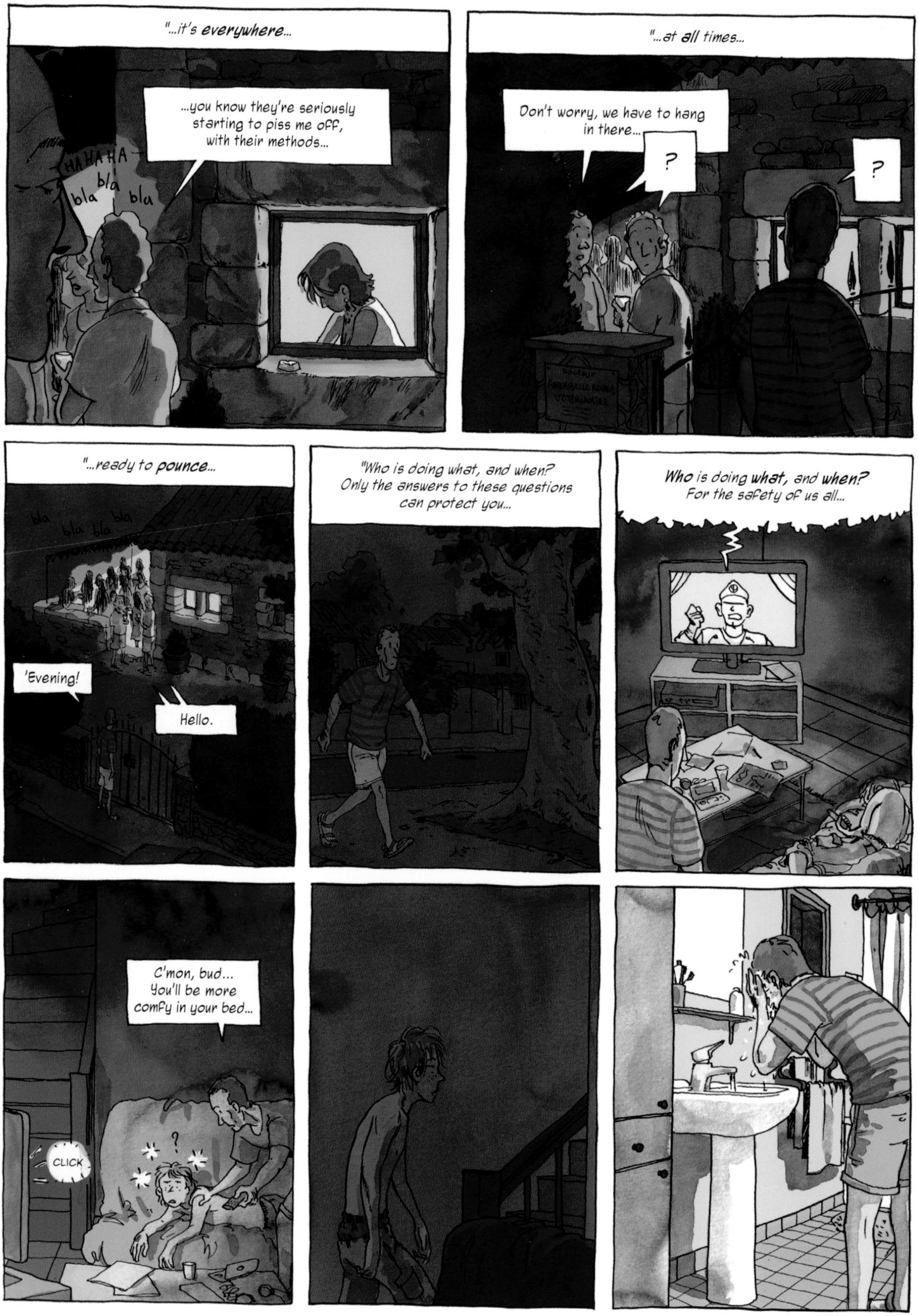

"...it's **everywhere**...
HAHAHA
bla
bla
bla
...you know they're seriously starting to piss me off, with their methods...
"...at **all** times...
Don't worry, we have to hang in there...
?
?
"...ready to **pounce**...
bla
bla bla bla
'Evening!
Hello.
"Who is doing what, and when? Only the answers to these questions can protect you...
Who is doing **what**, and **when?** For the safety of us all...
C'mon, bud... You'll be more comfy in your bed...
?
CLICK

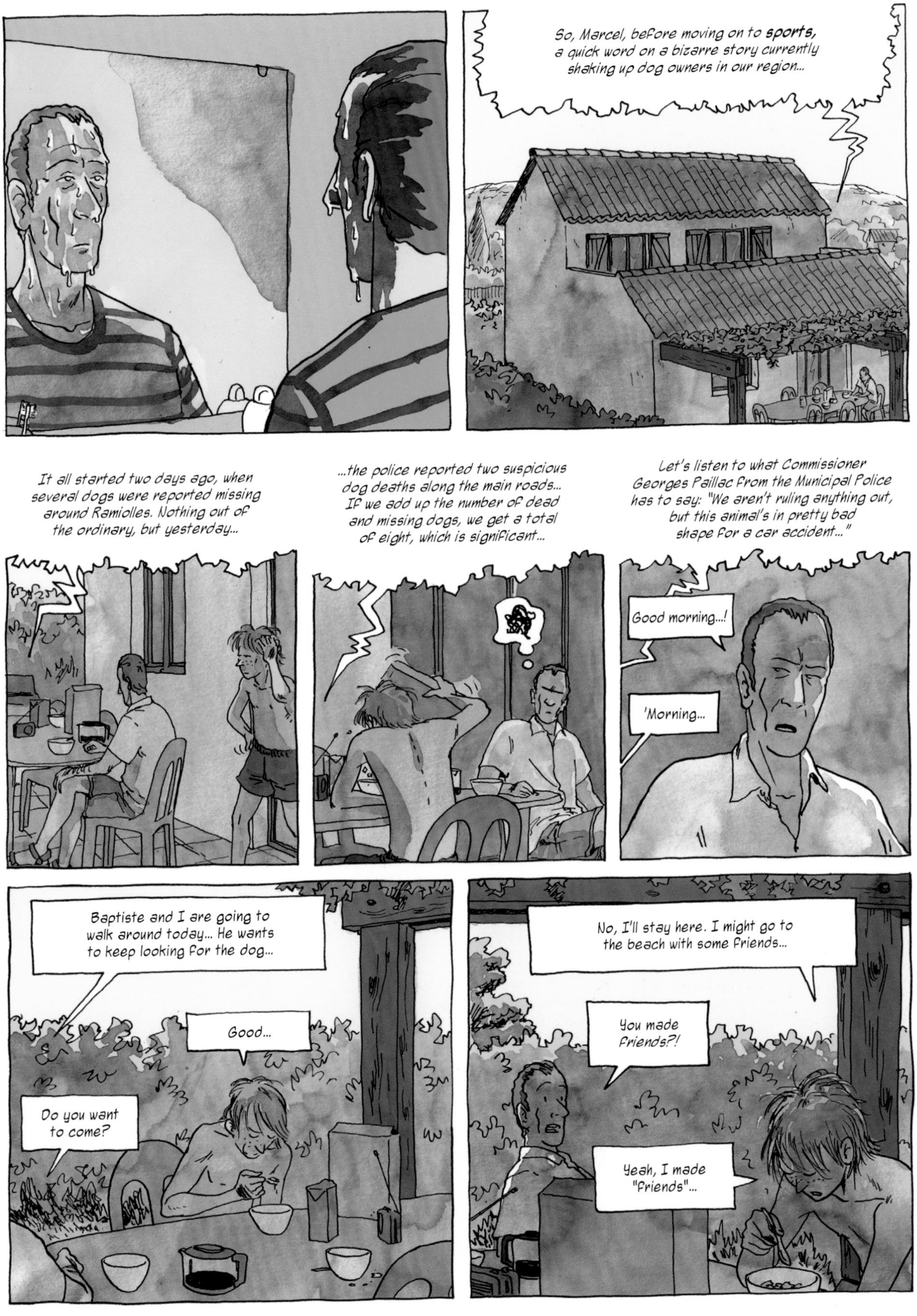

So, Marcel, before moving on to **sports,** a quick word on a bizarre story currently shaking up dog owners in our region...
It all started two days ago, when several dogs were reported missing around Ramiolles. Nothing out of the ordinary, but yesterday...
...the police reported two suspicious dog deaths along the main roads... If we add up the number of dead and missing dogs, we get a total of eight, which is significant...
Let's listen to what Commissioner Georges Paillac from the Municipal Police has to say: "We aren't ruling anything out, but this animal's in pretty bad shape for a car accident..."
Good morning...!
'Morning...
Baptiste and I are going to walk around today... He wants to keep looking for the dog...
Good...
Do you want to come?
No, I'll stay here. I might go to the beach with some friends...
You made friends?!
Yeah, I made "friends"...

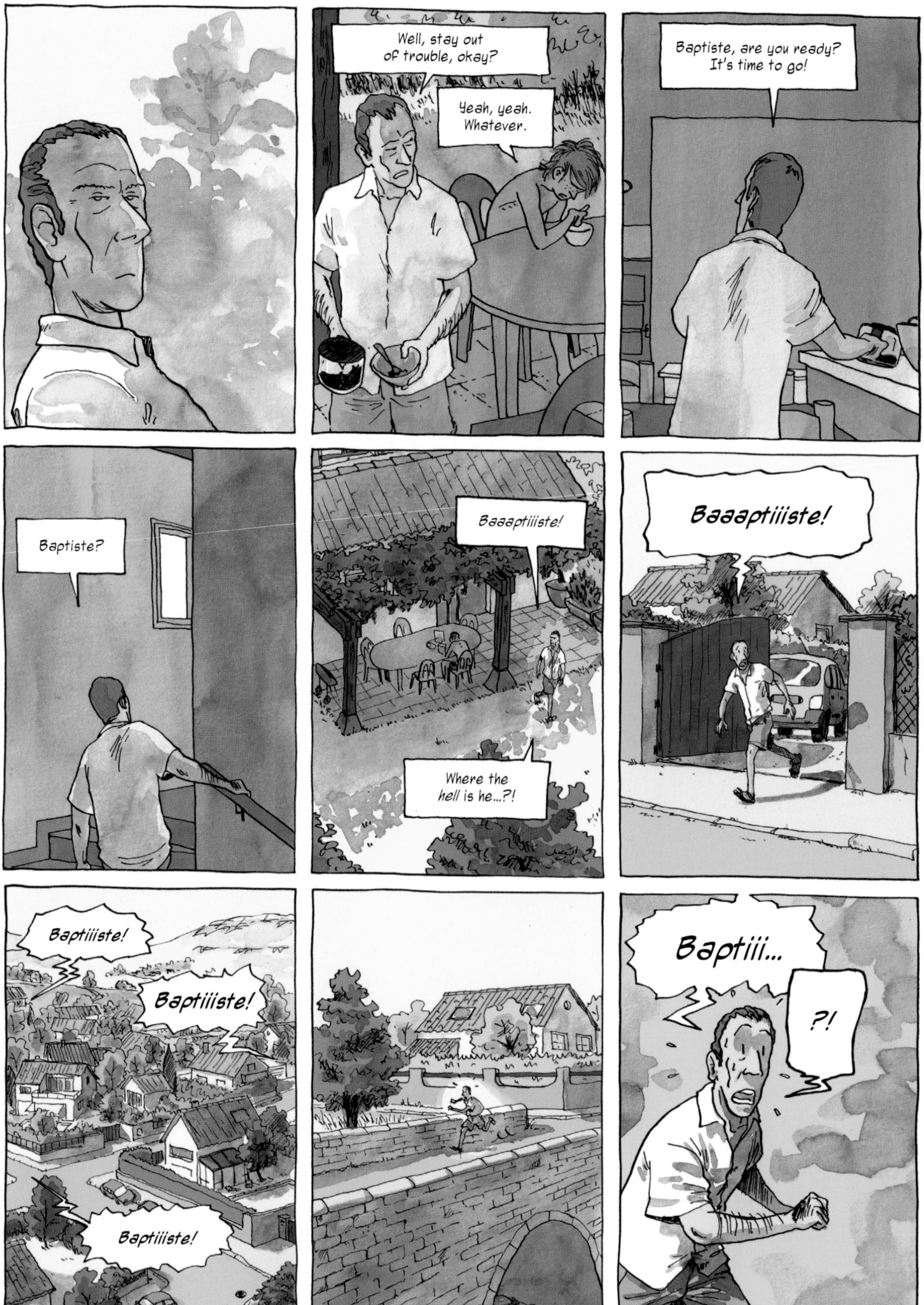

Well, stay out of trouble, okay?
Yeah, yeah. Whatever.
Baptiste, are you ready? It's time to go!
Baptiste?
Baaaptiiiste!
Where the hell is he...?!
Baaaptiiiste!
Baptiiiste!
Baptiiiste!
Baptiiiste!
Baptiii...
?!

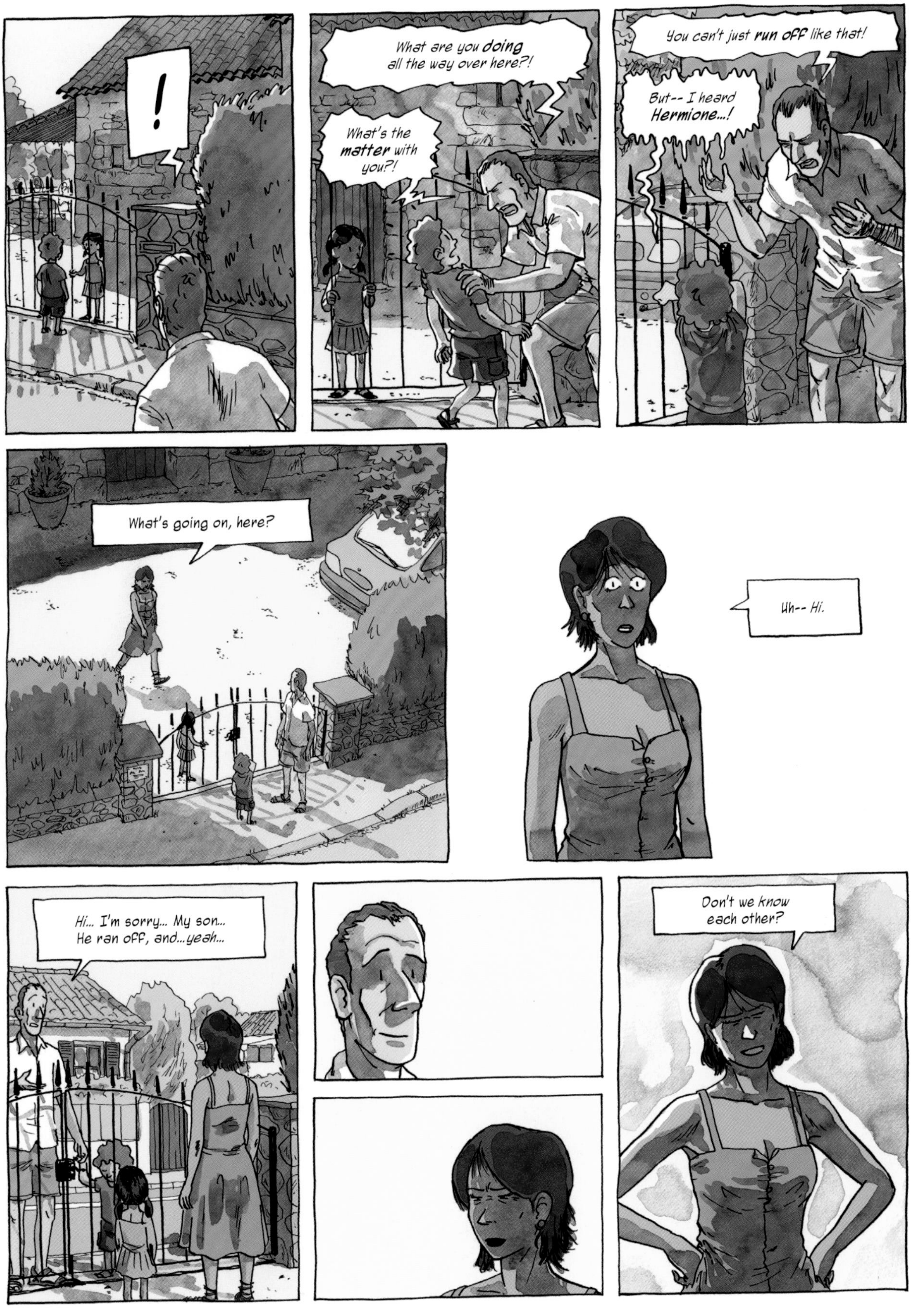
!
What are you doing all the way over here?!
What's the matter with you?!
You can't just run off like that!
But-- I heard Hermione...!
What's going on, here?
Uh-- Hi.
Hi... I'm sorry... My son... He ran off, and...yeah...
Don't we know each other?

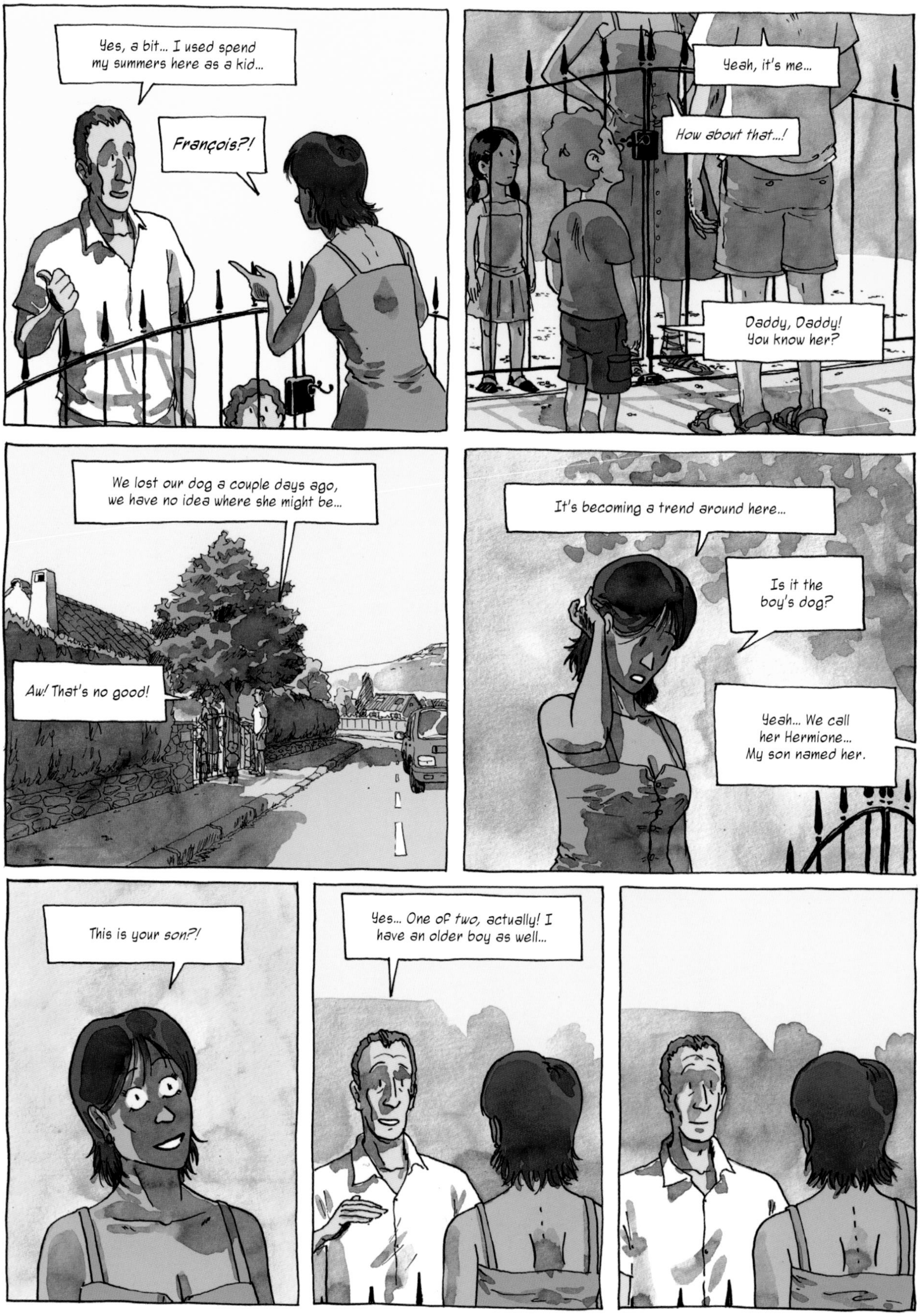
Yes, a bit... I used spend my summers here as a kid...
François?!
Yeah, it's me...
How about that...!
Daddy, Daddy! You know her?
We lost our dog a couple days ago, we have no idea where she might be...
Aw! That's no good!
It's becoming a trend around here...
Is it the boy's dog?
Yeah... We call her Hermione... My son named her.
This is your son?!
Yes... One of two, actually! I have an older boy as well...

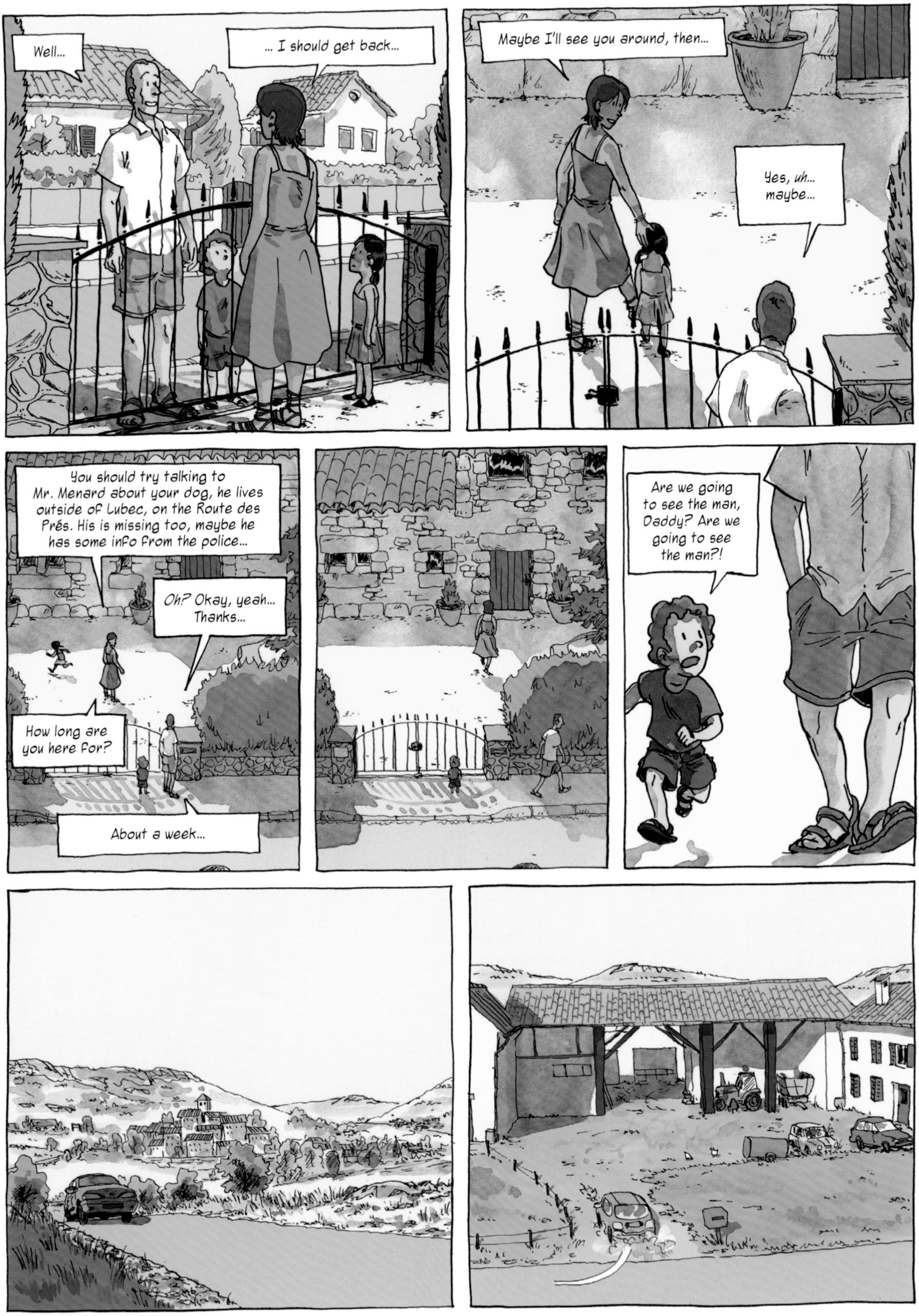
Well...
... I should get back...
Maybe I'll see you around, then...
Yes, uh... maybe...
You should try talking to Mr. Menard about your dog, he lives outside of Lubec, on the Route des Prés. His is missing too, maybe he has some info from the police...
Oh? Okay, yeah... Thanks...
How long are you here for?
About a week...
Are we going to see the man, Daddy? Are we going to see the man?!

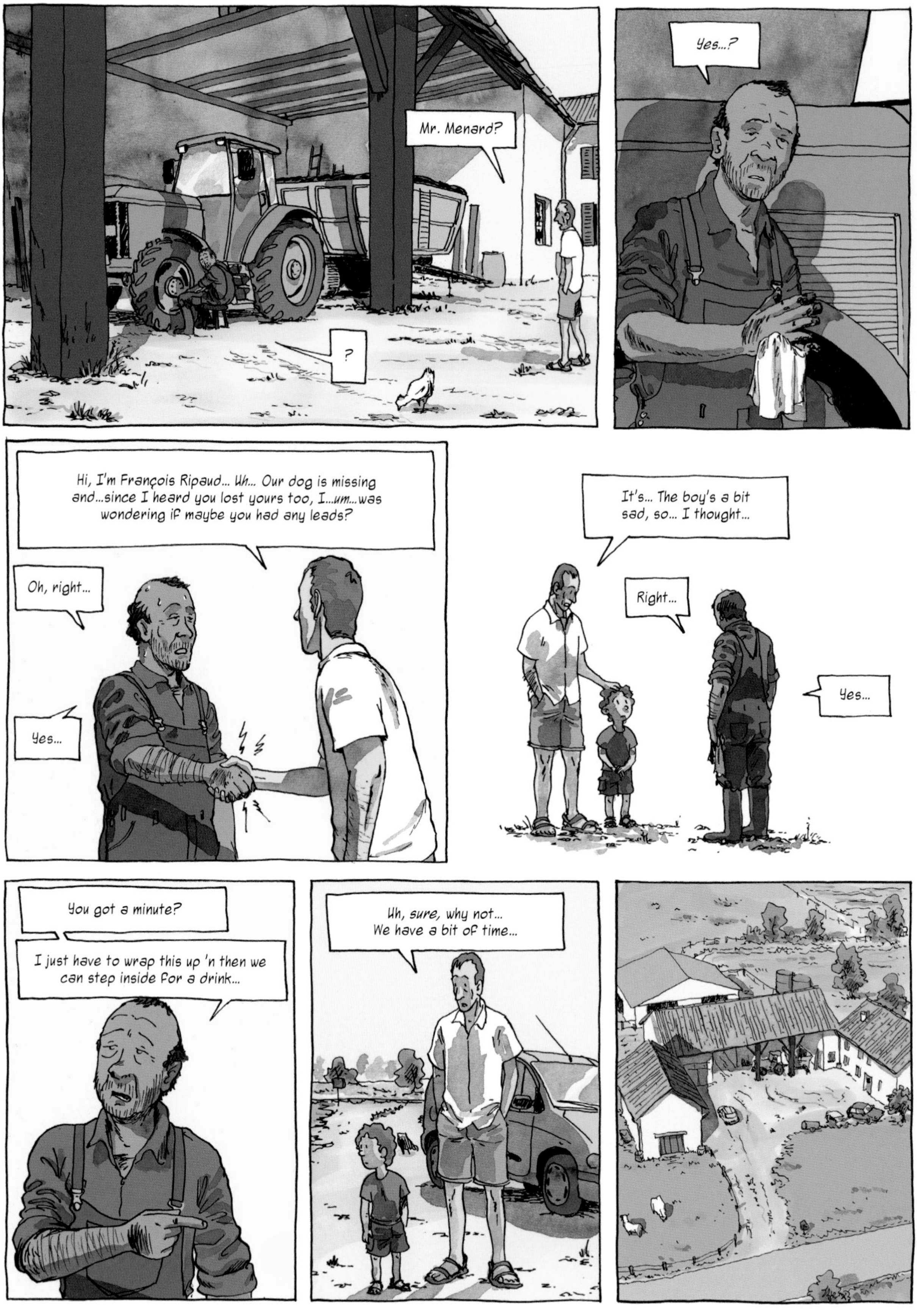
Mr. Menard?
?
Yes...?
Hi, I'm François Ripaud... Uh... Our dog is missing and...since I heard you lost yours too, I...um...was wondering if maybe you had any leads?
Oh, right...
Yes...
It's... The boy's a bit sad, so... I thought...
Right...
Yes...
You got a minute?
I just have to wrap this up 'n then we can step inside for a drink...
Uh, sure, why not... We have a bit of time...

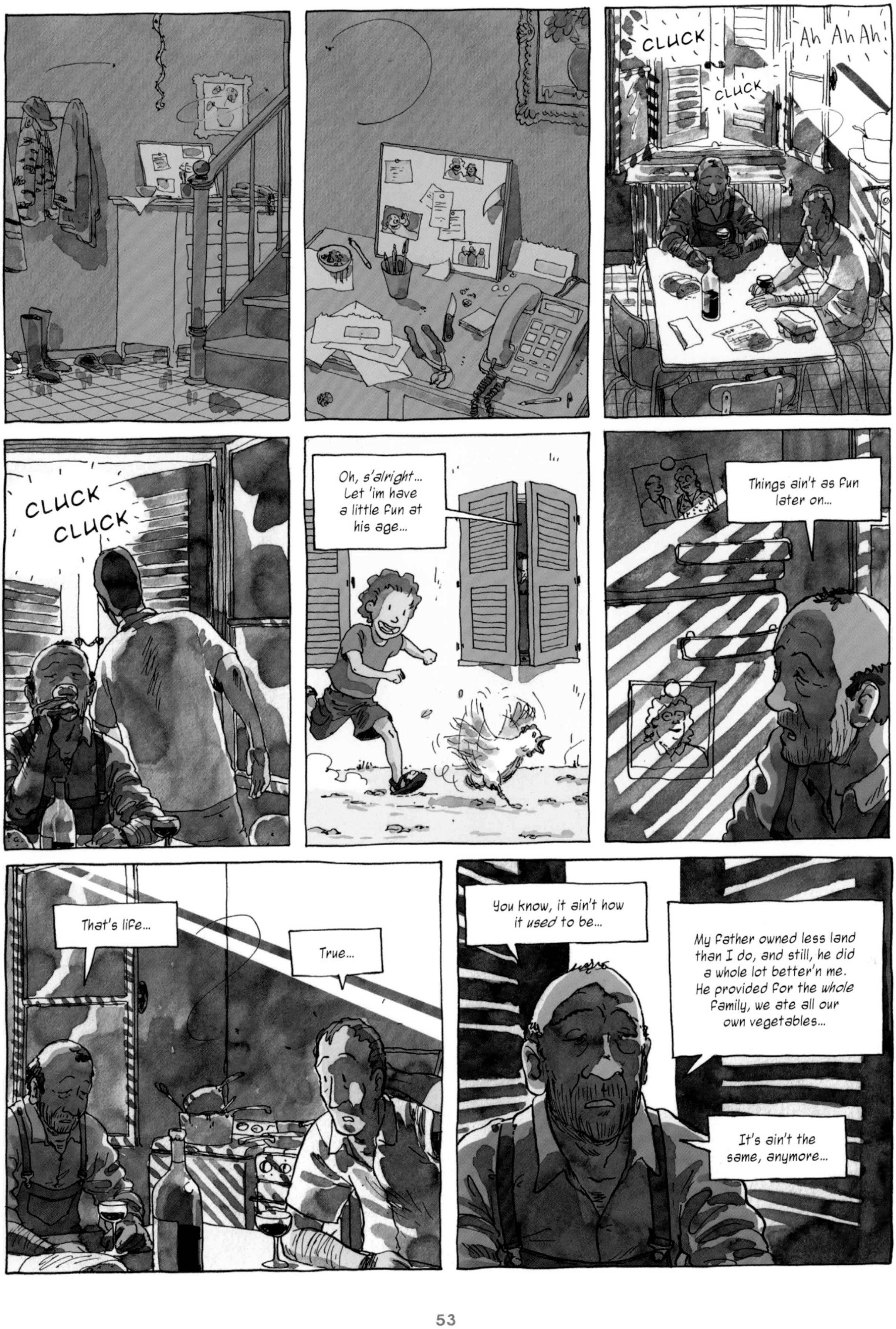
CLUCK
CLUCK
Ah Ah Ah!
CLUCK
CLUCK
Oh, s'alright... Let 'im have a little fun at his age...
Things ain't as fun later on...
That's life...
True...
You know, it ain't how it used to be...
My father owned less land than I do, and still, he did a whole lot better'n me. He provided for the whole family, we ate all our own vegetables...
It's ain't the same, anymore...

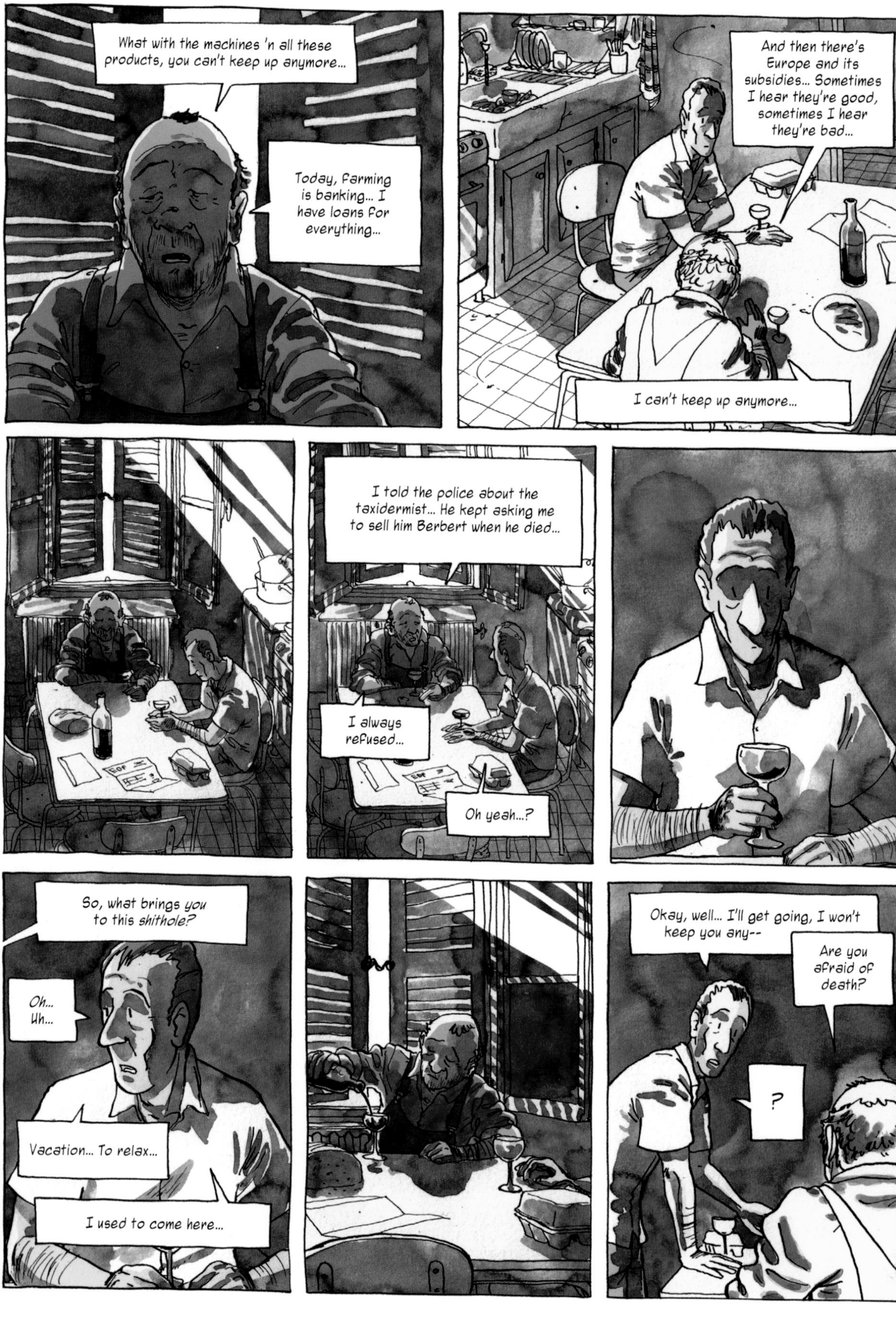

What with the machines 'n all these products, you can't keep up anymore...
Today, farming is banking... I have loans for everything...
And then there's Europe and its subsidies... Sometimes I hear they're good, sometimes I hear they're bad...
I can't keep up anymore...
I told the police about the taxidermist... He kept asking me to sell him Berbert when he died...
I always refused...
Oh yeah...?
So, what brings *you* to this *shithole?*
Oh... Uh...
Vacation... To relax...
I used to come here...
Okay, well... I'll get going, I won't keep you any--
Are you afraid of death?
?

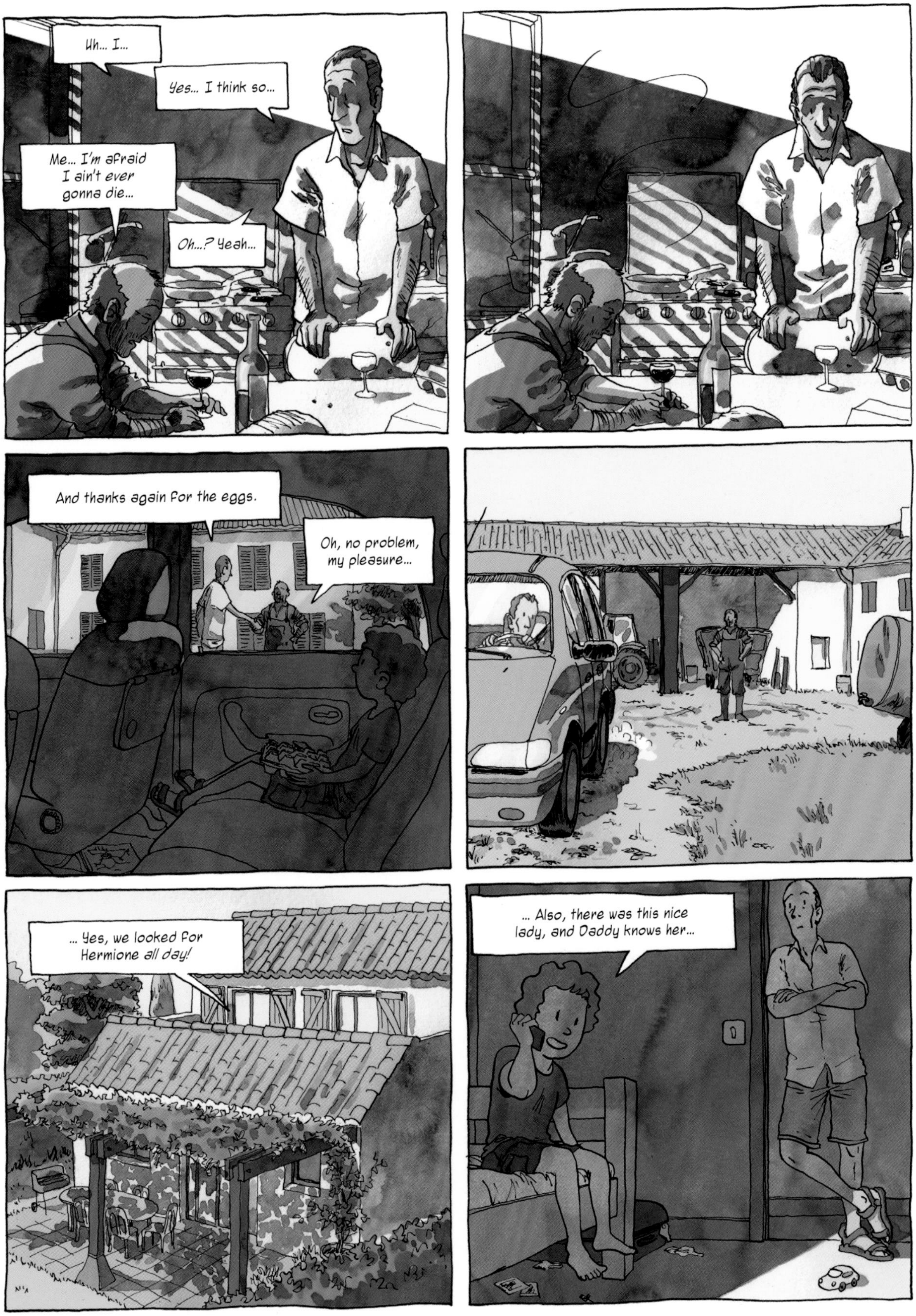

Uh... I...
Yes... I think so...
Me... I'm afraid I ain't ever gonna die...
Oh...? Yeah...
And thanks again for the eggs.
Oh, no problem, my pleasure...
... Yes, we looked for Hermione all day!
... Also, there was this nice lady, and Daddy knows her...

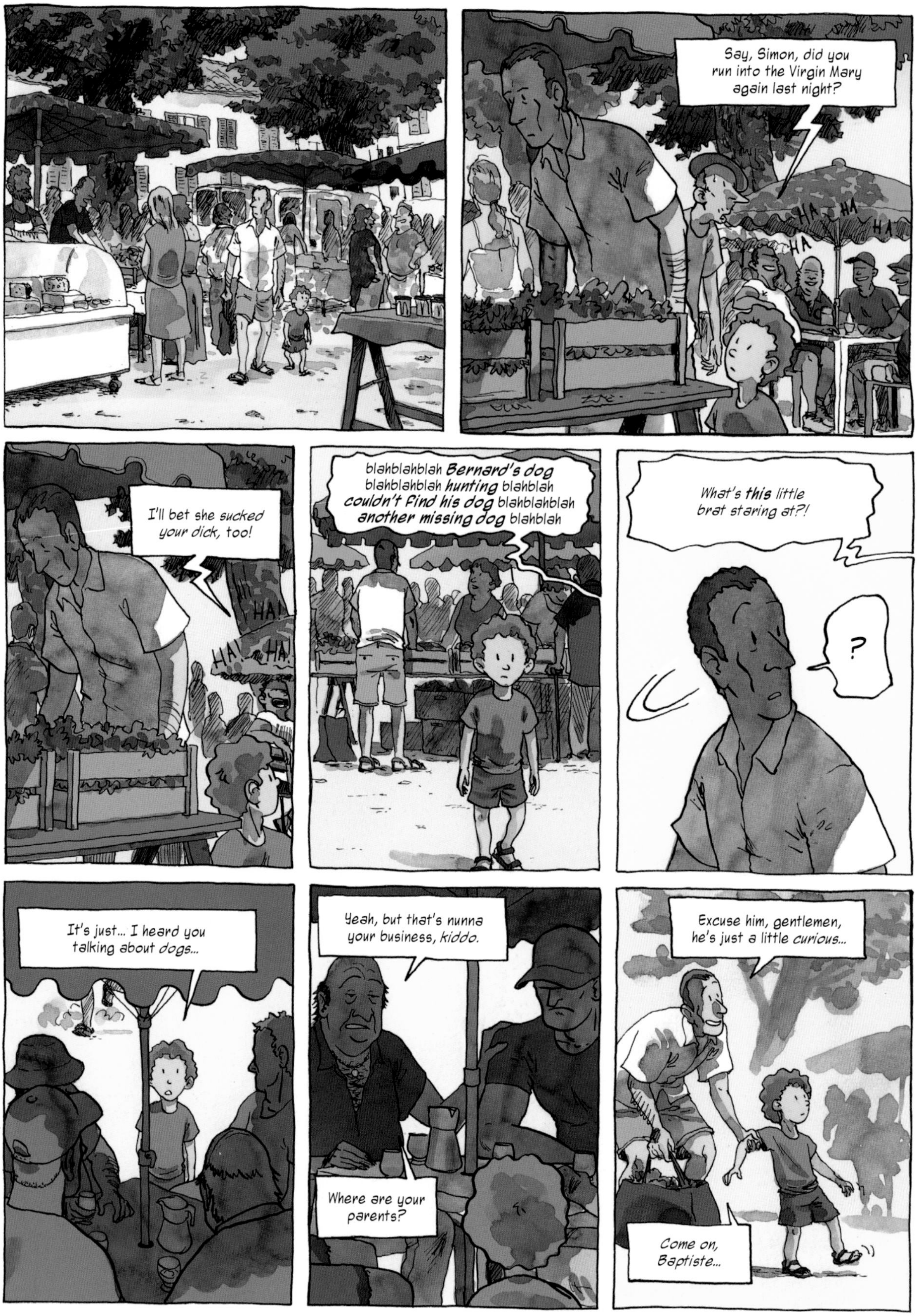
Say, Simon, did you run into the Virgin Mary again last night?
HA HA HA HA
I'll bet she sucked your dick, too!
HA! HA! HA!
blahblahblah Bernard's dog blahblahblah hunting blahblah couldn't find his dog blahblahblah another missing dog blahblah
What's this little brat staring at?!
?
It's just... I heard you talking about dogs...
Yeah, but that's nunna your business, kiddo.
Where are your parents?
Excuse him, gentlemen, he's just a little curious...
Come on, Baptiste...

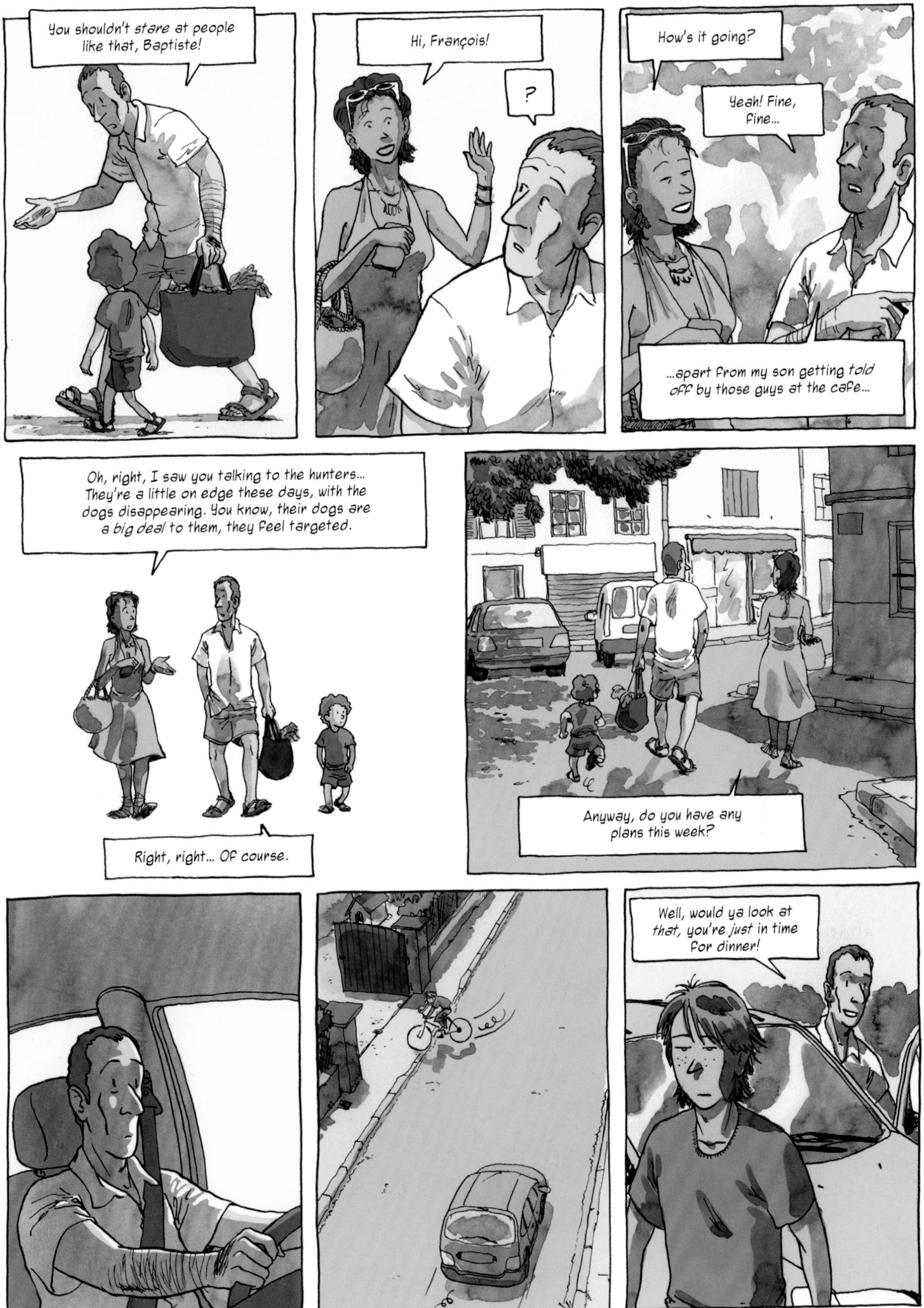
You shouldn't *stare* at people like that, Baptiste!
Hi, François!
?
How's it going?
Yeah! Fine, fine...
...apart from my son getting *told off* by those guys at the cafe...
Oh, right, I saw you talking to the hunters... They're a little on edge these days, with the dogs disappearing. You know, their dogs are a *big deal* to them, they feel targeted.
Right, right... Of course.
Anyway, do you have any plans this week?
Well, would ya look at *that*, you're *just* in time for dinner!

...who beat the Toulouse team four to zero. In other news, it seems like murder may be the cause behind the case of the disappearing dogs...

Let's hear what Annabelle Roland has to say, she's the veterinarian in charge of the autopsies...

"The remains found in the stomachs show that they have definitely been poisoned, probably with meatballs...

"Some bodies nevertheless have no traces of poison... These are perhaps accidents that have nothing to do with our case." Well, that's it for today's news. And now, it's time for Valerie and her "oldies"...

CLIC

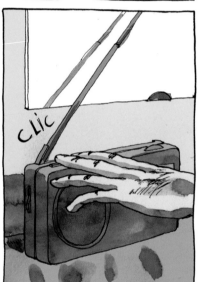

Fiiiisshhhhhhhhh

Sssssshhhhhhhhhhhh

58

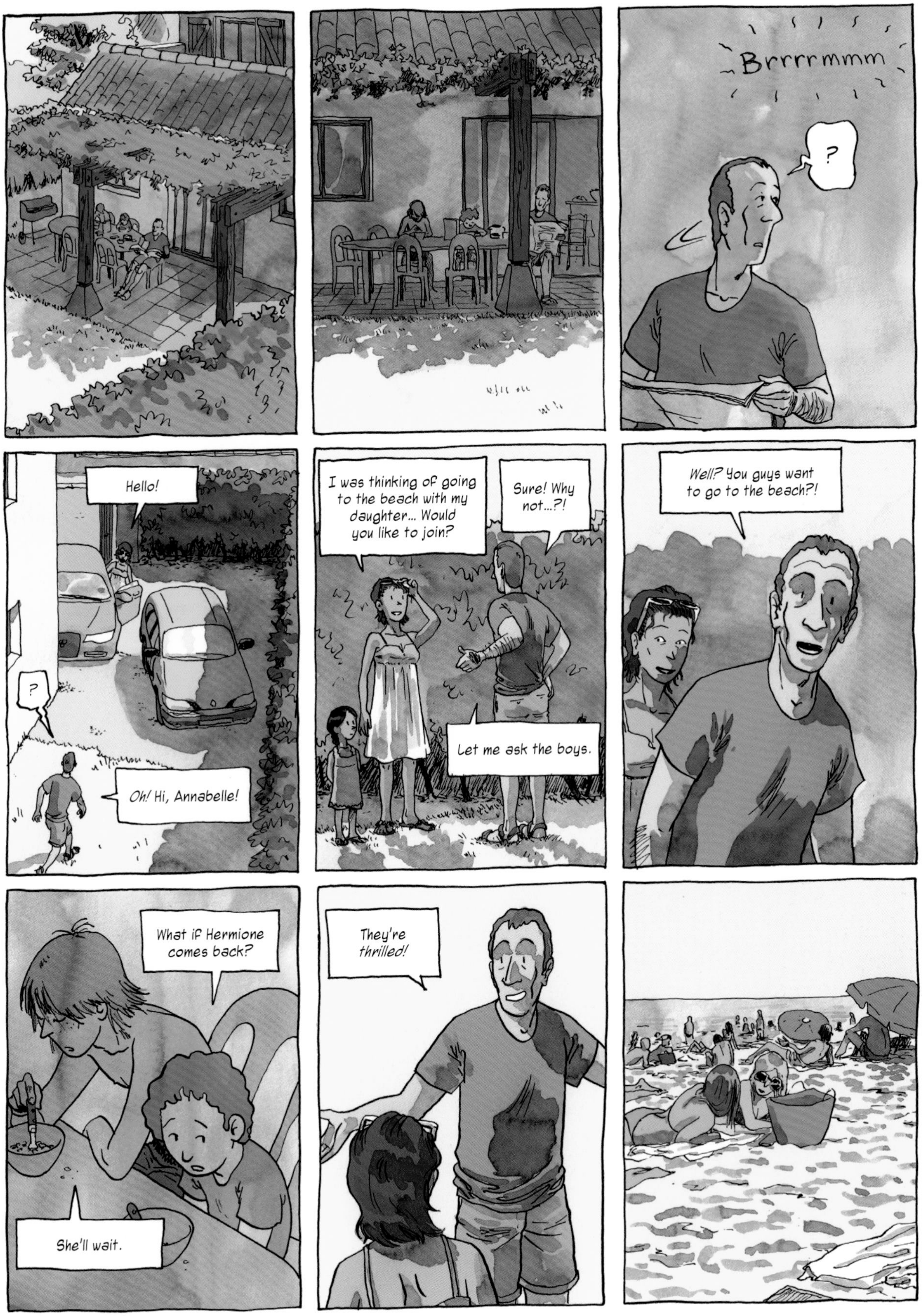
Brrrrmmm
?
Hello!
?
Oh! Hi, Annabelle!
I was thinking of going to the beach with my daughter... Would you like to join?
Sure! Why not...?!
Let me ask the boys.
Well? You guys want to go to the beach?!
What if Hermione comes back?
She'll wait.
They're thrilled!

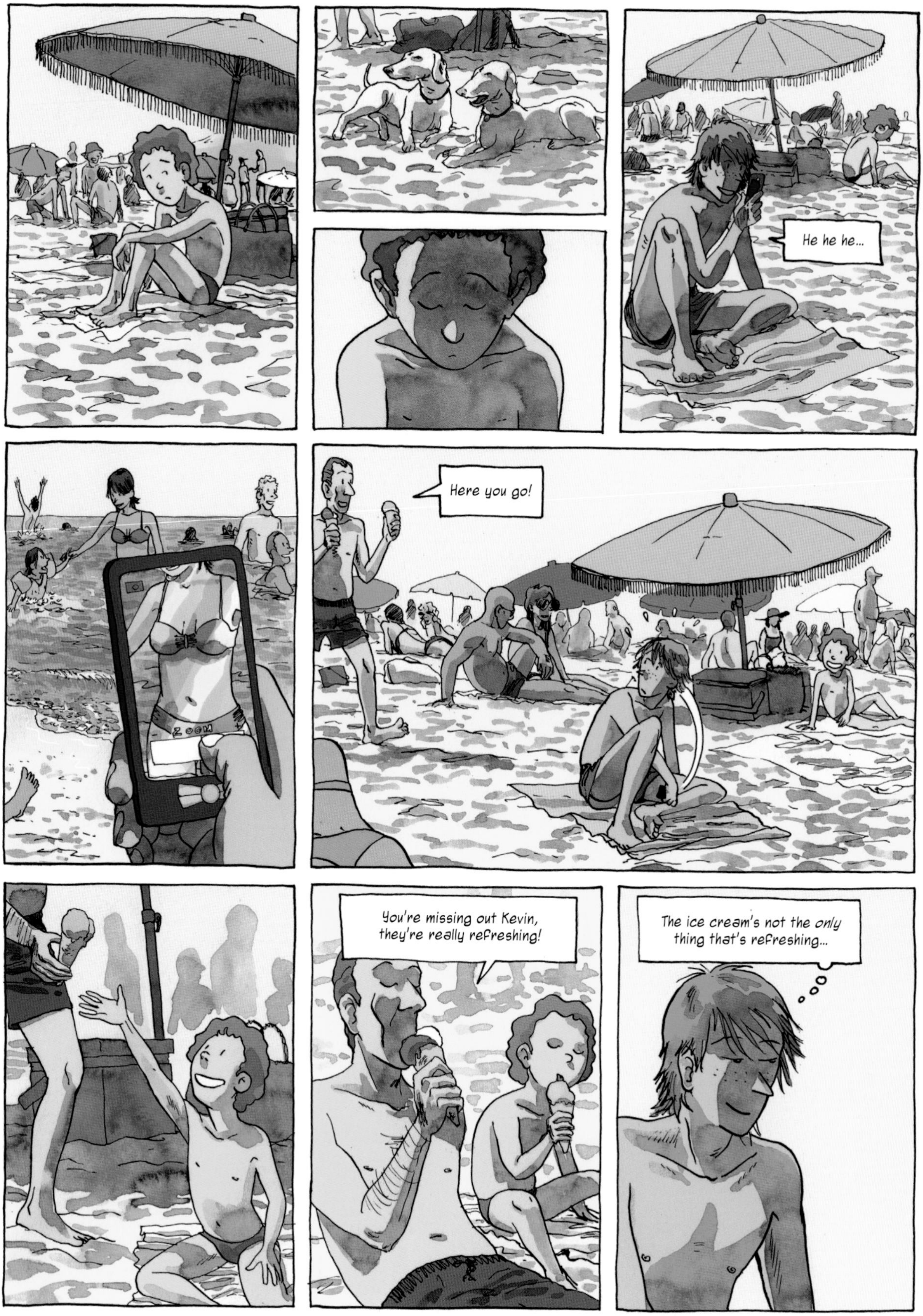

He he he...
ZOOM
Here you go!
You're missing out Kevin, they're really refreshing!
The ice cream's not the *only* thing that's refreshing...

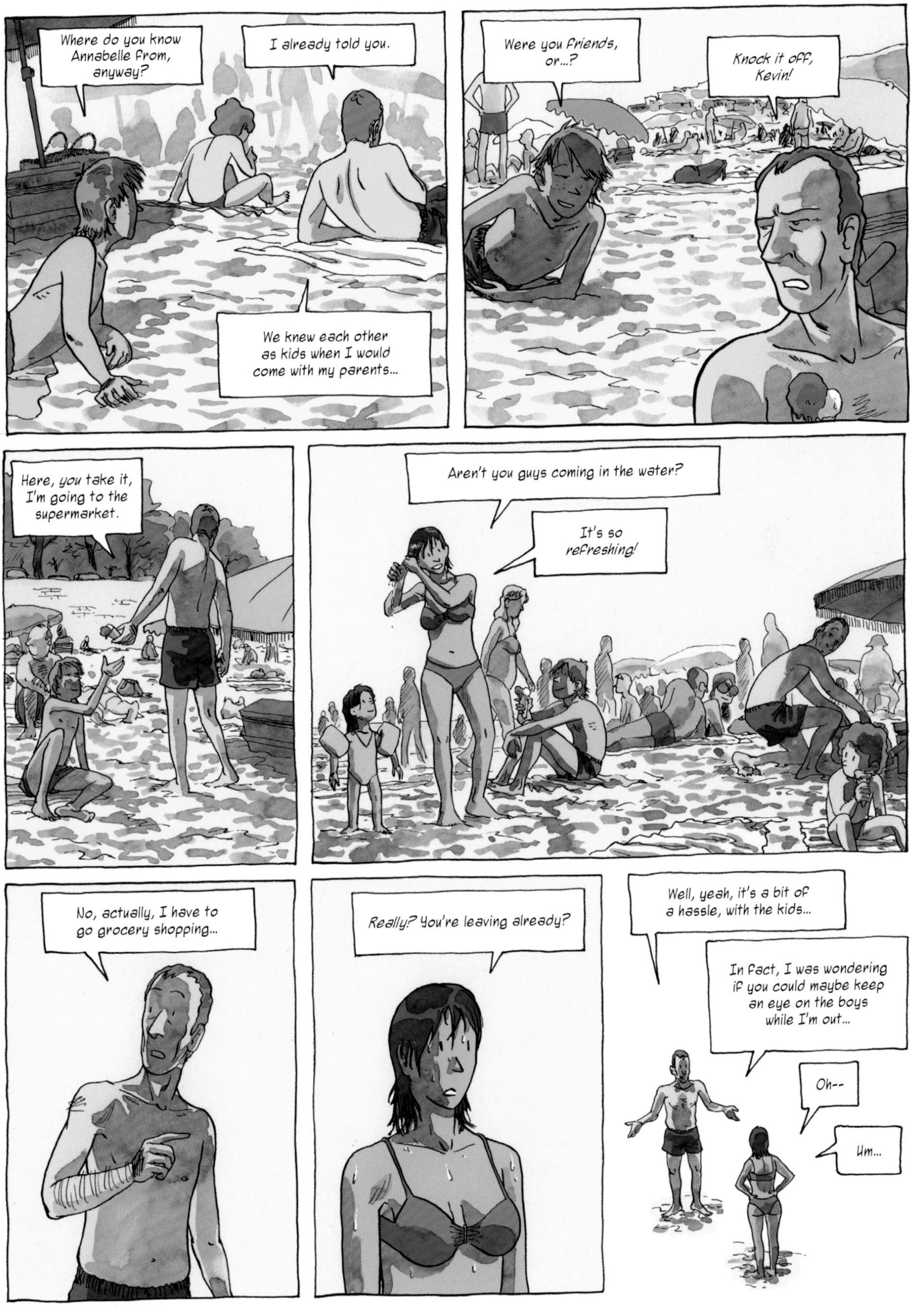
Where do you know Annabelle from, anyway?
I already told you.
We knew each other as kids when I would come with my parents...
Were you friends, or...?
Knock it off, Kevin!
Here, you take it, I'm going to the supermarket.
Aren't you guys coming in the water?
It's so refreshing!
No, actually, I have to go grocery shopping...
Really? You're leaving already?
Well, yeah, it's a bit of a hassle, with the kids...
In fact, I was wondering if you could maybe keep an eye on the boys while I'm out...
Oh--
Um...

Yeah, sure... Well, if you're going to the supermarket, do you think you could get me a few things? I'll make a list.

Uh... Yeah, of course...

Thanks, I really appreciate it...

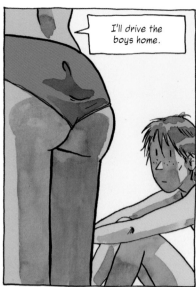

I'll drive the boys home.

You call *this* vacation...? I can't even have a moment to myself.

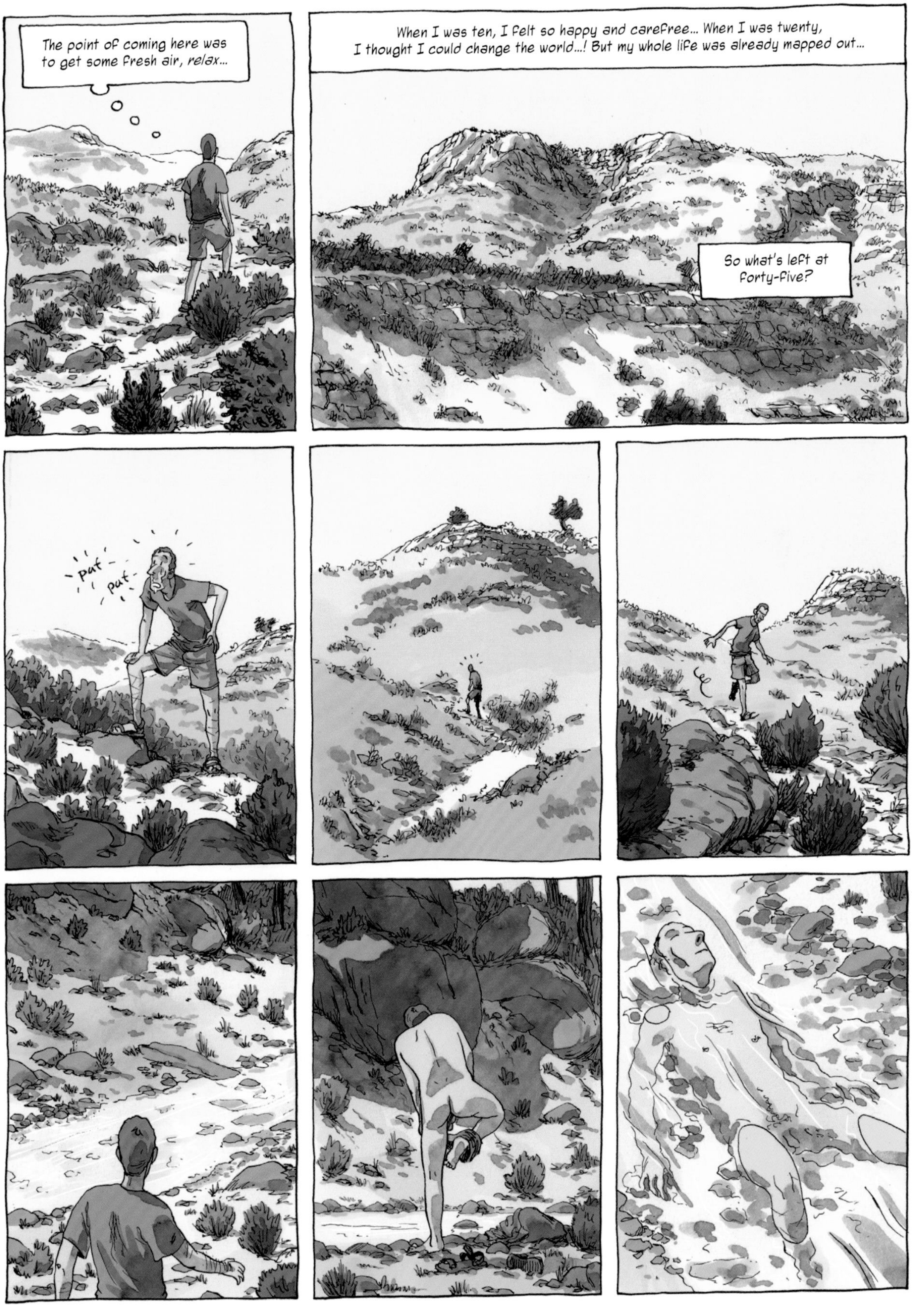
The point of coming here was to get some fresh air, *relax*...
When I was ten, I felt so happy and carefree... When I was twenty, I thought I could change the world...! But my whole life was already mapped out...
So what's left at forty-five?
pat
pat

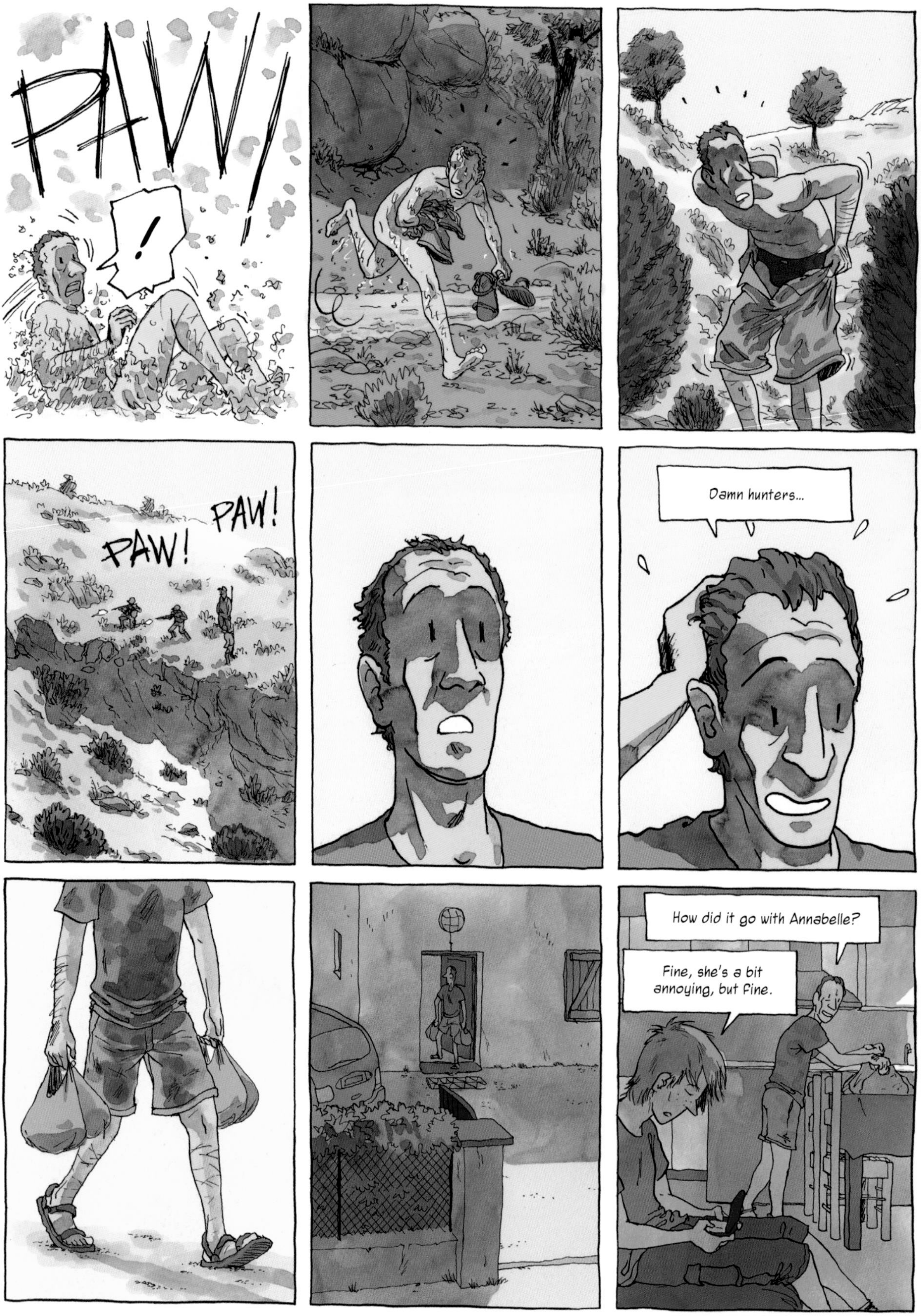
PAW!
!
PAW!
PAW!
Damn hunters...
How did it go with Annabelle?
Fine, she's a bit annoying, but fine.

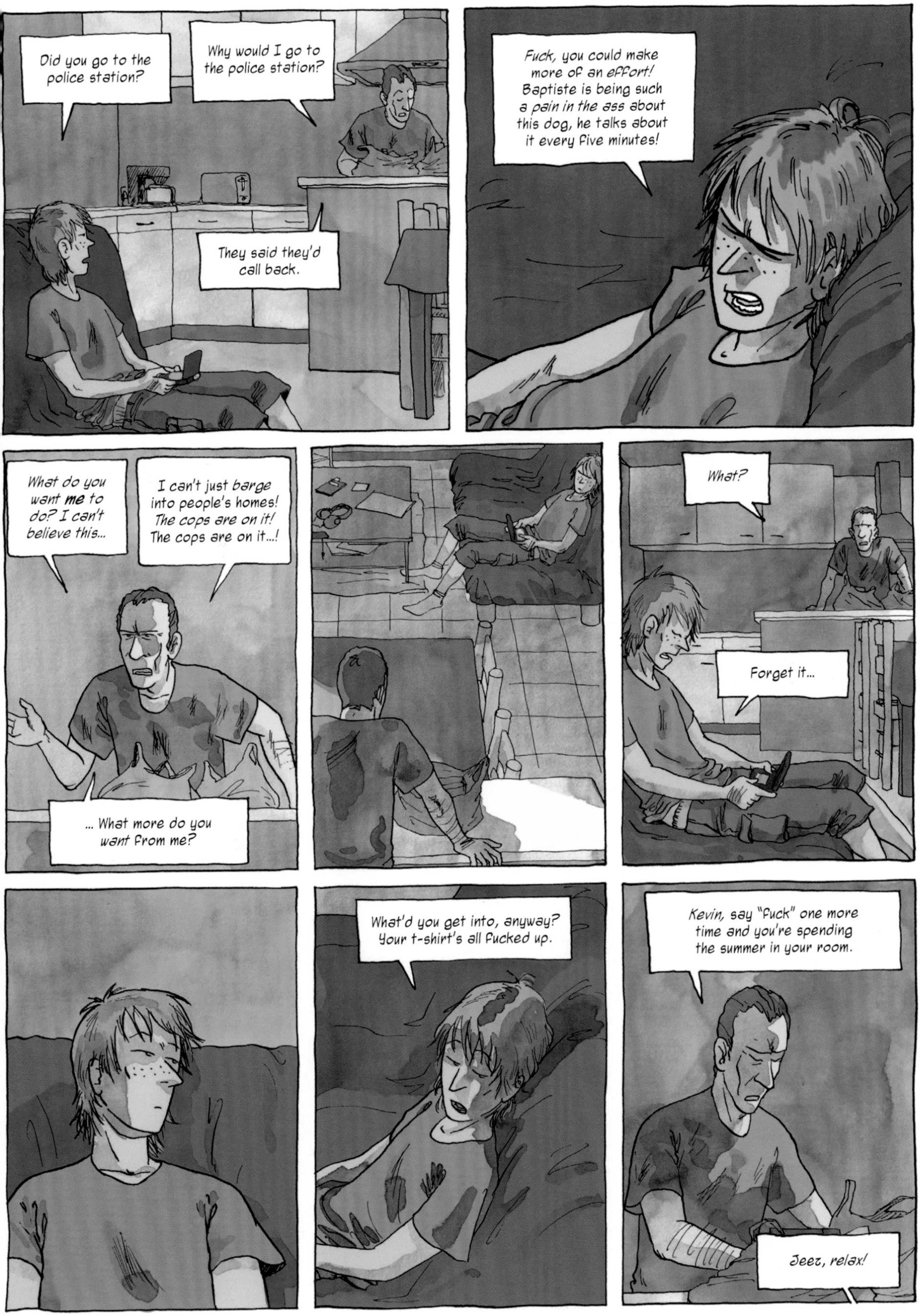
Did you go to the police station?
Why would I go to the police station?
They said they'd call back.
Fuck, you could make more of an effort! Baptiste is being such a pain in the ass about this dog, he talks about it every five minutes!
What do you want me to do? I can't believe this...
I can't just barge into people's homes! The cops are on it! The cops are on it...!
... What more do you want from me?
What?
Forget it...
What'd you get into, anyway? Your t-shirt's all fucked up.
Kevin, say "fuck" one more time and you're spending the summer in your room.
Jeez, relax!

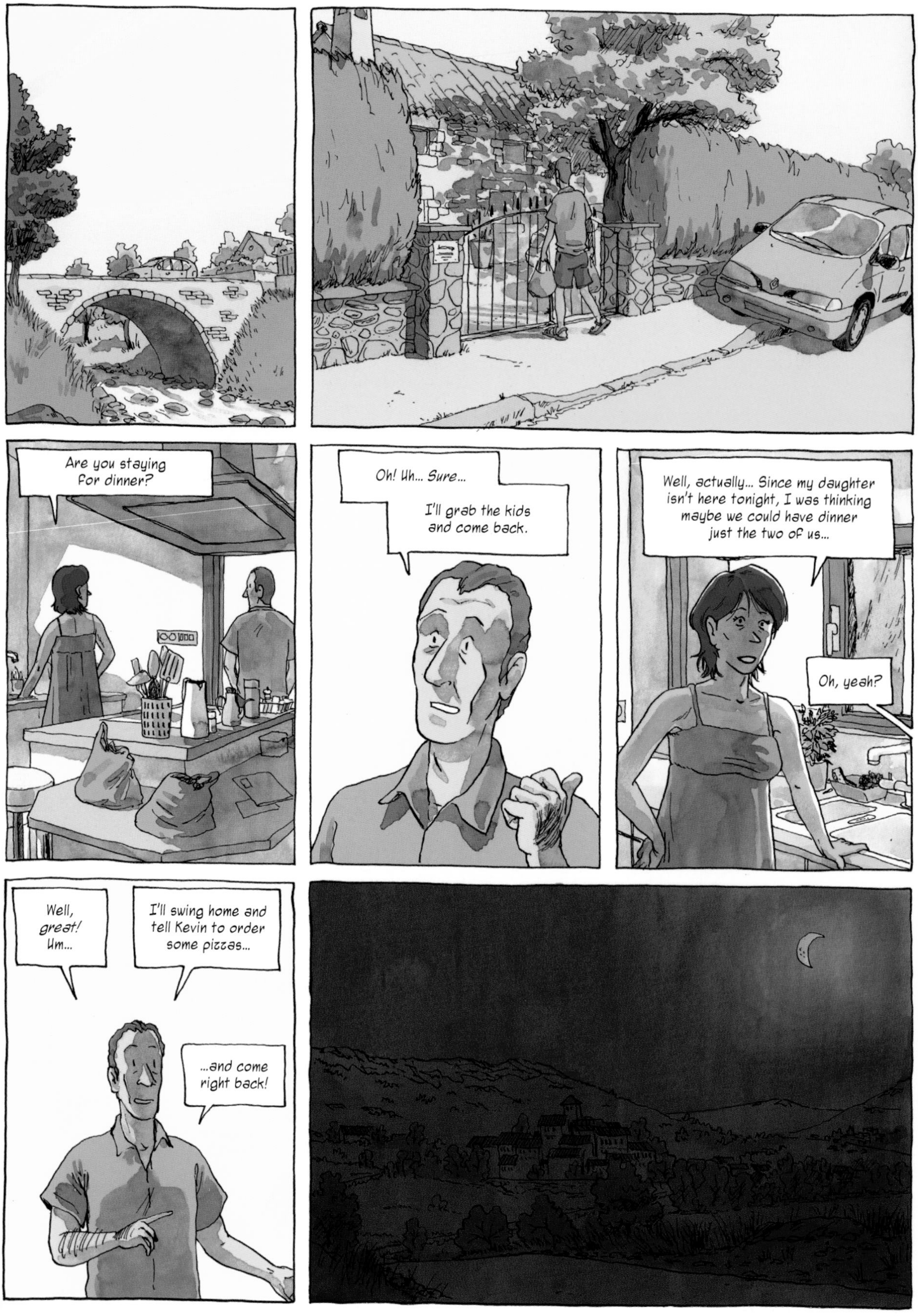
Are you staying for dinner?
Oh! Uh... Sure...
I'll grab the kids and come back.
Well, actually... Since my daughter isn't here tonight, I was thinking maybe we could have dinner just the two of us...
Oh, yeah?
Well, great! Um...
I'll swing home and tell Kevin to order some pizzas...
...and come right back!

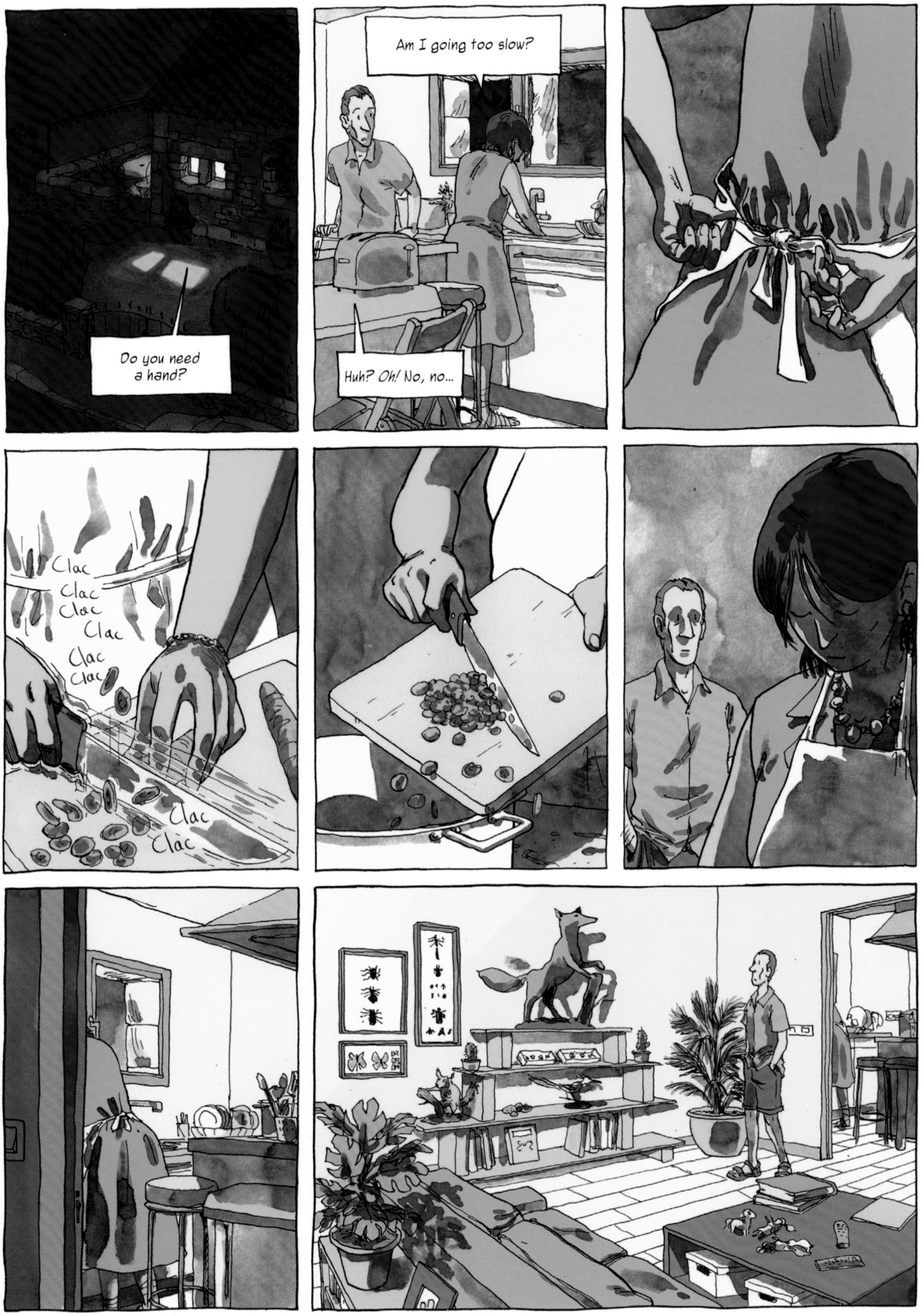
Do you need
a hand?
Am I going too slow?
Huh? Oh! No, no...
Clac
Clac
Clac
Clac
Clac
Clac
Clac
Clac

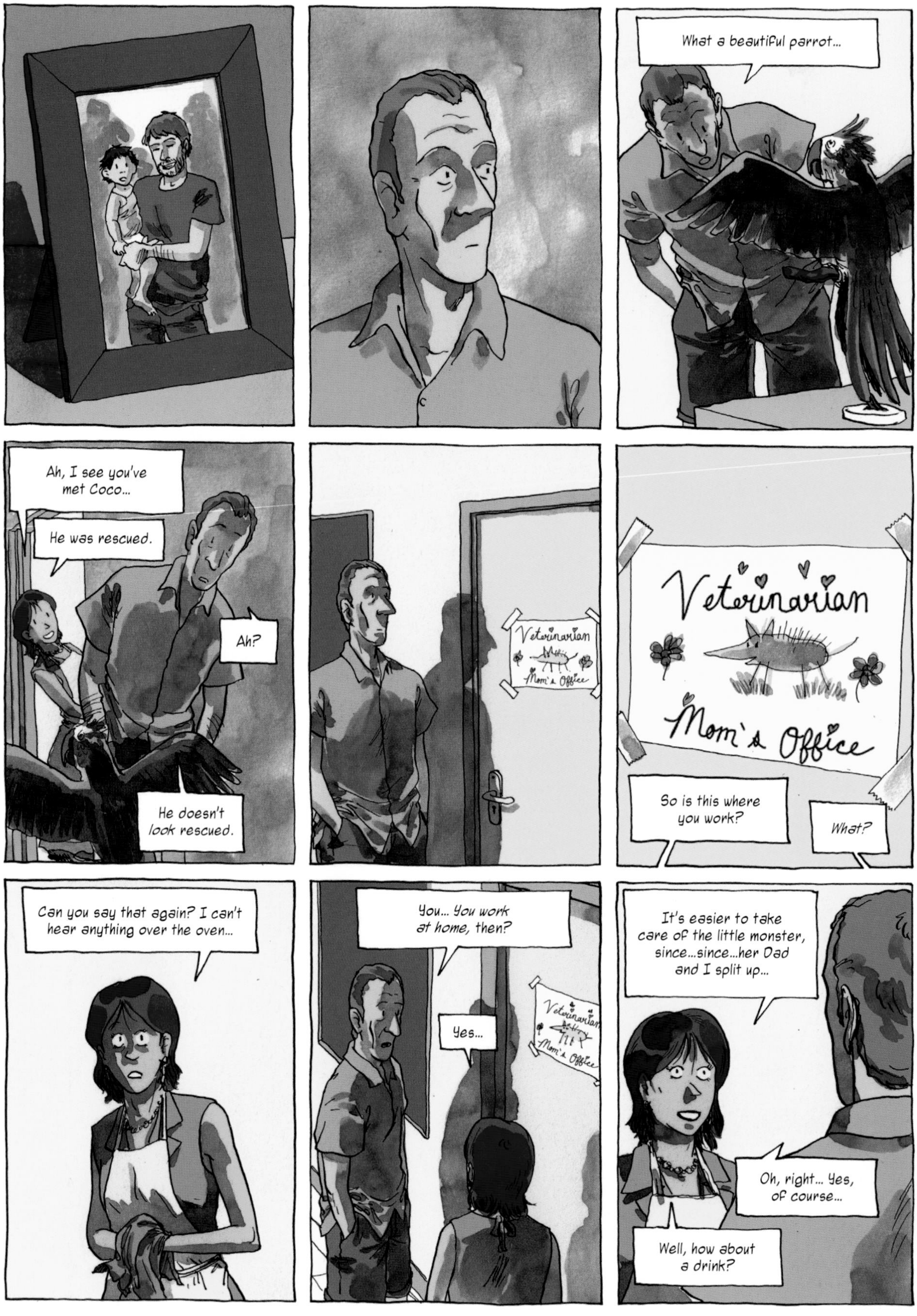
What a beautiful parrot...
Ah, I see you've met Coco...
He was rescued.
Ah?
He doesn't look rescued.
Veterinarian
Mom's Office
Veterinarian
Mom's Office
So is this where you work?
What?
Can you say that again? I can't hear anything over the oven...
You... You work at home, then?
Yes...
Veterinarian
Mom's Office
It's easier to take care of the little monster, since...since...her Dad and I split up...
Oh, right... Yes, of course...
Well, how about a drink?

She's pretty...

Almost as pretty as before...

...then again, her smile has faded...

She looks good in that dress.

She has a nice voice...

But she looks sad...
You can see it in her eyes...

The eyes always give you away.

By the way, where was your *parrot* rescued from?

Oh, it's a strange story...

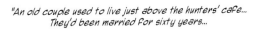

"An old couple used to live just above the hunters' cafe...
They'd been married for sixty years...

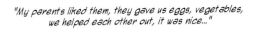

"My parents liked them, they gave us eggs, vegetables, we helped each other out, it was nice..."

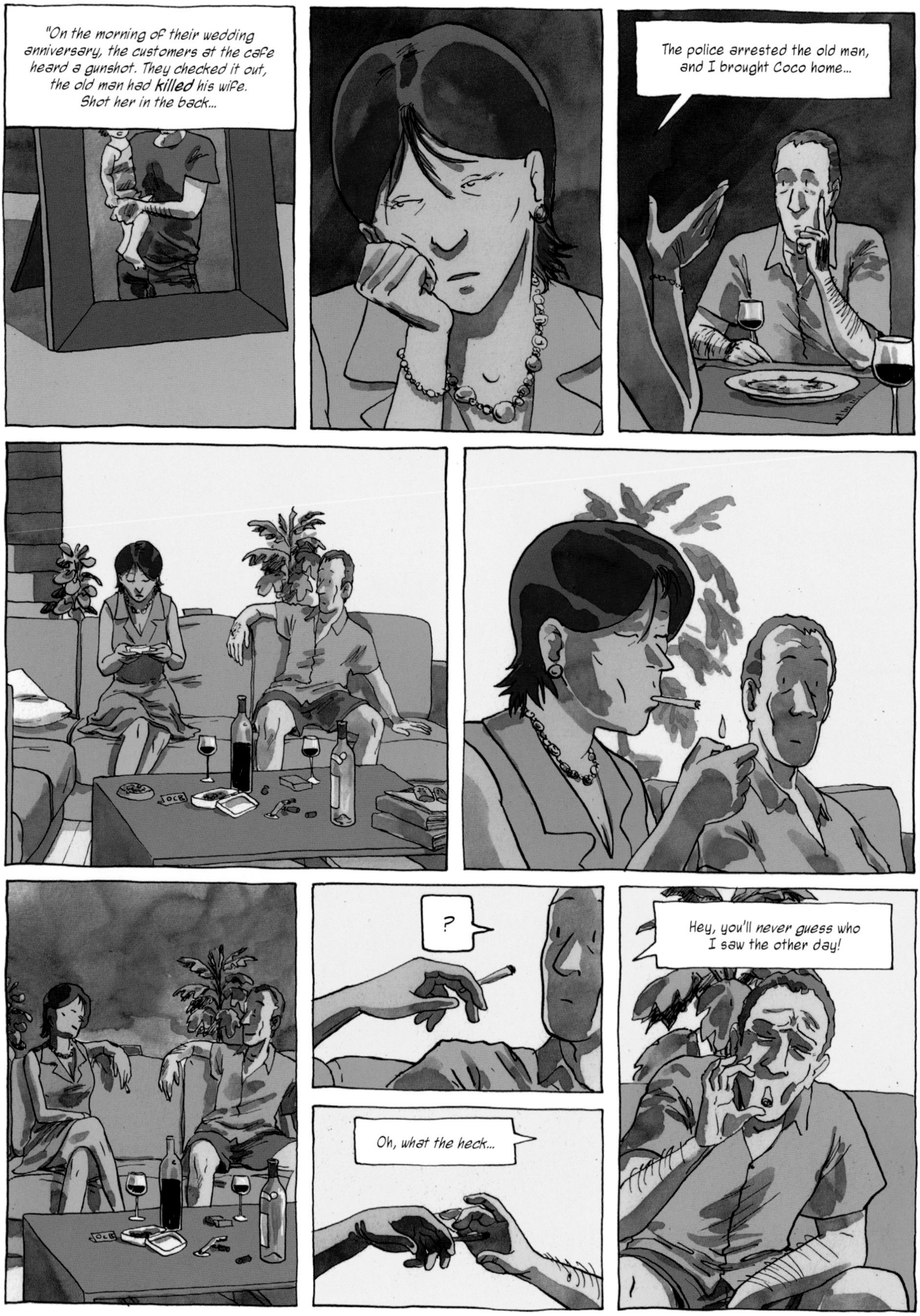
"On the morning of their wedding anniversary, the customers at the cafe heard a gunshot. They checked it out, the old man had **killed** his wife. Shot her in the back...
The police arrested the old man, and I brought Coco home...
OCB
?
Oh, what the heck...
Hey, you'll *never guess* who I saw the other day!

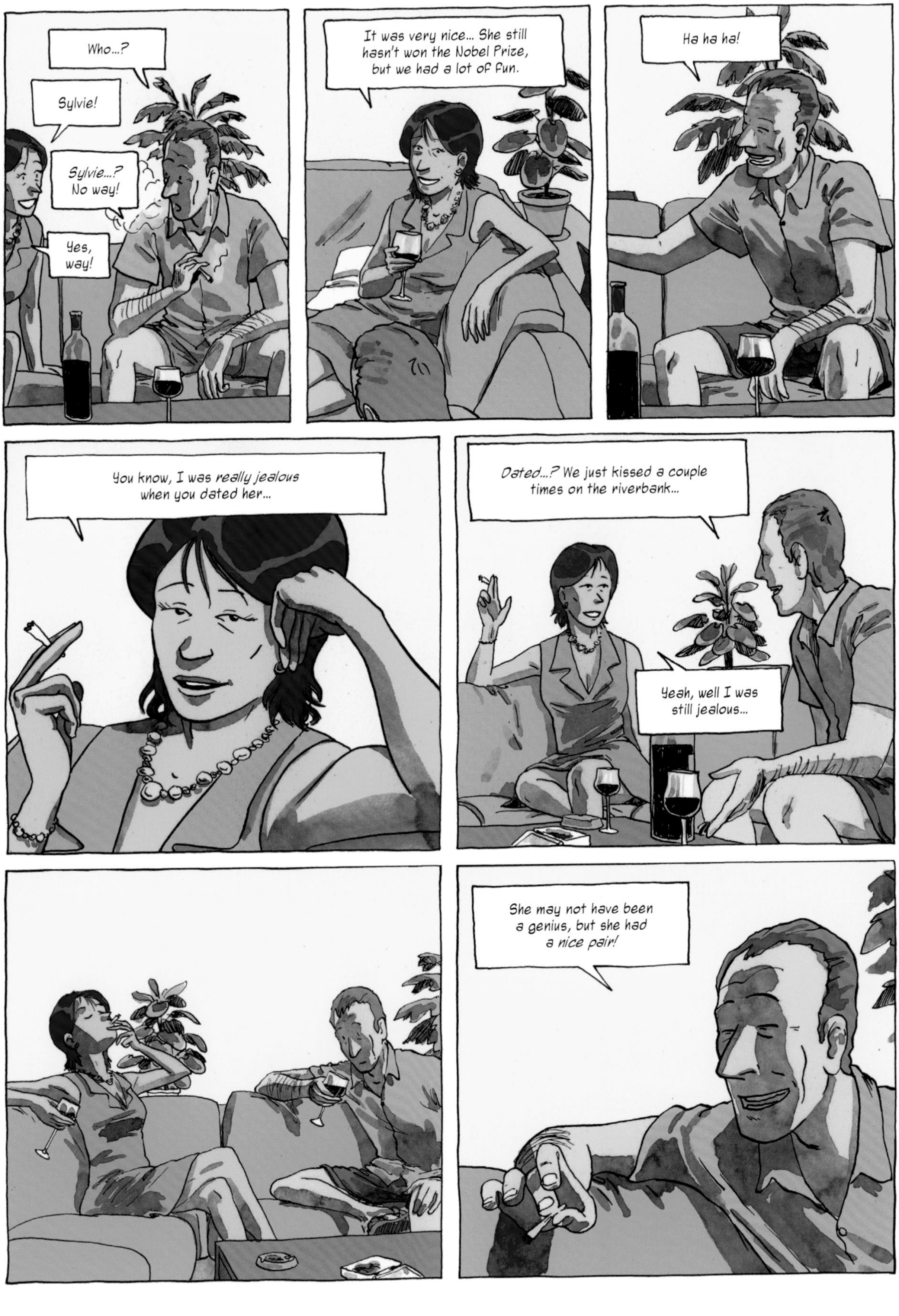
Who...?
Sylvie!
Sylvie...? No way!
Yes, way!
It was very nice... She still hasn't won the Nobel Prize, but we had a lot of fun.
Ha ha ha!
You know, I was *really jealous* when you dated her...
Dated...? We just kissed a couple times on the riverbank...
Yeah, well I was still jealous...
She may not have been a genius, but she had a *nice pair!*

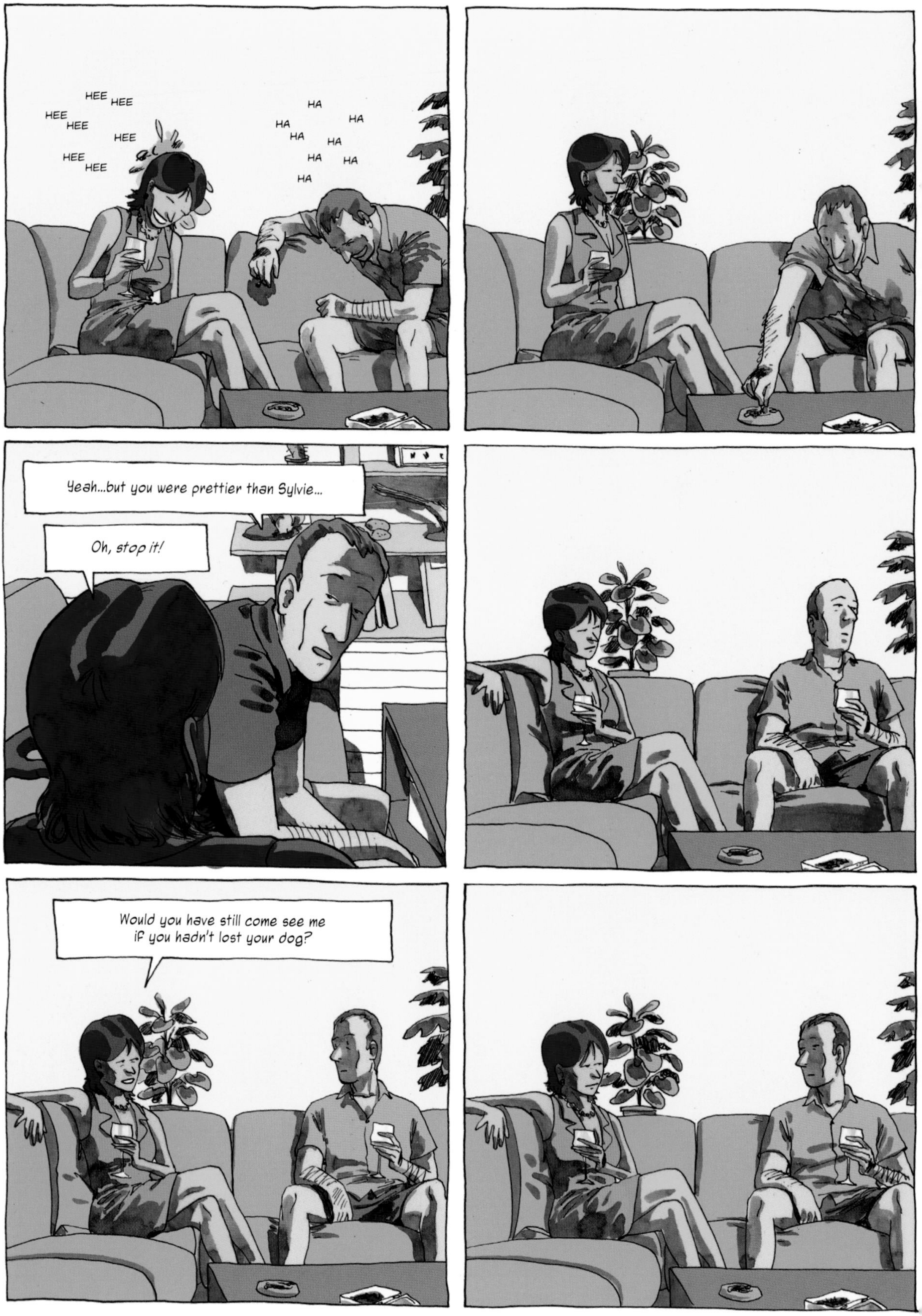
HEE HEE
HEE
HEE
HEE
HEE
HEE
HA
HA
HA
HA
HA
HA
HA
HA
Yeah...but you were prettier than Sylvie...
Oh, stop it!
Would you have still come see me if you hadn't lost your dog?

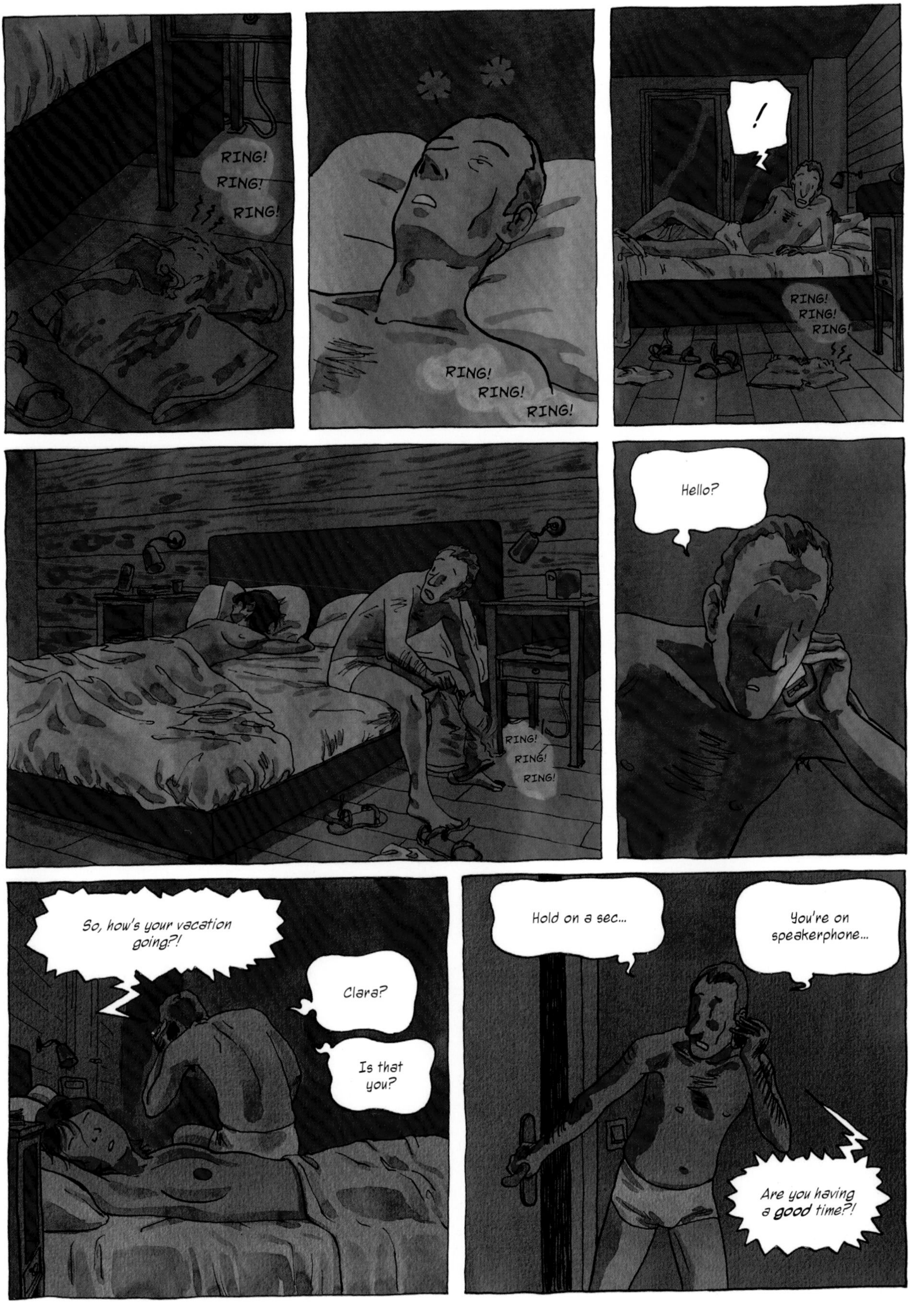
RING! RING! RING!
RING! RING! RING!
!
RING! RING! RING!
RING! RING! RING!
Hello?
So, how's your vacation going?!
Clara?
Is that you?
Hold on a sec...
You're on speakerphone...
Are you having a **good** time?!

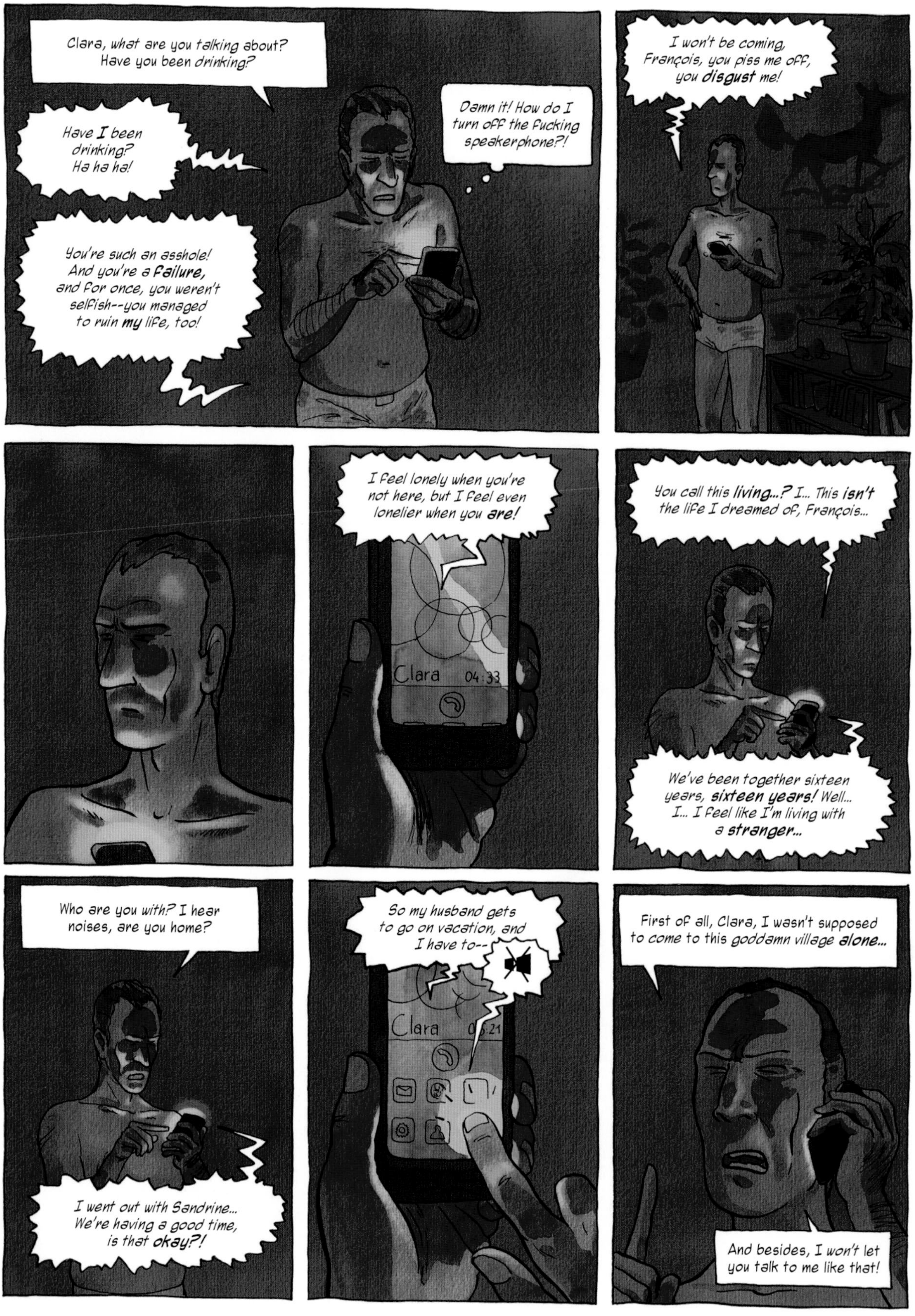
Clara, what are you talking about? Have you been drinking?
Have I been drinking? Ha ha ha!
You're such an asshole! And you're a failure, and for once, you weren't selfish--you managed to ruin my life, too!
Damn it! How do I turn off the fucking speakerphone?!
I won't be coming, François, you piss me off, you disgust me!
I feel lonely when you're not here, but I feel even lonelier when you are!
Clara 04:33
You call this living...? I... This isn't the life I dreamed of, François...
We've been together sixteen years, sixteen years! Well... I... I feel like I'm living with a stranger...
Who are you with? I hear noises, are you home?
I went out with Sandrine... We're having a good time, is that okay?!
So my husband gets to go on vacation, and I have to--
Clara
First of all, Clara, I wasn't supposed to come to this goddamn village alone...
And besides, I won't let you talk to me like that!

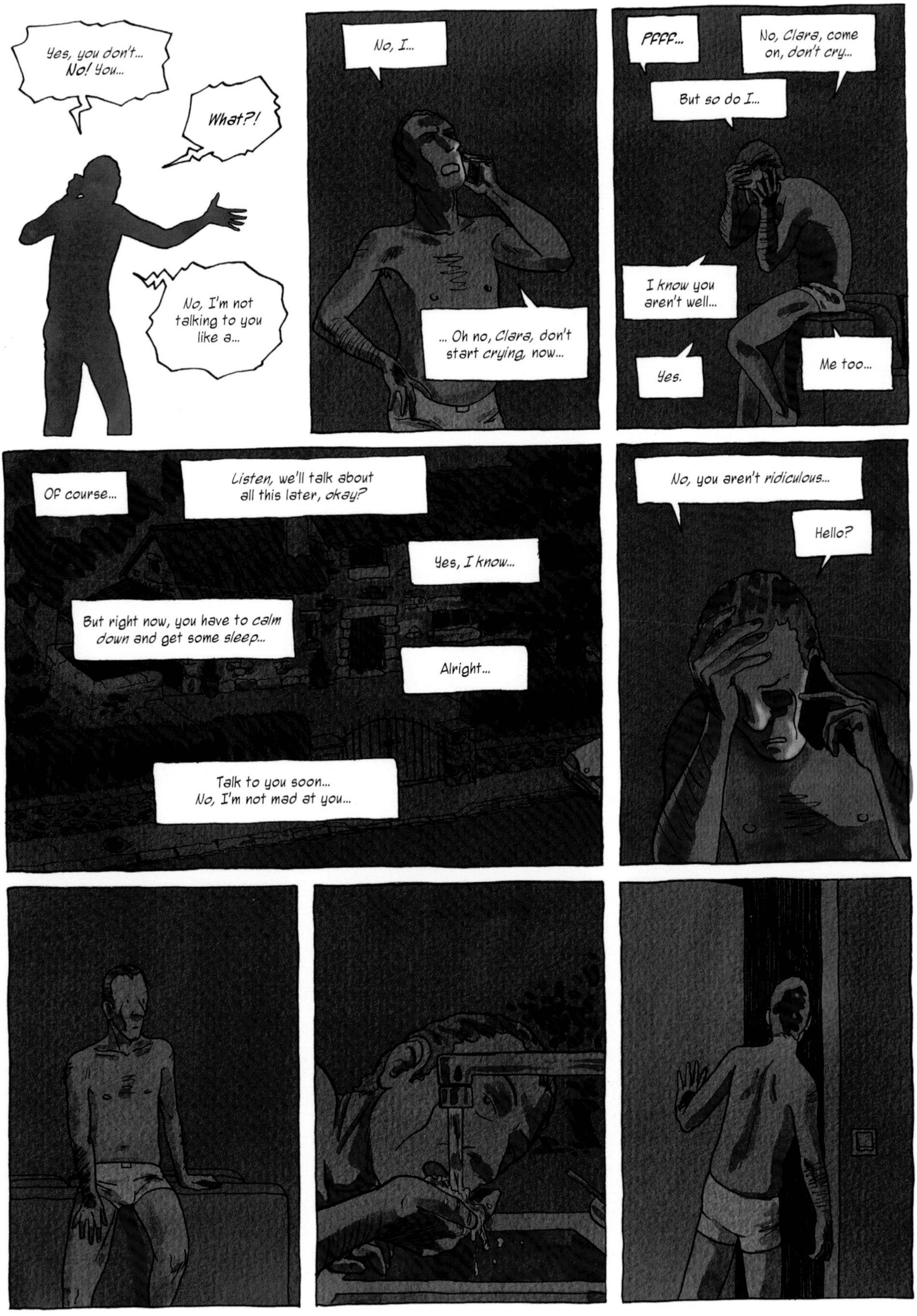
Yes, you don't...
No! You...
What?!
No, I'm not talking to you like a...
No, I...
... Oh no, Clara, don't start crying, now...
PFFF...
No, Clara, come on, don't cry...
But so do I...
I know you aren't well...
Yes.
Me too...
Of course...
Listen, we'll talk about all this later, okay?
Yes, I know...
But right now, you have to calm down and get some sleep...
Alright...
Talk to you soon... No, I'm not mad at you...
No, you aren't ridiculous...
Hello?

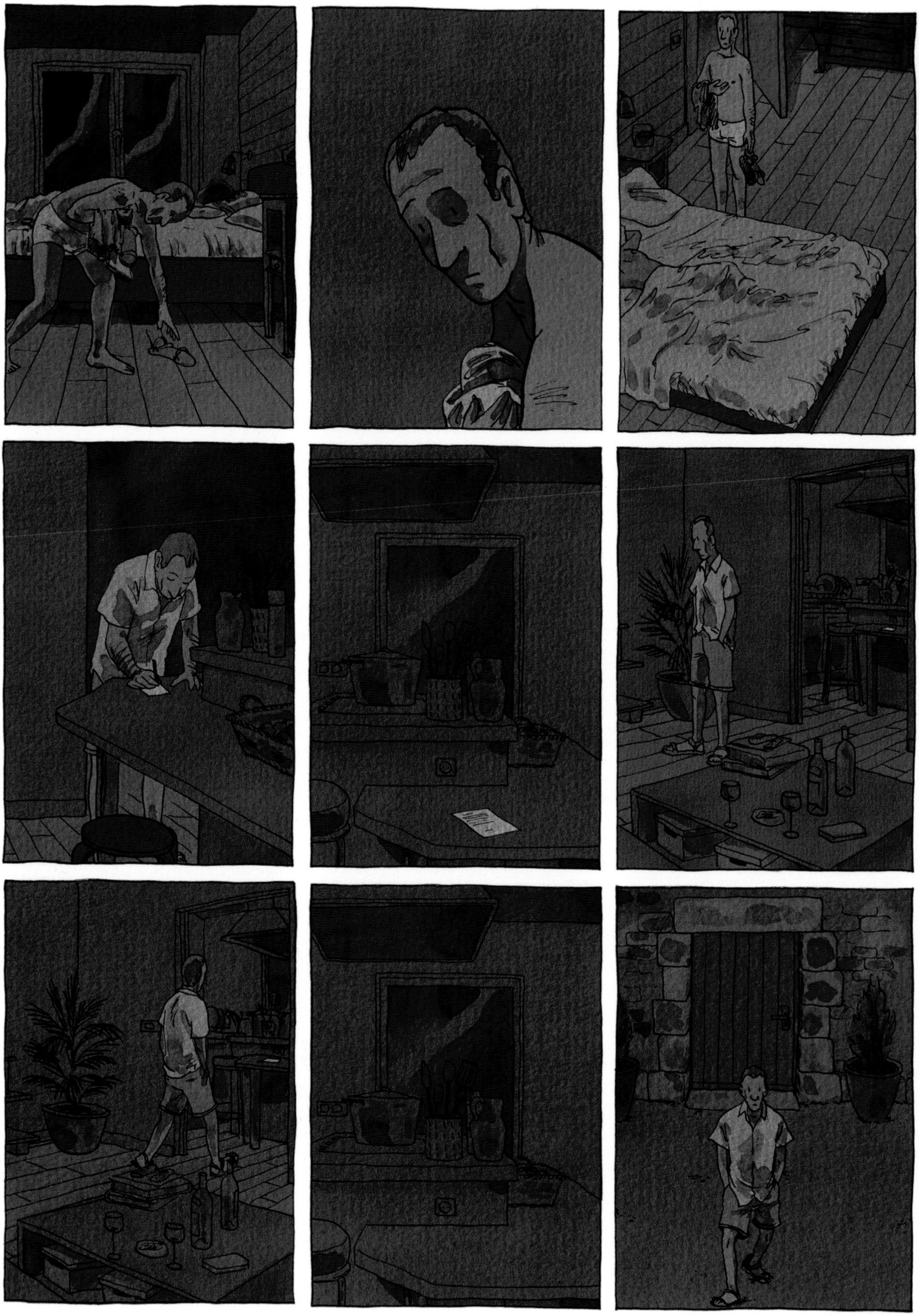

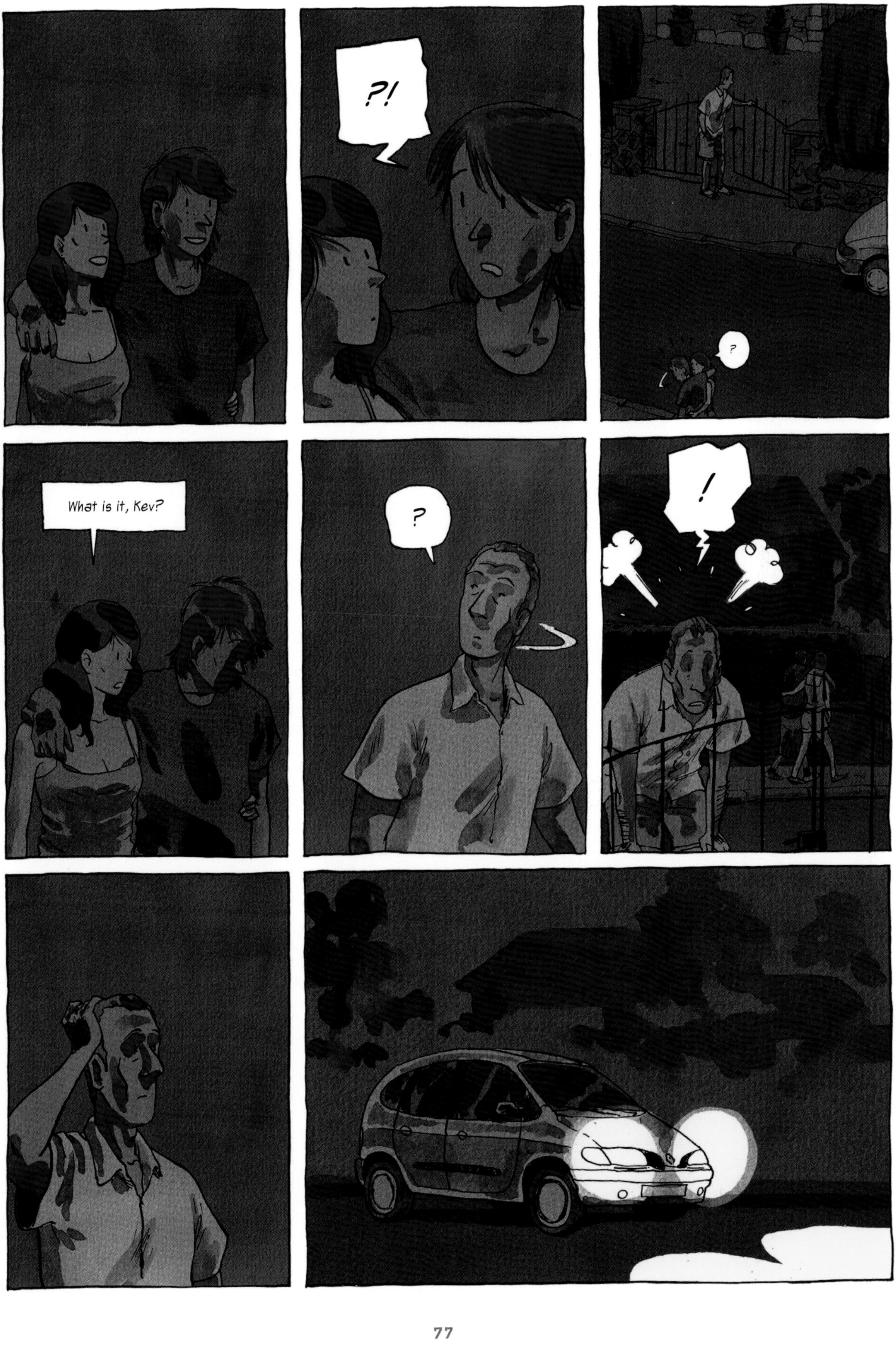
?!
?
What is it, Kev?
?
!

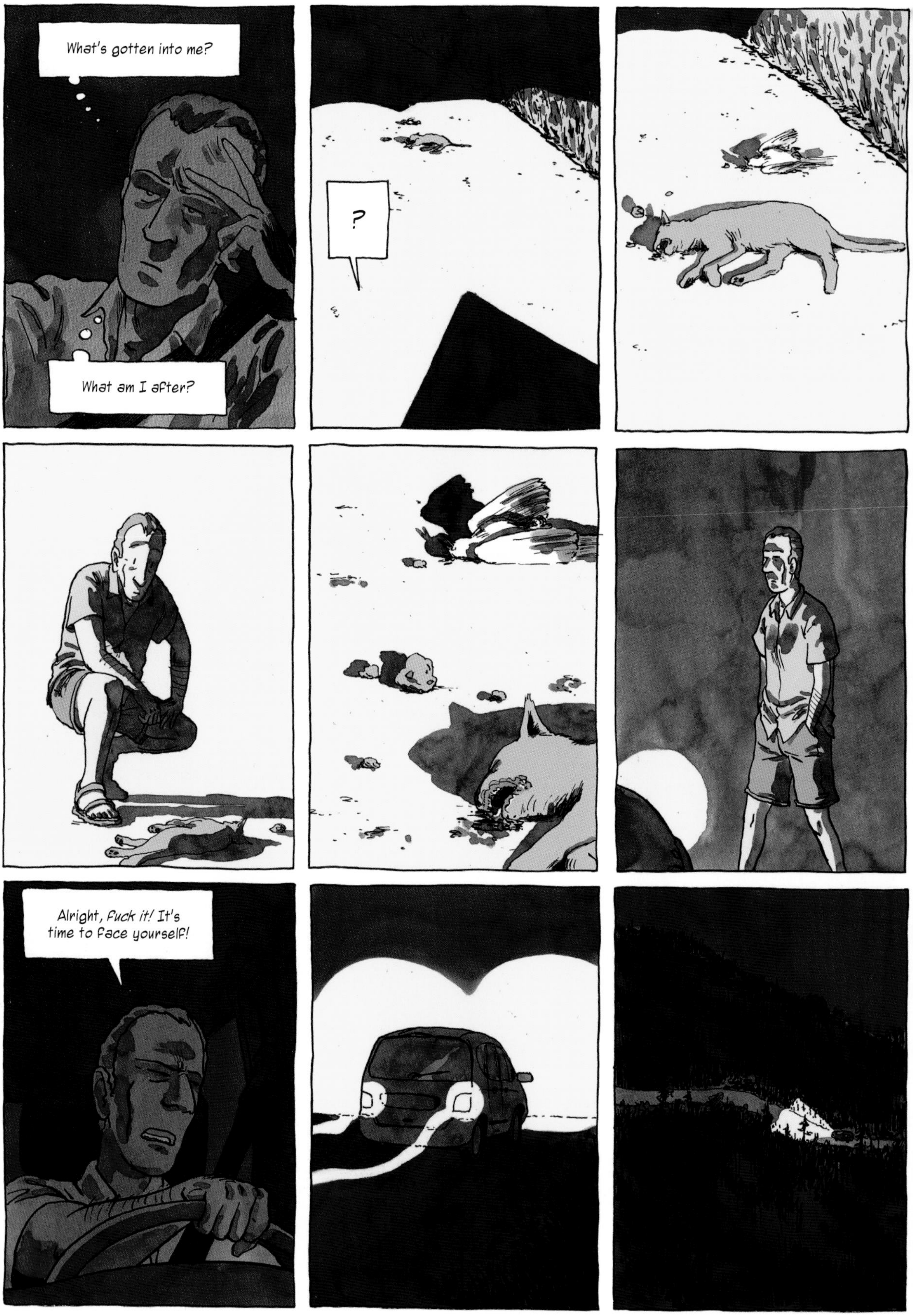
What's gotten into me?
What am I after?
?
Alright, *fuck it!* It's time to face yourself!

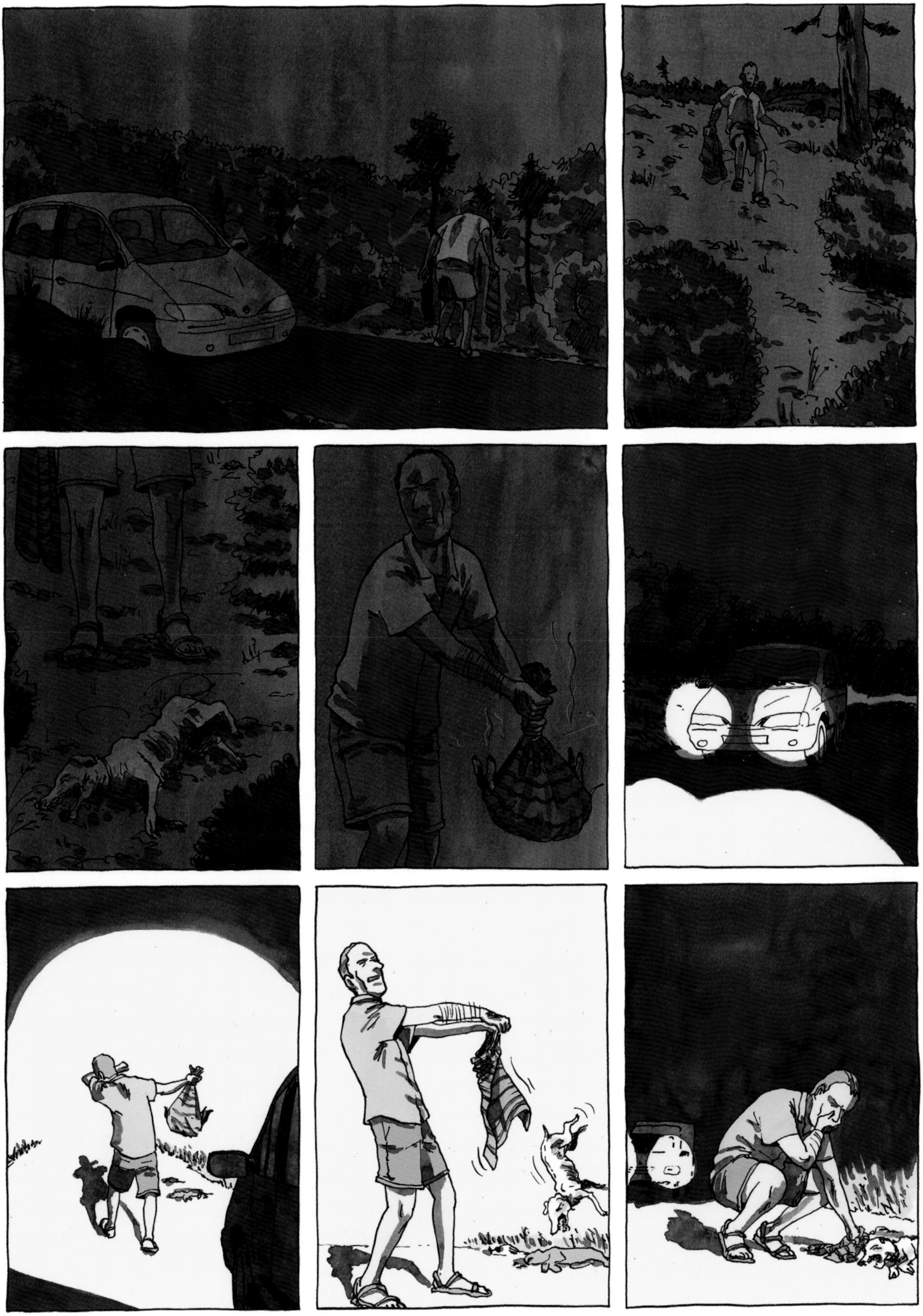

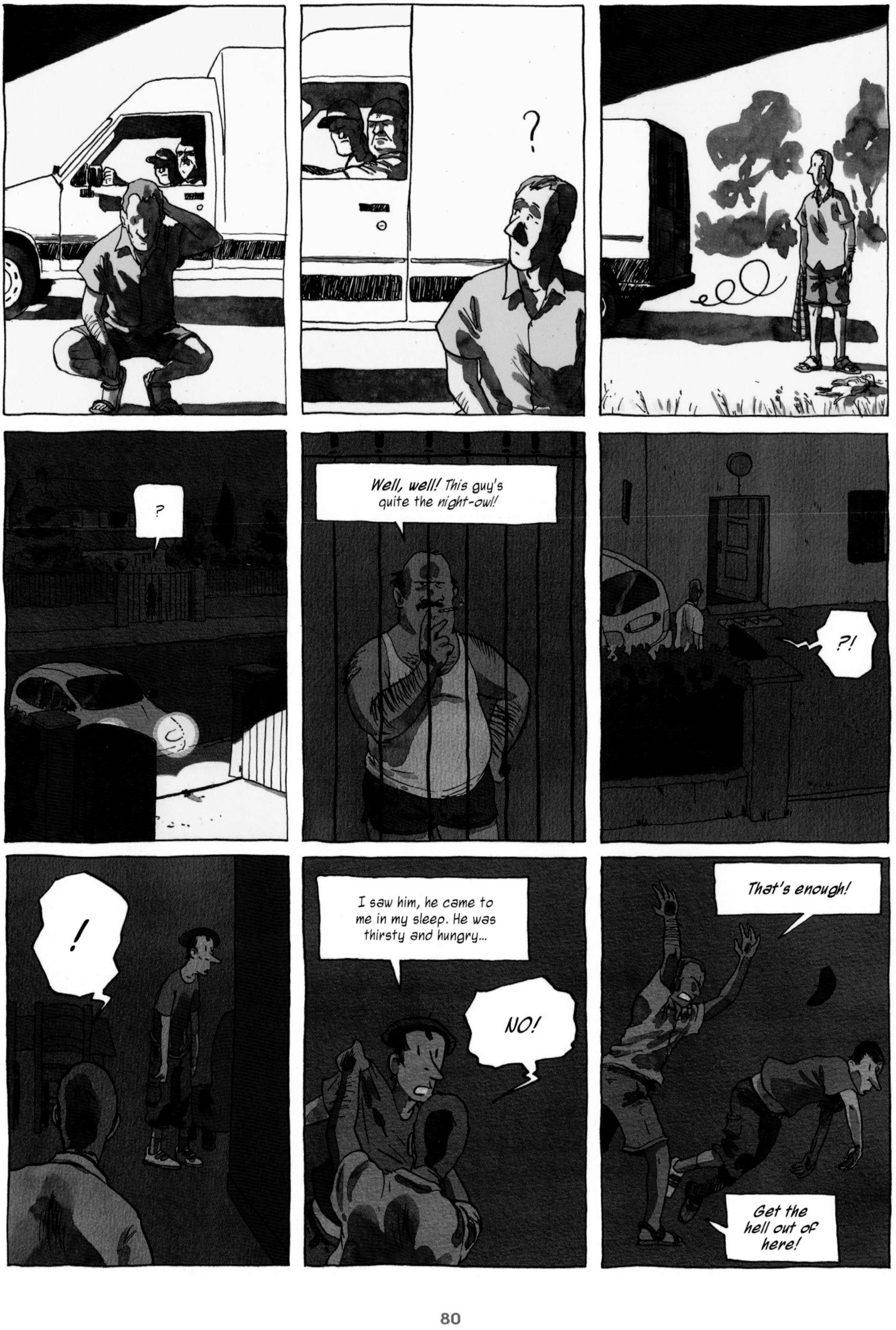
?
?
Well, well! This guy's quite the night-owl!
?!
!
I saw him, he came to me in my sleep. He was thirsty and hungry...
NO!
That's enough!
Get the hell out of here!

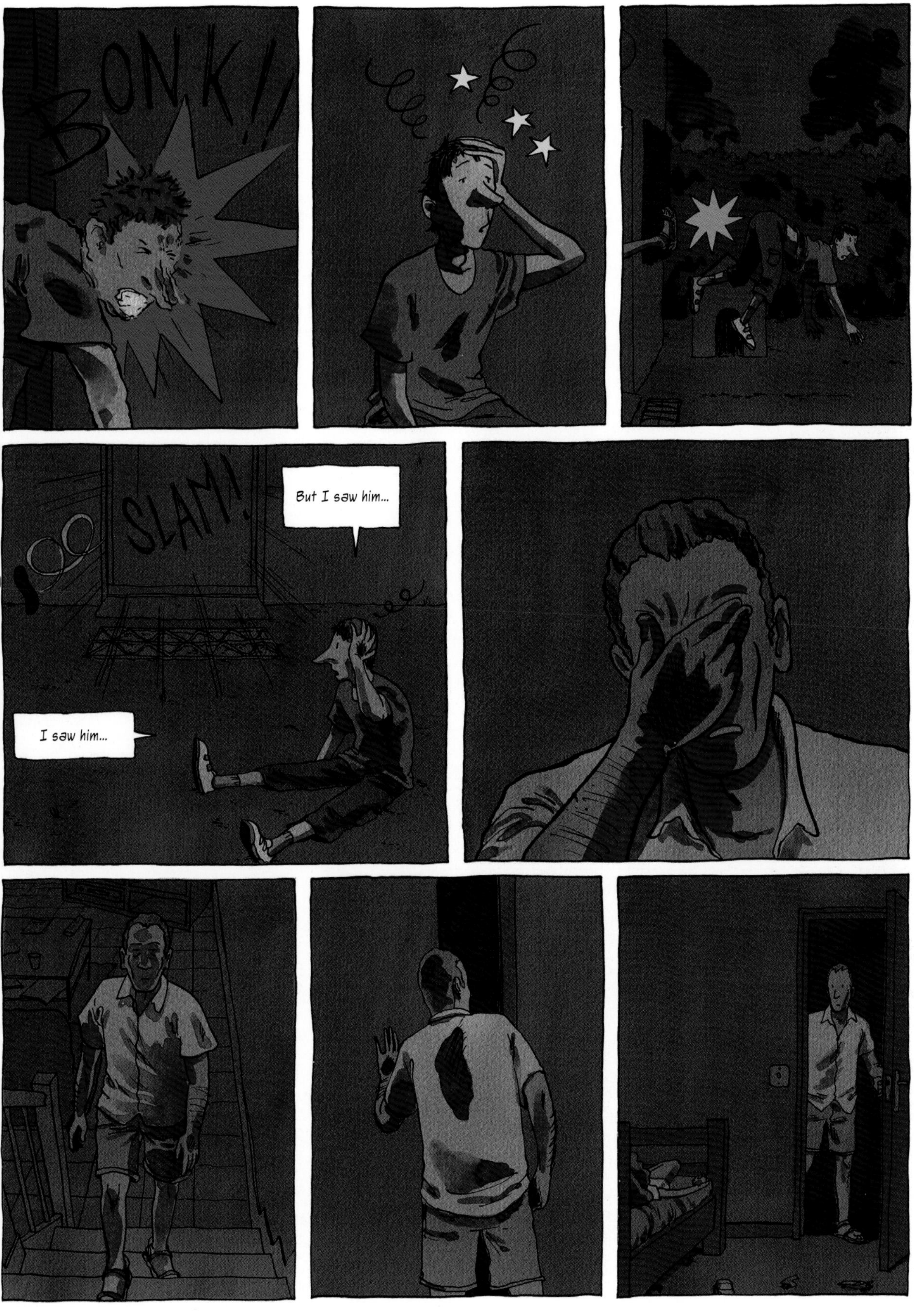
BONK!!
SLAM!
But I saw him...
I saw him...

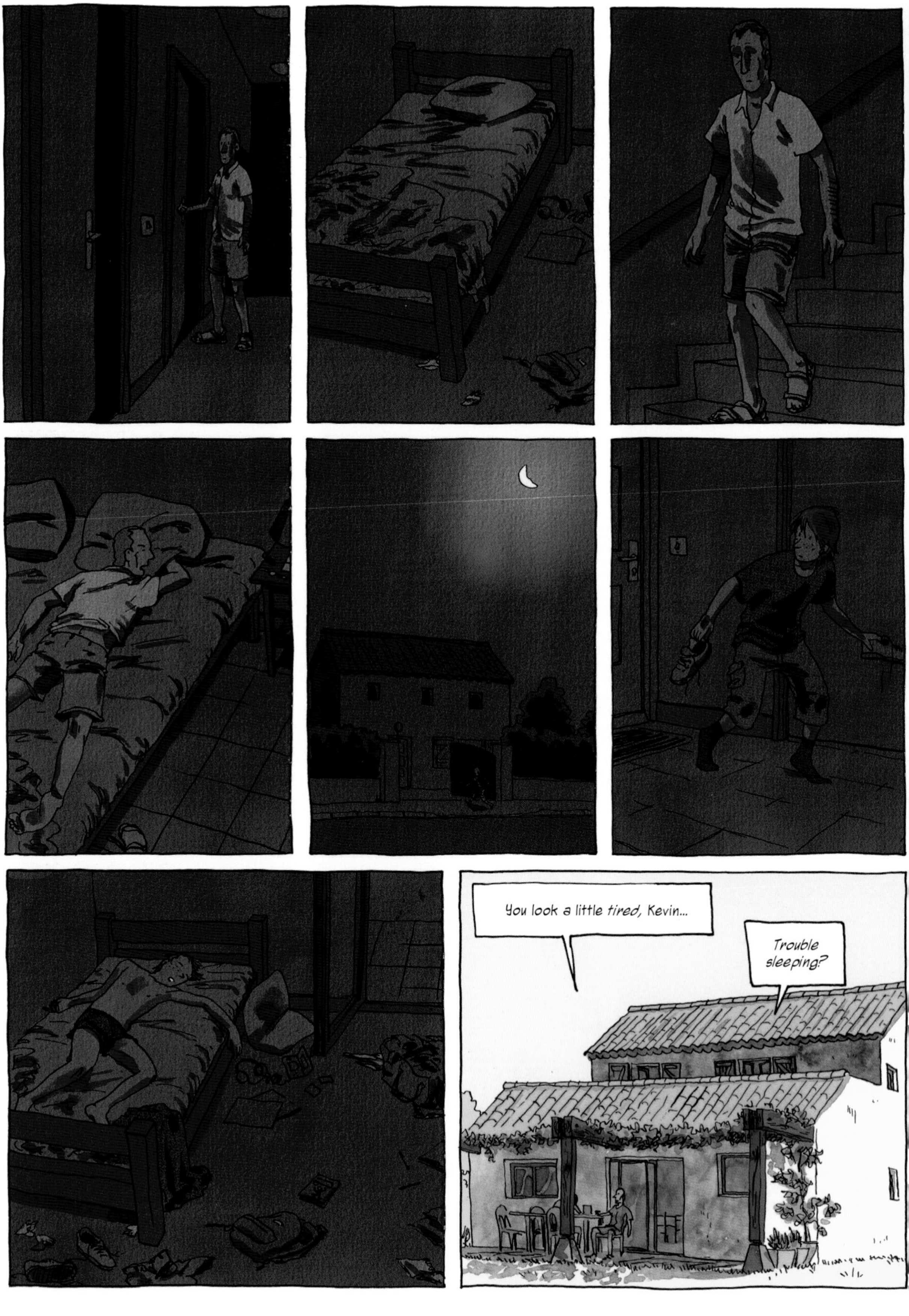
You look a little *tired*, Kevin...
Trouble sleeping?

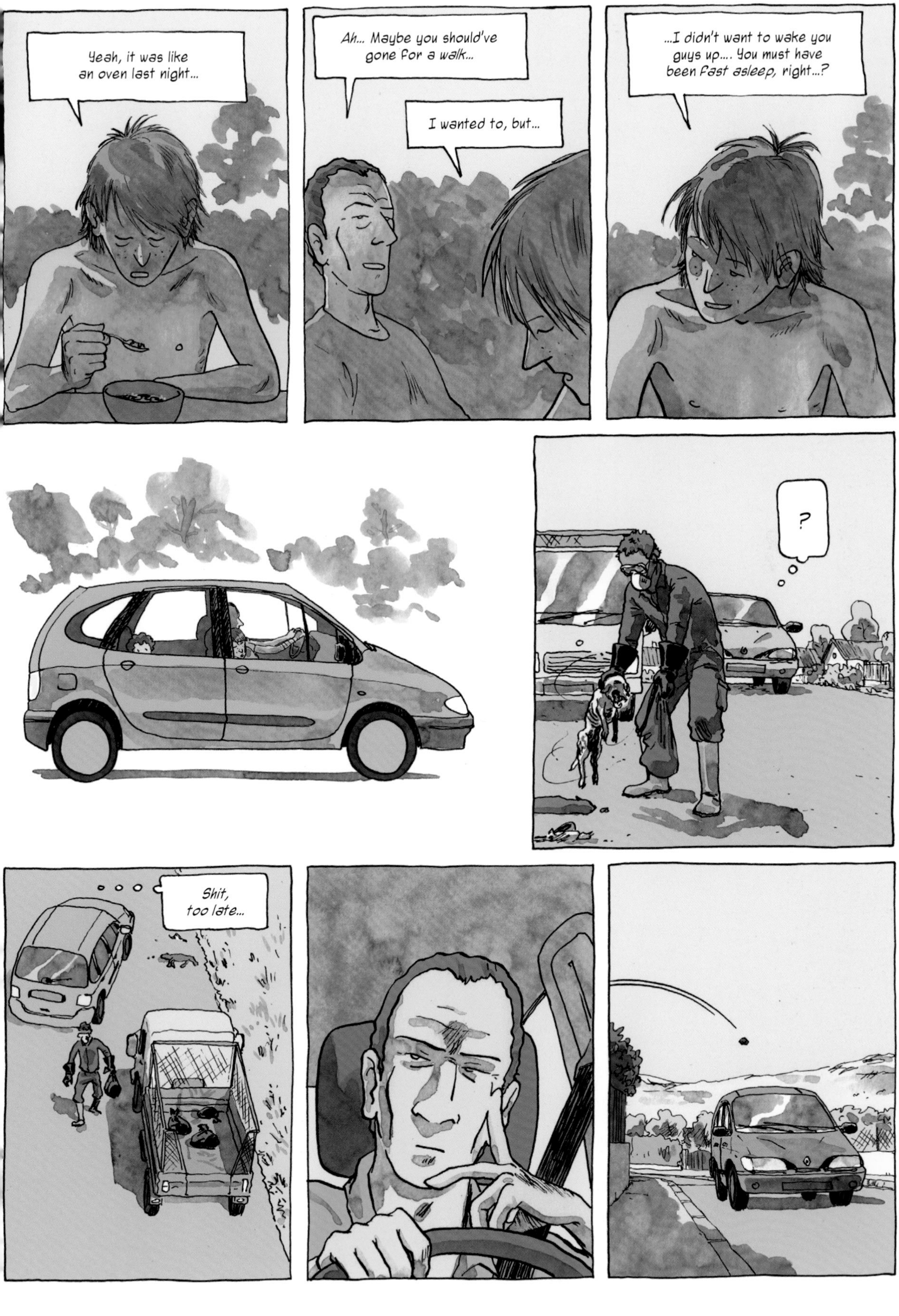
Yeah, it was like an oven last night...
Ah... Maybe you should've gone for a walk...
I wanted to, but...
...I didn't want to wake you guys up.... You must have been fast asleep, right...?
?
Shit, too late...

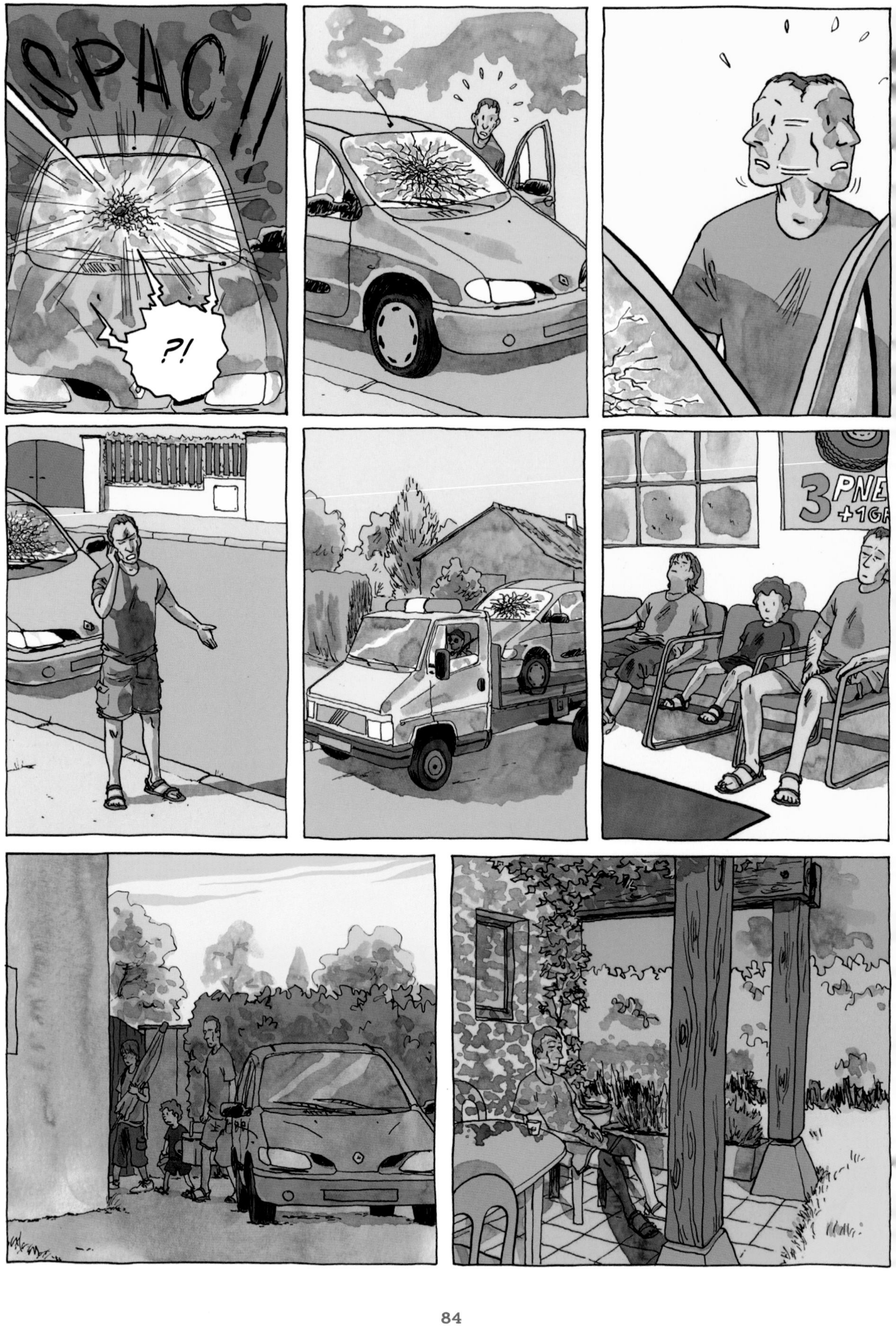
SPAC!!
?!

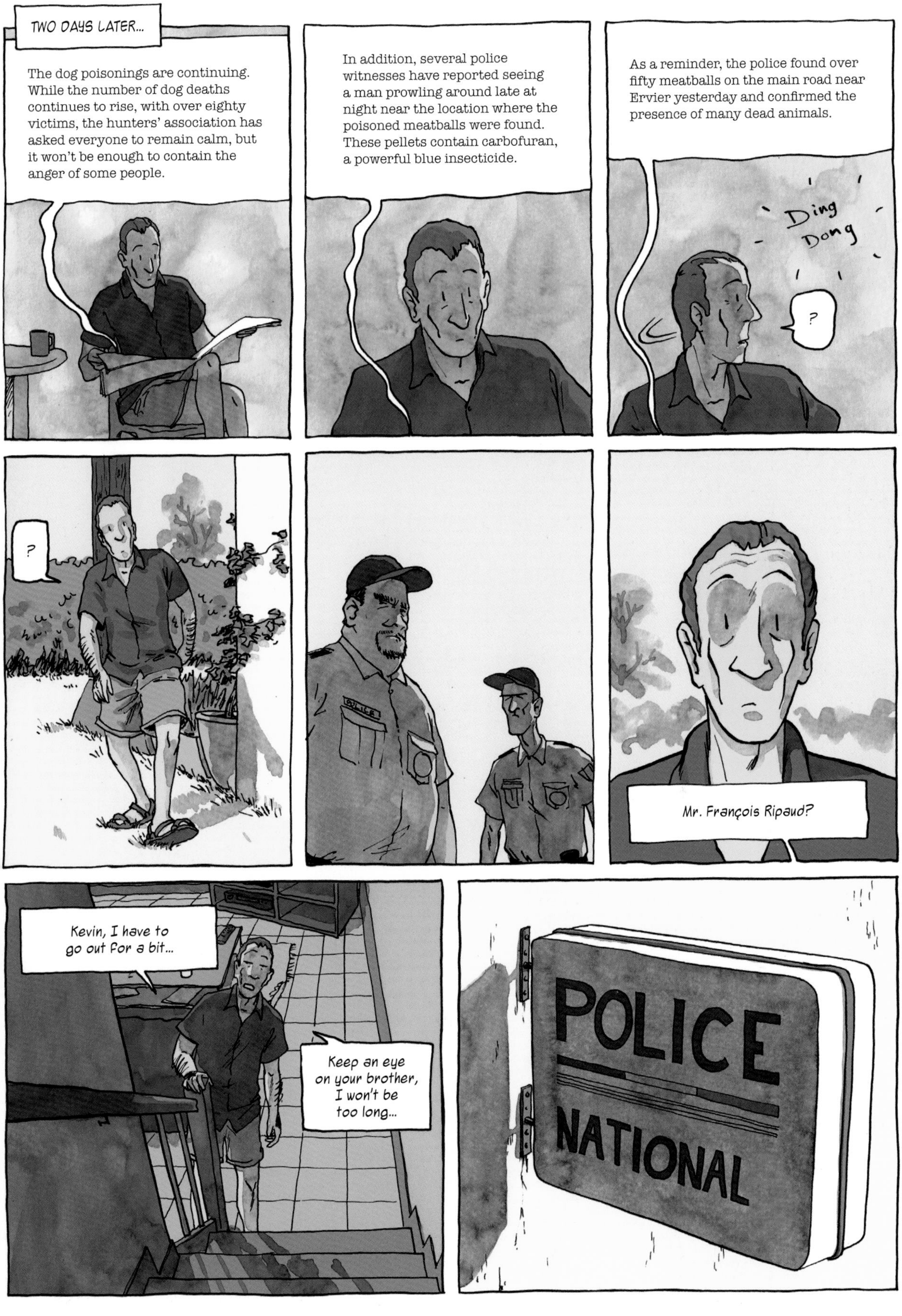
TWO DAYS LATER...
The dog poisonings are continuing. While the number of dog deaths continues to rise, with over eighty victims, the hunters' association has asked everyone to remain calm, but it won't be enough to contain the anger of some people.
In addition, several police witnesses have reported seeing a man prowling around late at night near the location where the poisoned meatballs were found. These pellets contain carbofuran, a powerful blue insecticide.
As a reminder, the police found over fifty meatballs on the main road near Ervier yesterday and confirmed the presence of many dead animals.
Ding Dong
?
?
Mr. François Ripaud?
Kevin, I have to go out for a bit...
Keep an eye on your brother, I won't be too long...
POLICE
NATIONAL

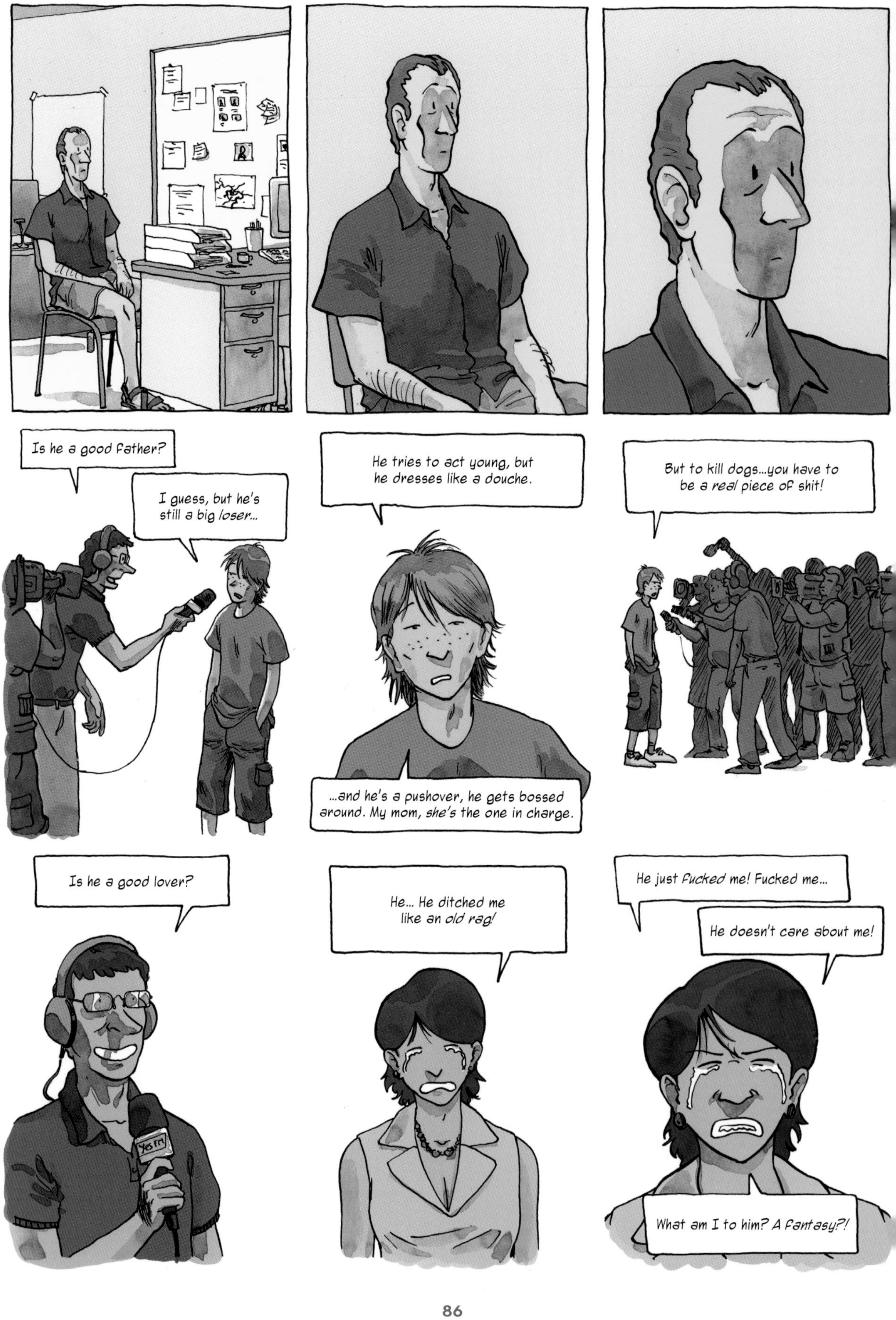
Is he a good father?
I guess, but he's still a big *loser*...
He tries to act young, but he dresses like a douche.
...and he's a pushover, he gets bossed around. My mom, *she's* the one in charge.
But to kill dogs...you have to be a *real* piece of shit!
Is he a good lover?
Yes FM
He... He ditched me like an *old rag!*
He just *fucked* me! Fucked me...
He doesn't care about me!
What am I to him? A *fantasy?!*

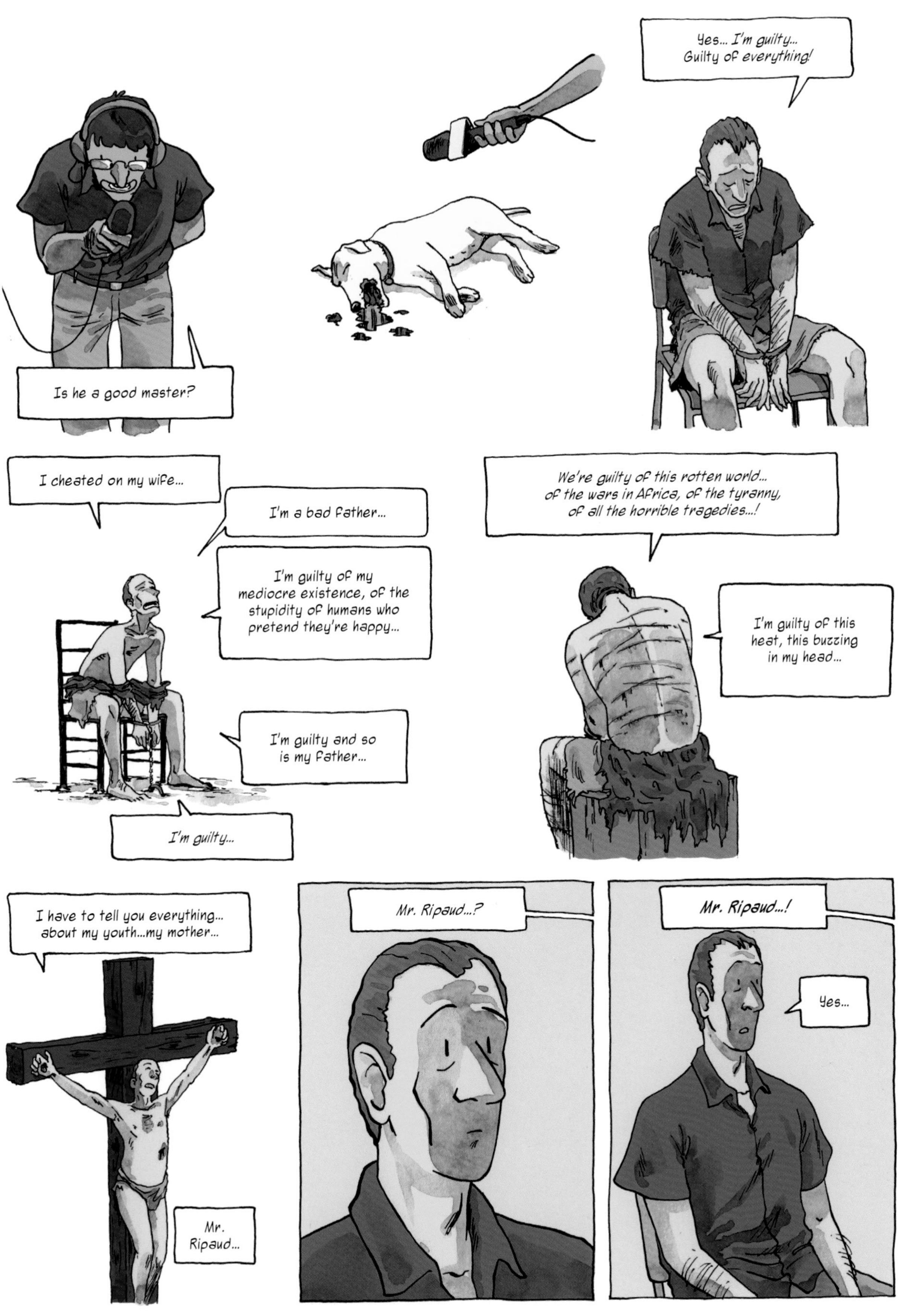
Is he a good master?
Yes... I'm guilty... Guilty of everything!
I cheated on my wife...
I'm a bad father...
I'm guilty of my mediocre existence, of the stupidity of humans who pretend they're happy...
I'm guilty and so is my father...
I'm guilty...
We're guilty of this rotten world... of the wars in Africa, of the tyranny, of all the horrible tragedies...!
I'm guilty of this heat, this buzzing in my head...
I have to tell you everything... about my youth...my mother...
Mr. Ripaud...
Mr. Ripaud...?
Mr. Ripaud...!
Yes...

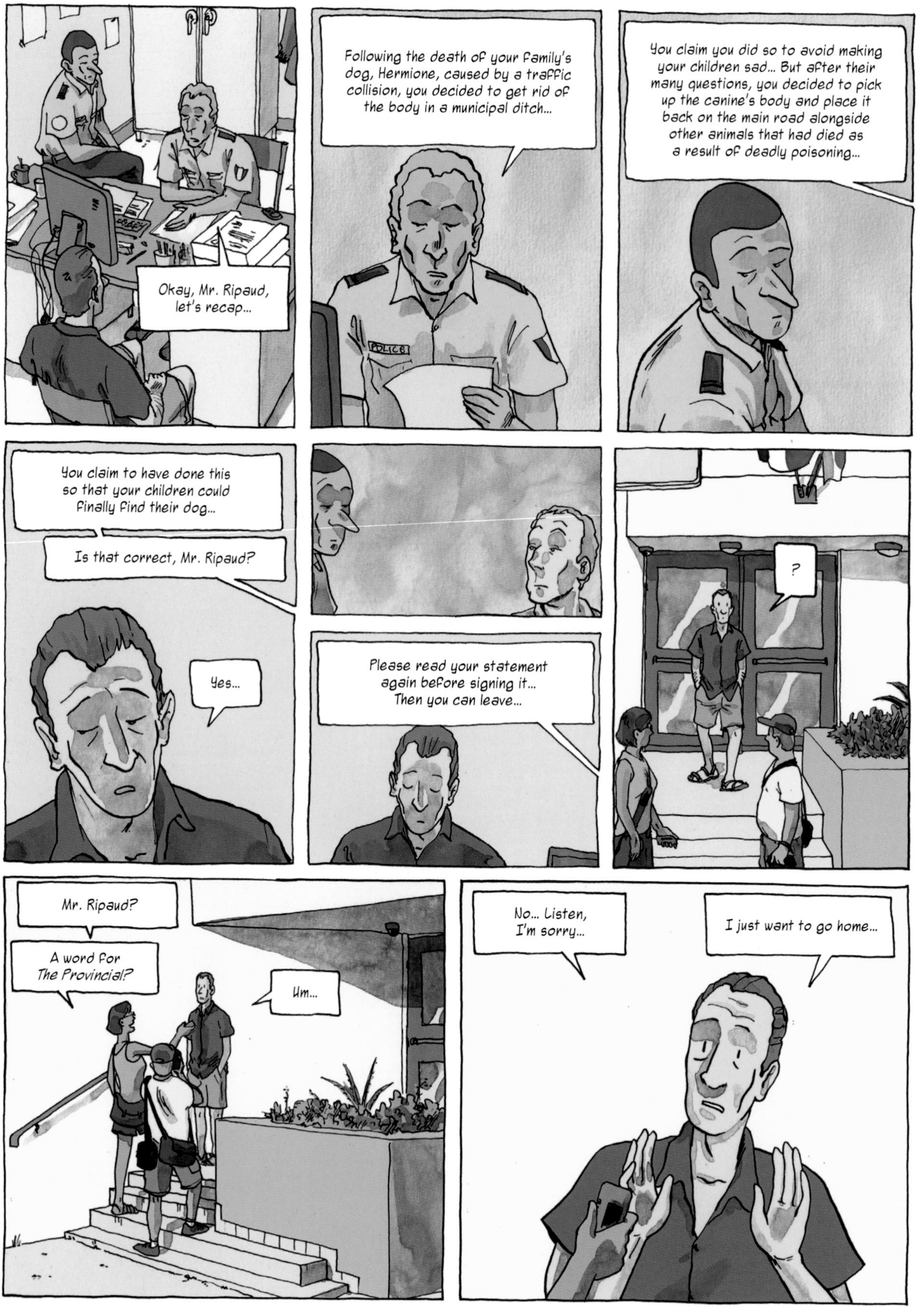
Okay, Mr. Ripaud, let's recap...
Following the death of your family's dog, Hermione, caused by a traffic collision, you decided to get rid of the body in a municipal ditch...
POLICE
You claim you did so to avoid making your children sad... But after their many questions, you decided to pick up the canine's body and place it back on the main road alongside other animals that had died as a result of deadly poisoning...
You claim to have done this so that your children could finally find their dog...
Is that correct, Mr. Ripaud?
Yes...
Please read your statement again before signing it... Then you can leave...
?
Mr. Ripaud?
A word for *The Provincial*?
Um...
No... Listen, I'm sorry...
I just want to go home...

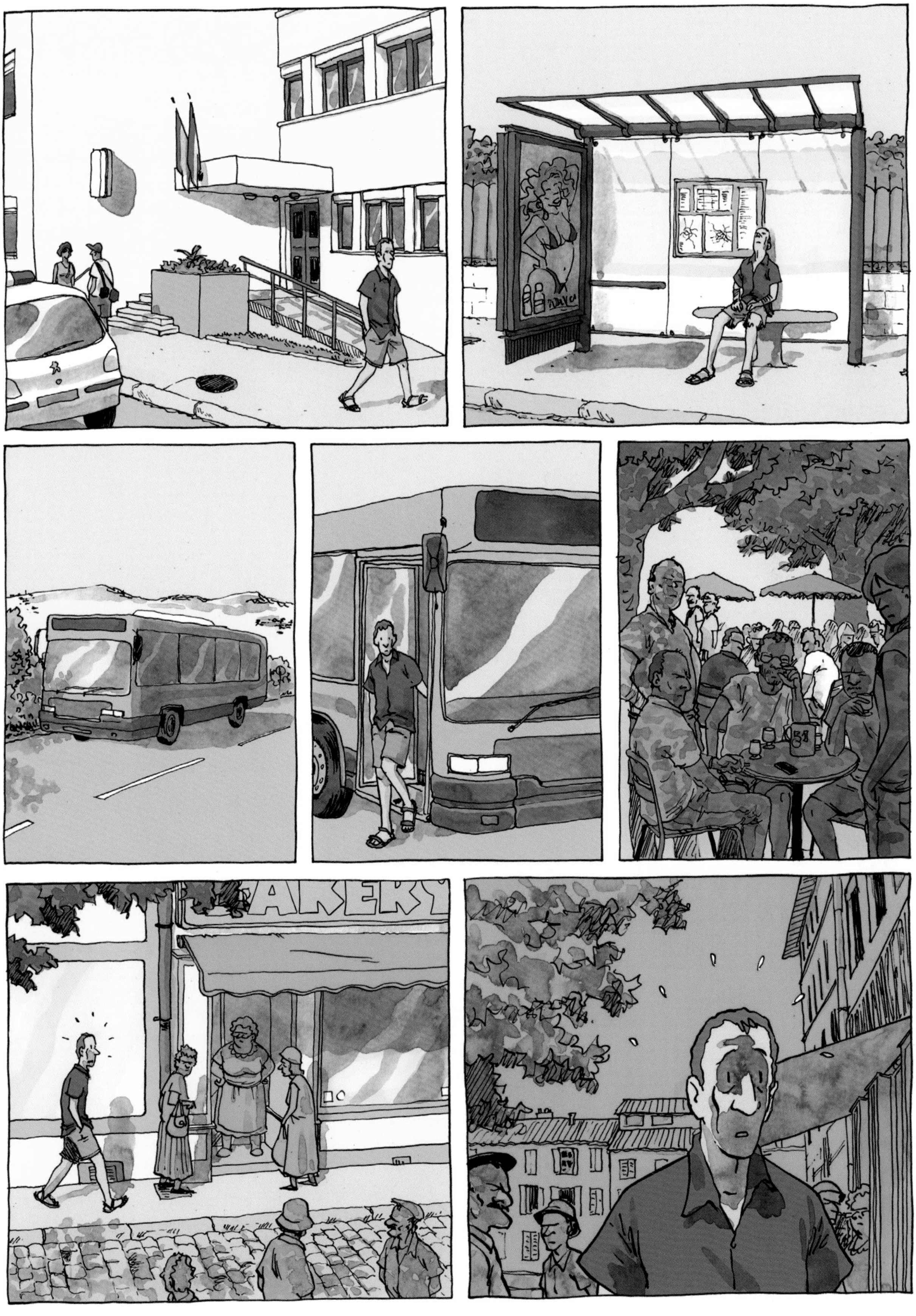
AKERY

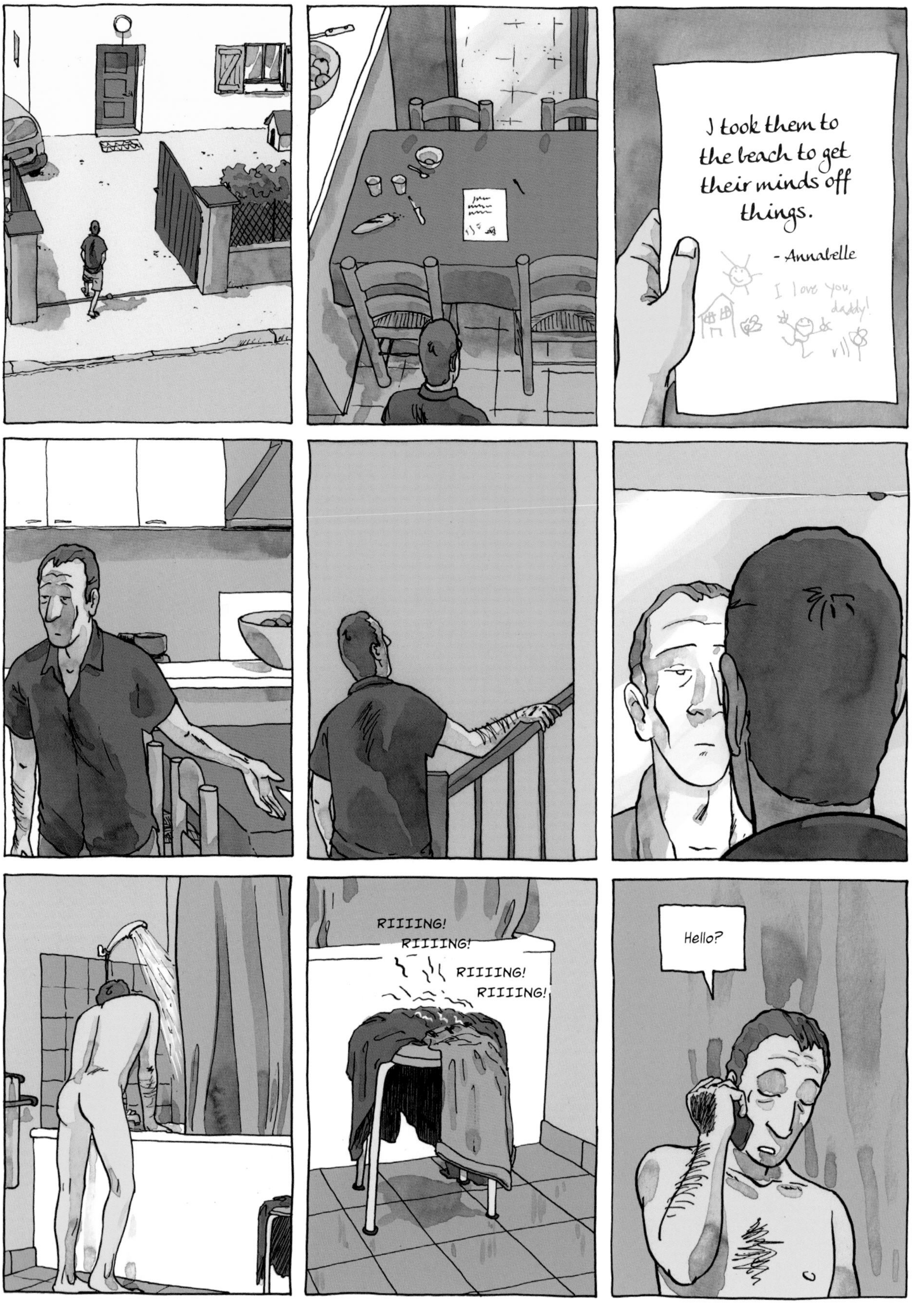

I took them to the beach to get their minds off things.
- Annabelle
I love you, daddy!
RIIIING!
RIIIING!
RIIIING!
RIIIING!
Hello?

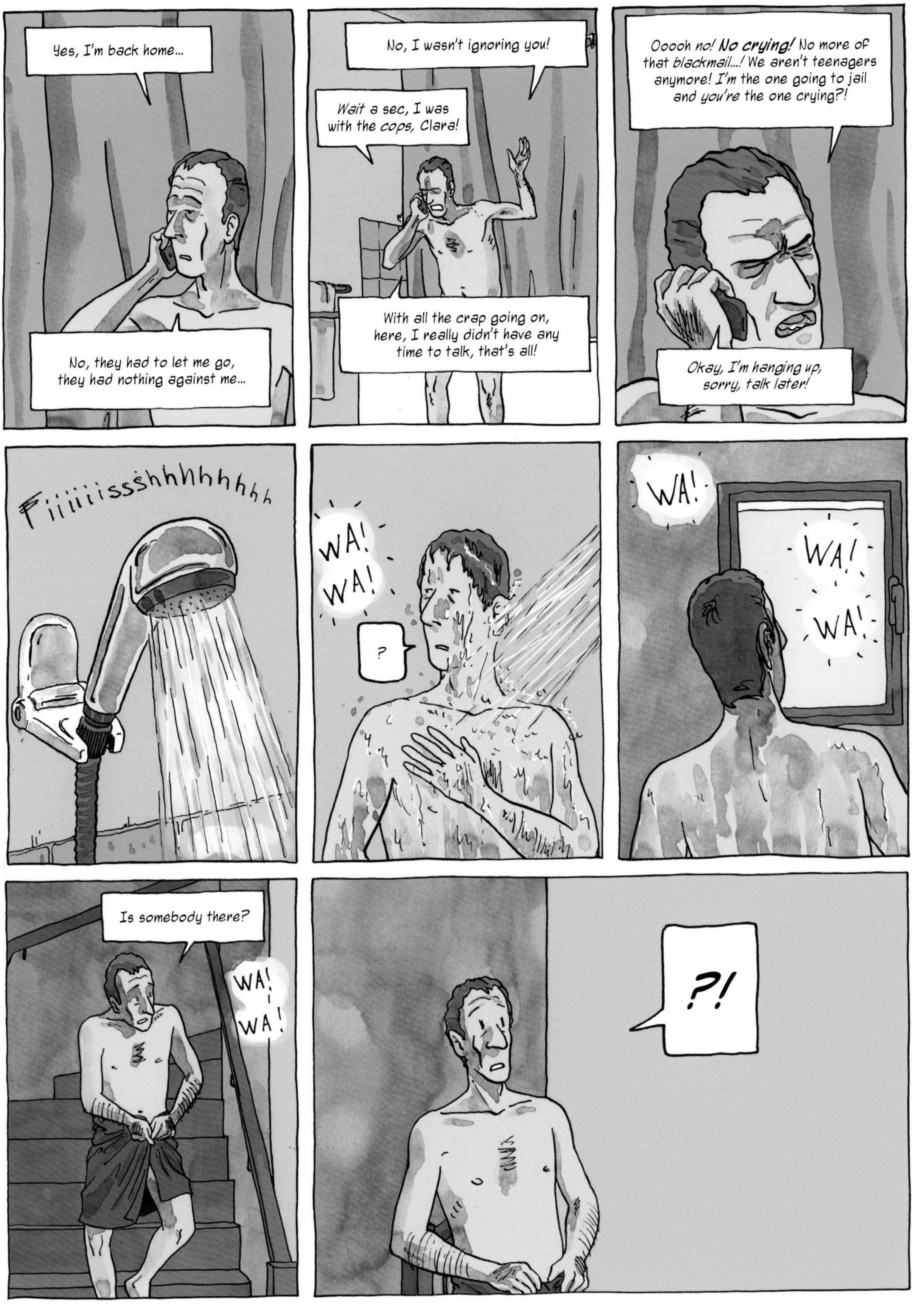
Yes, I'm back home...
No, they had to let me go, they had nothing against me...
No, I wasn't ignoring you!
Wait a sec, I was with the cops, Clara!
With all the crap going on, here, I really didn't have any time to talk, that's all!
Ooooh no! No crying! No more of that blackmail...! We aren't teenagers anymore! I'm the one going to jail and you're the one crying?!
Okay, I'm hanging up, sorry, talk later!
Fiiiiiissshhhhhhhh
WA!
WA!
?
WA!
WA!
WA!
Is somebody there?
WA!
WA!
?!

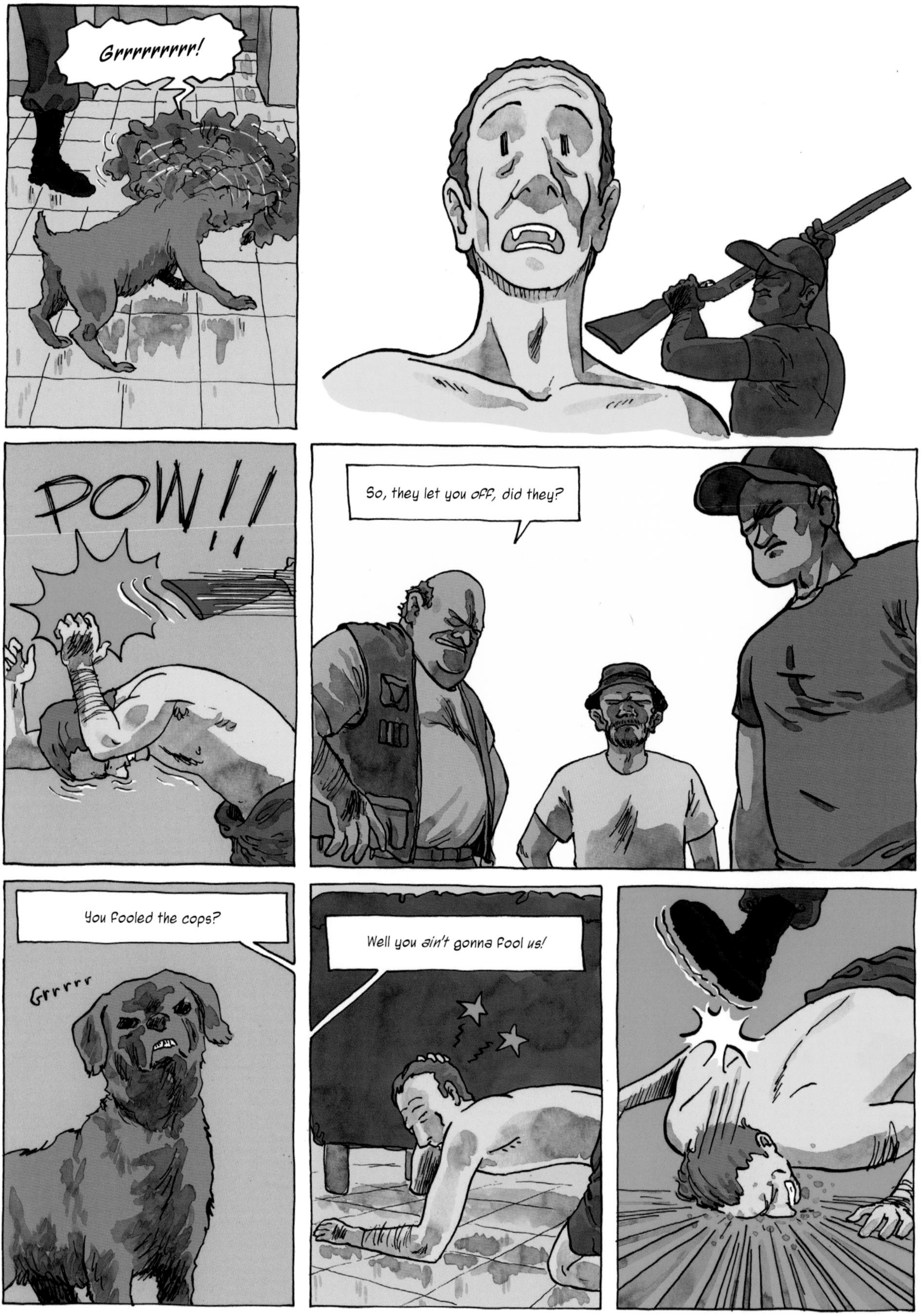
Grrrrrrrr!
POW!!
So, they let you off, did they?
You fooled the cops?
Grrrr
Well you ain't gonna fool us!

WA!
WA!
WA!
WA!
WA!
WA!
WA
WA
WA
WA
SAINT ANNE'S HOSPITAL
Hey...
Hey...

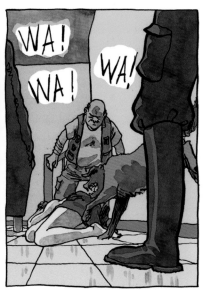

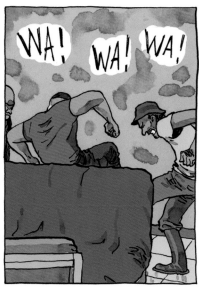

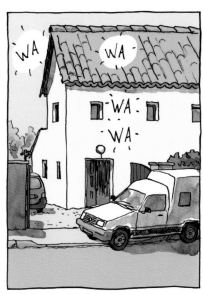

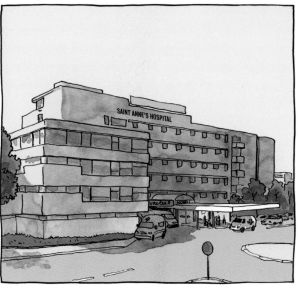

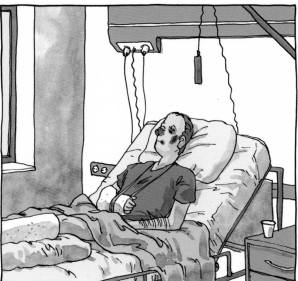

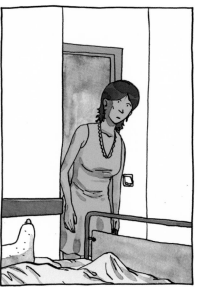

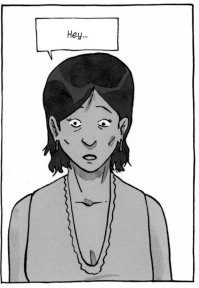

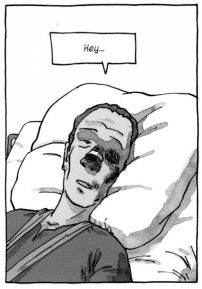

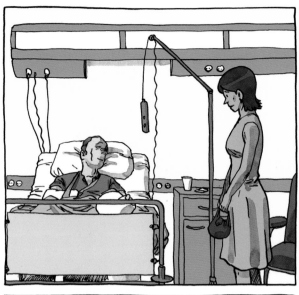

The boys are on the train. Your wife is picking them up at the station...

Oh...great.
Thank you...

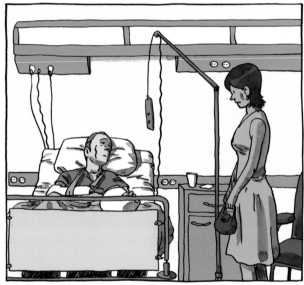

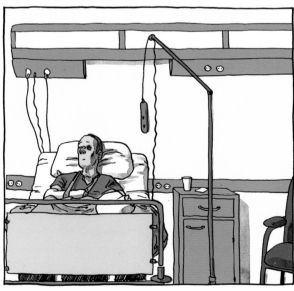

Mr. Ripaud?

SAINT ANNE'S HOSPITAL

94

Are you sure? You *really* don't want to file a complaint?

You should reconsider, sir, if you don't file a complaint, there's nothing we can do for you...

Listen, I think he's had enough. He just wants to go home and forget about all this...

Have it your way...

EMERGENCY ROOM ADMISSI

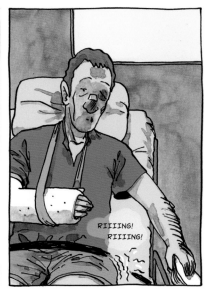

RIIIING! RIIIING!

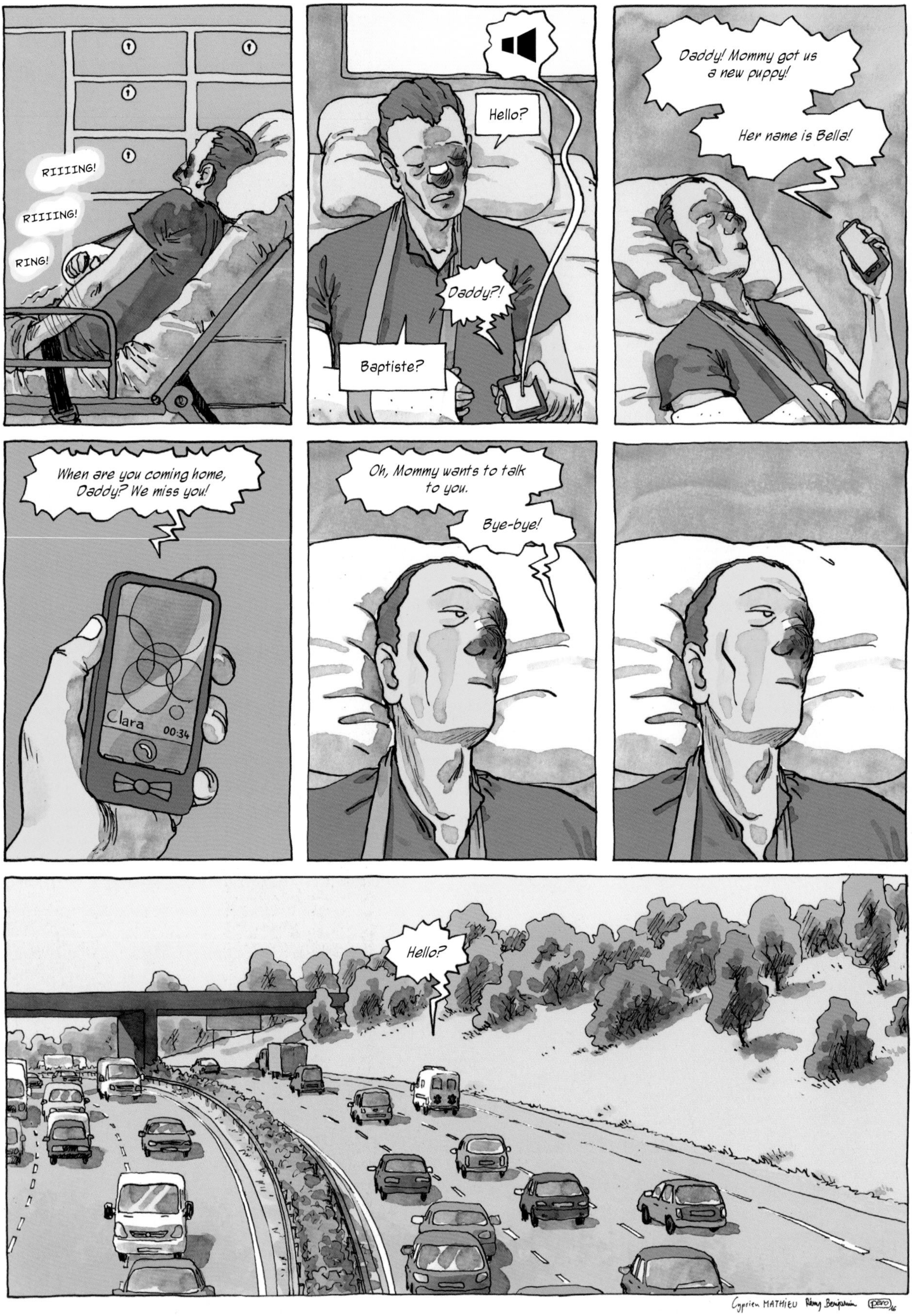
RIIIING!
RIIIING!
RING!
Hello?
Baptiste?
Daddy?!
Daddy! Mommy got us a new puppy!
Her name is Bella!
When are you coming home, Daddy? We miss you!
Clara
00:34
Oh, Mommy wants to talk to you.
Bye-bye!
Hello?
Cyprien MATHIEU Rémy Benjamin péro 16

BACK STORIES

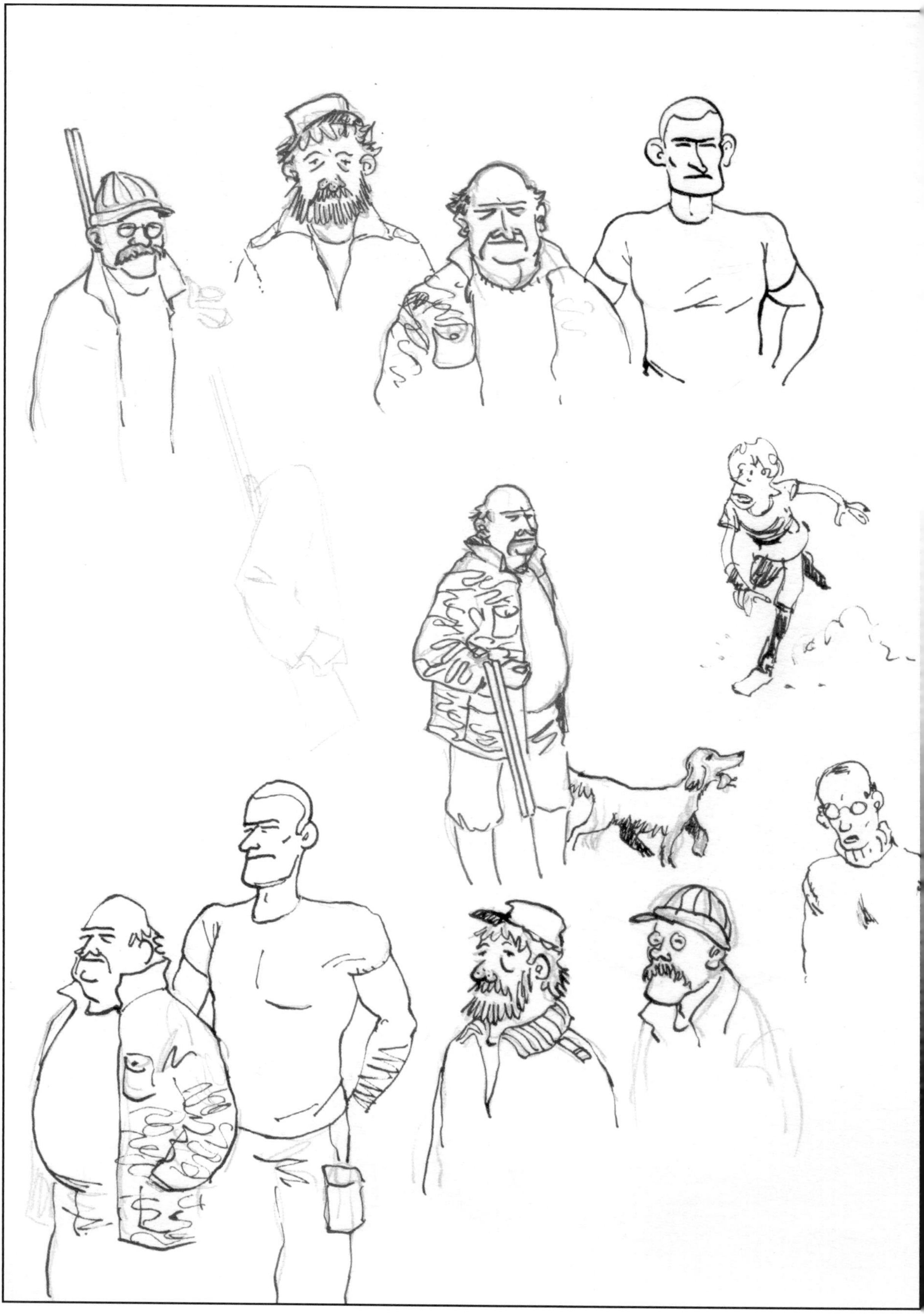

Character designs.

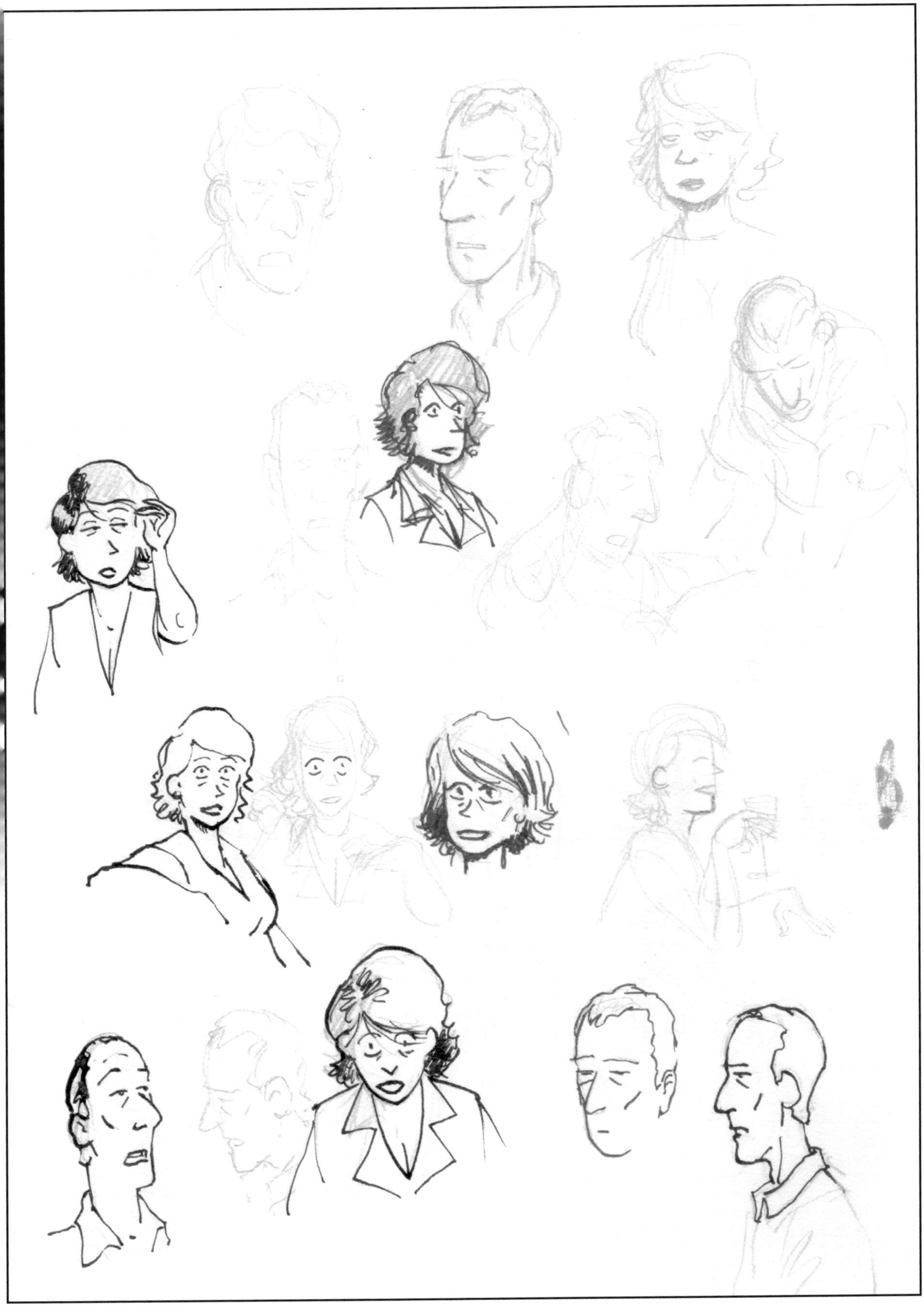

Character designs for François and Annabelle.

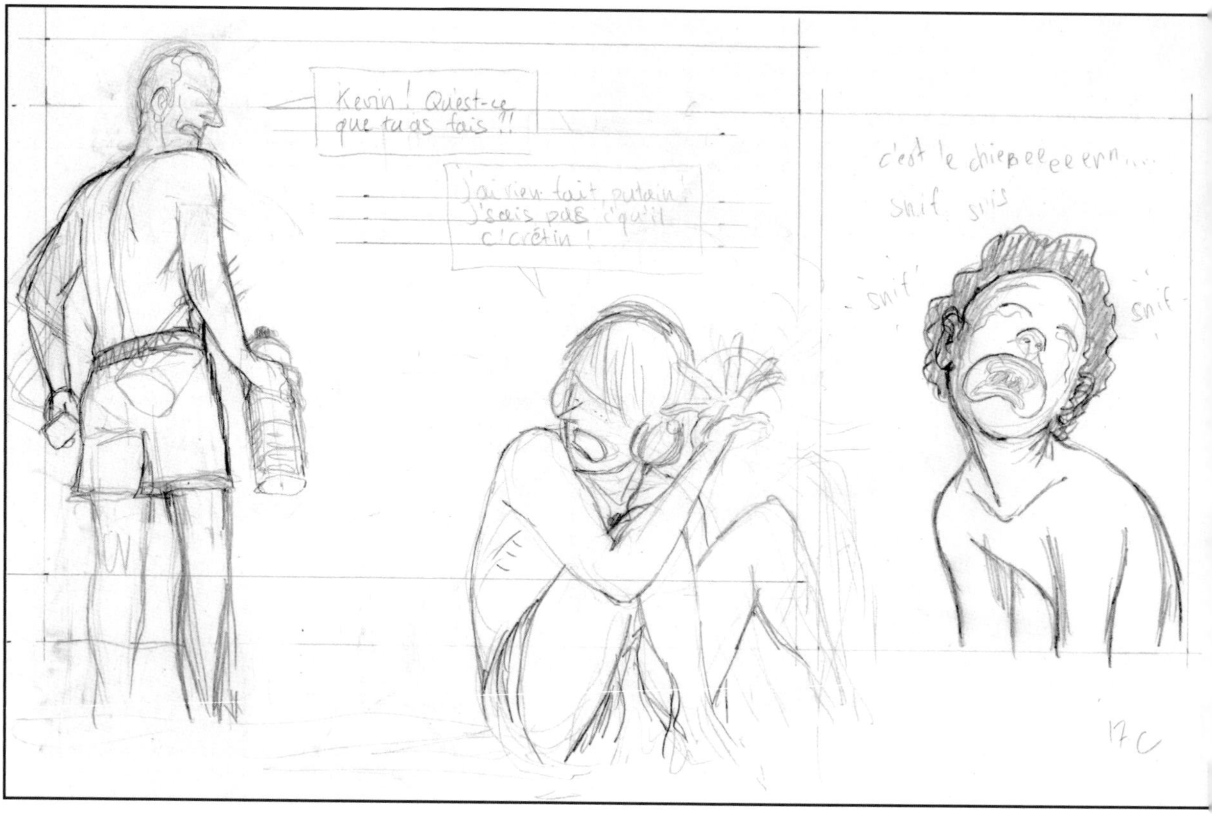
Kevin! Quest-ce que tuas fais !!
J'ai rien fait, putain! J'sais pas c'qu'il c'crétin!
c'est le chieeeeeeern....
snif
snif
snif
17c

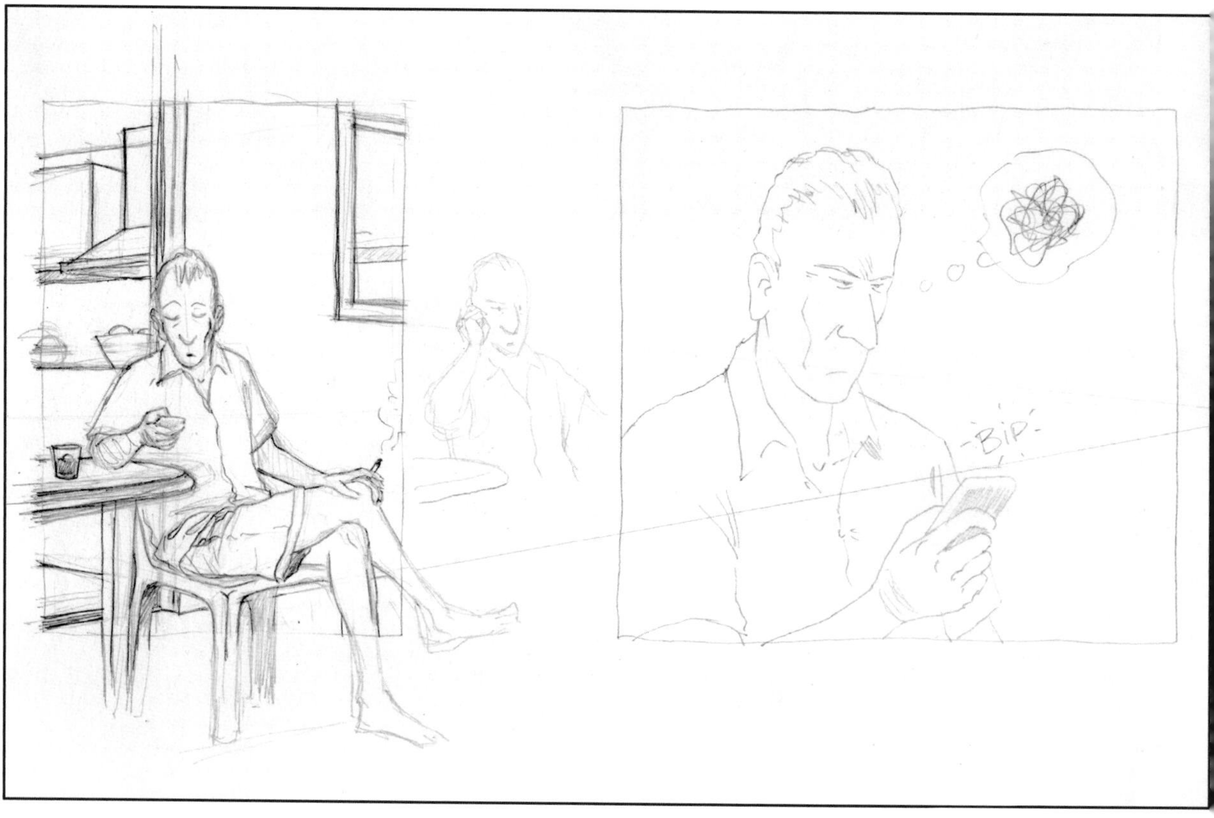
-BIP-

Layouts from pages 21 and 16.

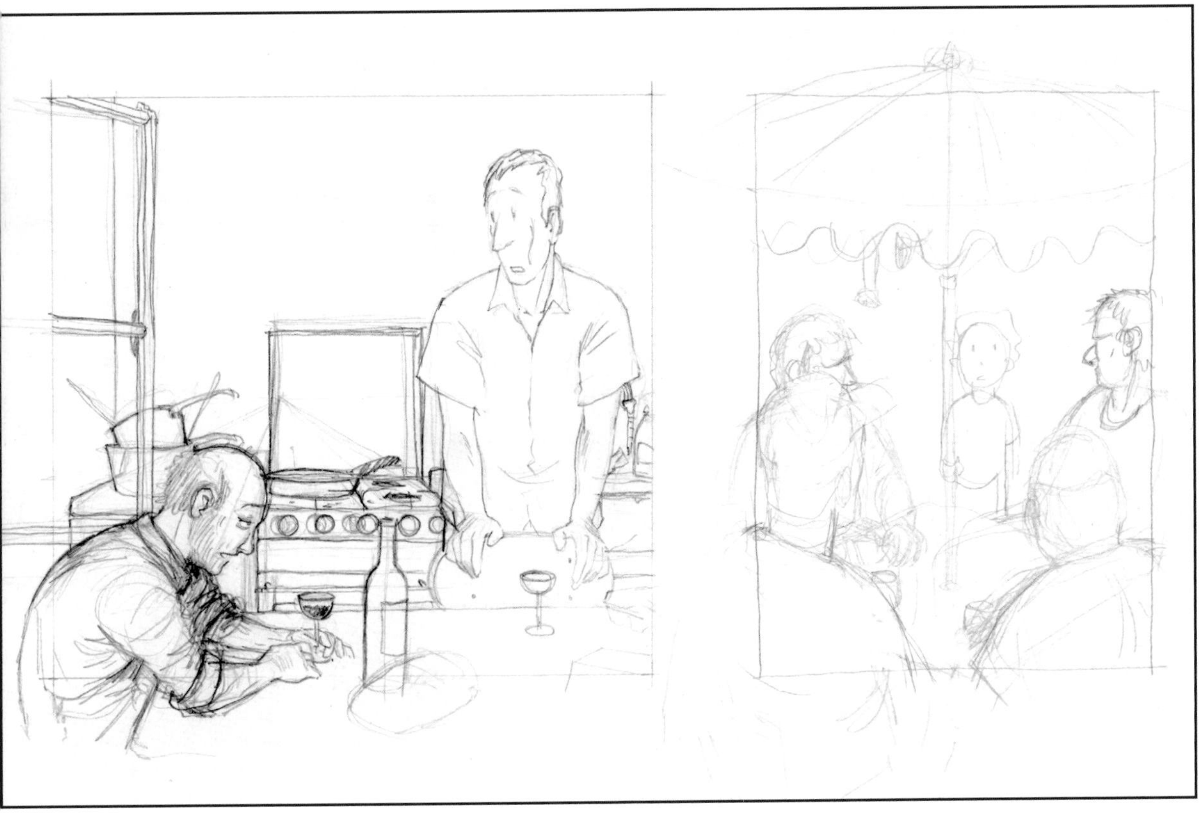

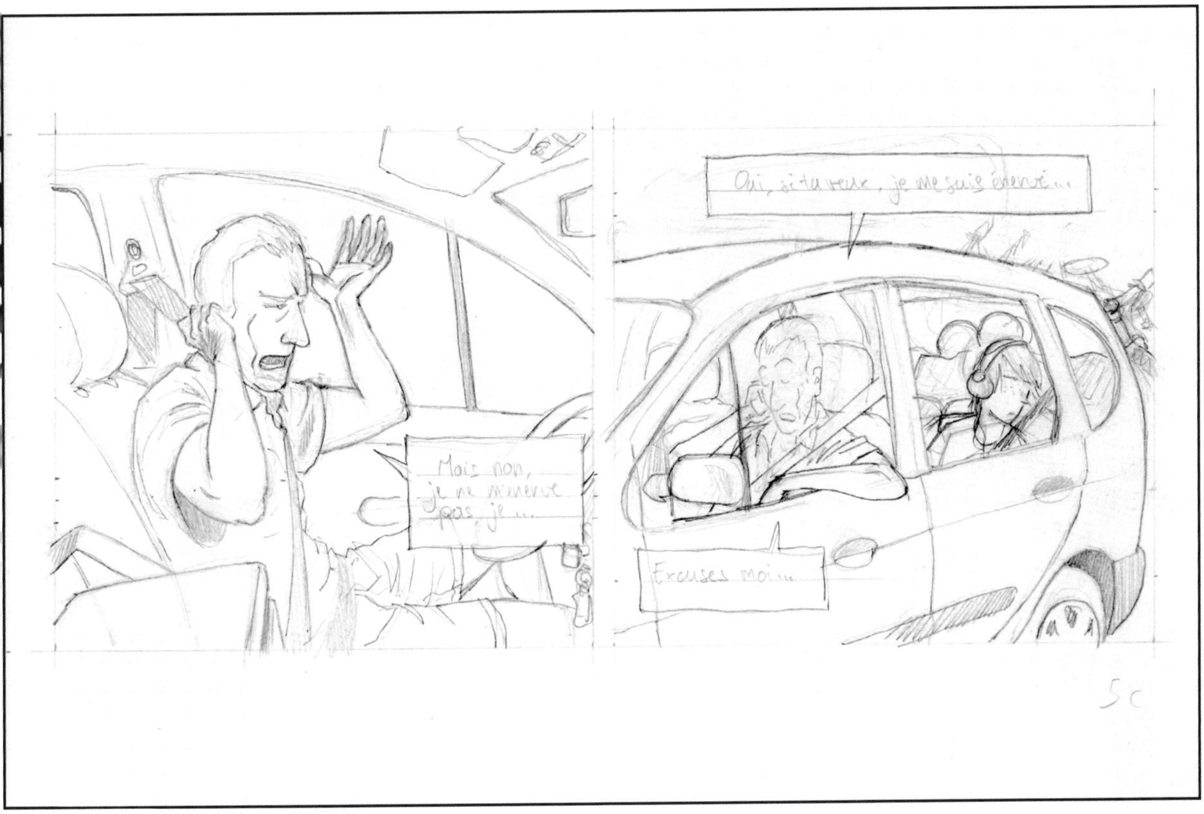
Mais non,
je ne m'énerve
pas, je ...
Oui, si tu veux, je me suis énervé...
Excuses moi...

Layouts from pages 55 and 9.

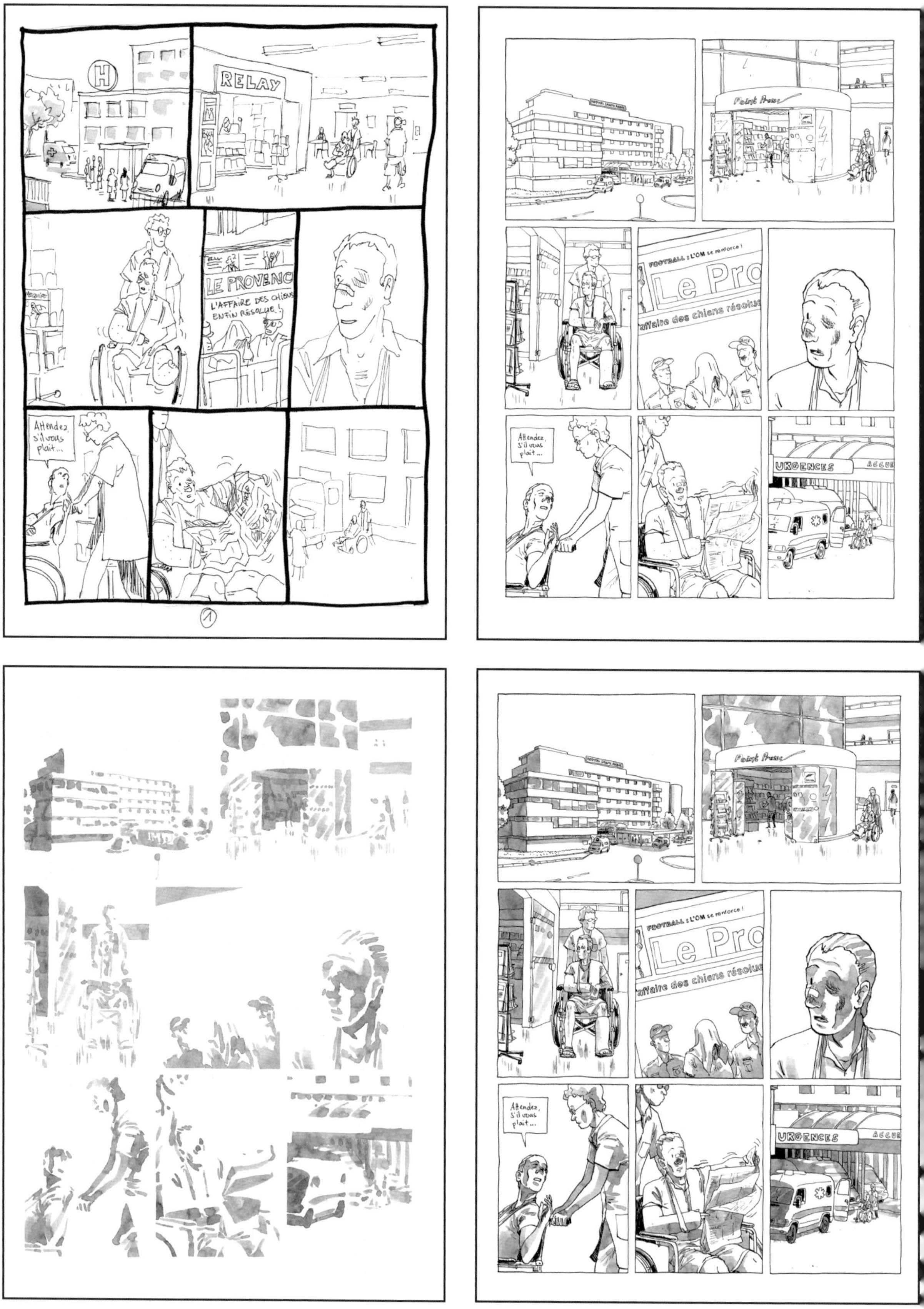
RELAY
LE PROVENC
L'AFFAIRE DES CHIENS ENFIN RÉSOLUE !
Attendez, s'il vous plait...
FOOTBALL : L'OM se renforce !
Le Pro
l'affaire des chiens résolu
Attendez, s'il vous plait...
URGENCES
FOOTBALL : L'OM se renforce !
Le Pro
l'affaire des chiens résolu
Attendez, s'il vous plait...
URGENCES

Various stages of page 5: storyboard (top left), India ink (top right), shading with wash or black watercolor (bottom left), digital superimposition of shading and line (bottom right).

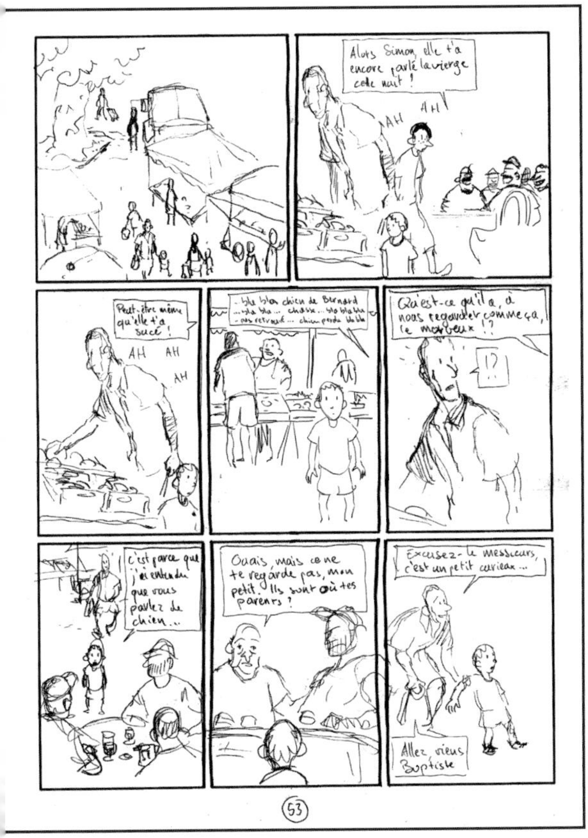

Alors Simon, elle t'a encore parlé la vierge cette nuit !
AH
AH
Peut-être même qu'elle t'a sucé !
AH AH
AH
… bla bla chien de Bernard … bla bla … chasse … bla bla bla … pas retrouvé … chien perdu bla bla
Qu'est-ce qu'il a, à nous regarder comme ça, le morveux !?
!?
C'est parce que j'ai entendu que vous parlez de chien…
Ouais, mais ce ne te regarde pas, mon petit. Ils sont où tes parents ?
Excusez-le messieurs, c'est un petit curieux…
Allez viens Baptiste
53

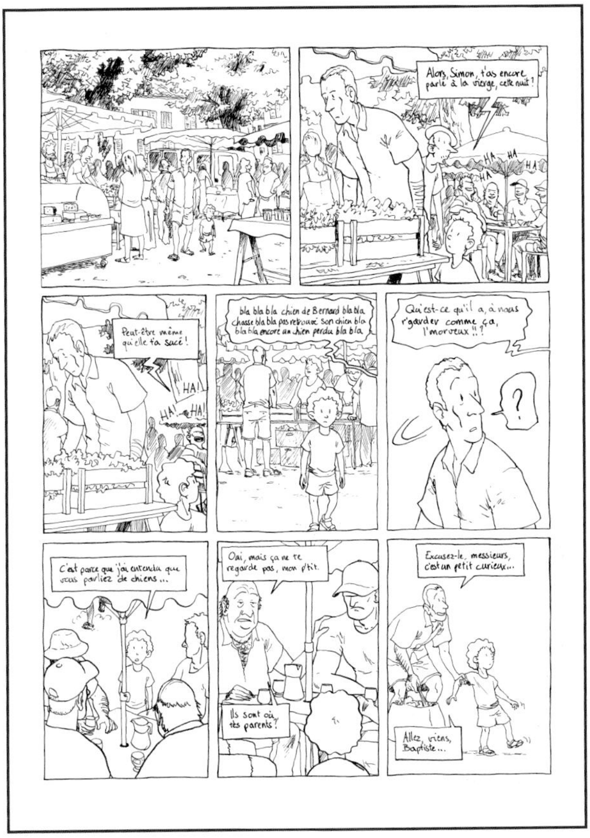

Alors, Simon, t'as encore parlé à la vierge, cette nuit !
HA HA HA HA
Peut-être même qu'elle t'a sucé !
HA!
HA! HA!
bla bla bla chien de Bernard bla bla chasse bla bla pas retrouvé son chien bla bla bla encore un chien perdu bla bla
Qu'est-ce qu'il a, à nous r'garder comme ça, l'morveux !!?
?
C'est parce que j'ai entendu que vous parliez de chiens…
Oai, mais ça ne te regarde pas, mon p'tit.
Ils sont où, tes parents?
Excusez-le, messieurs, c'est un petit curieux…
Allez, viens, Baptiste…

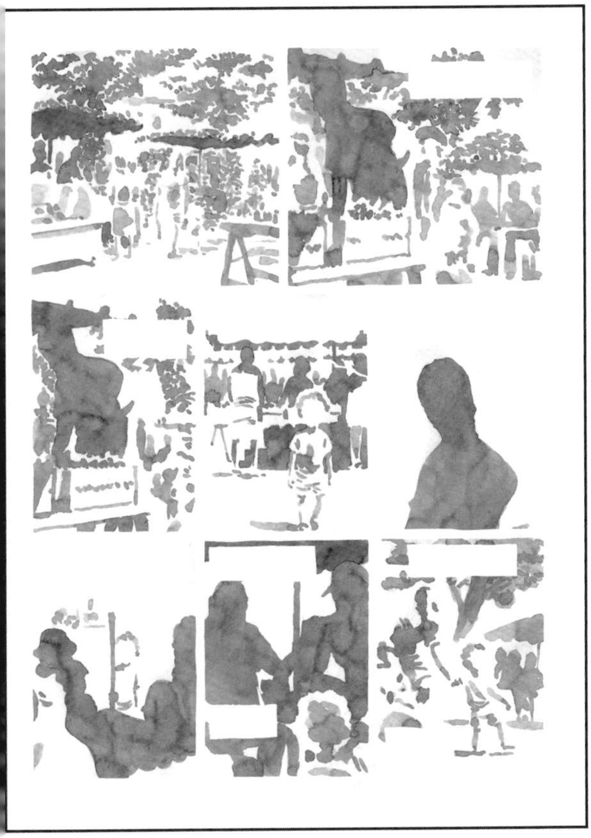

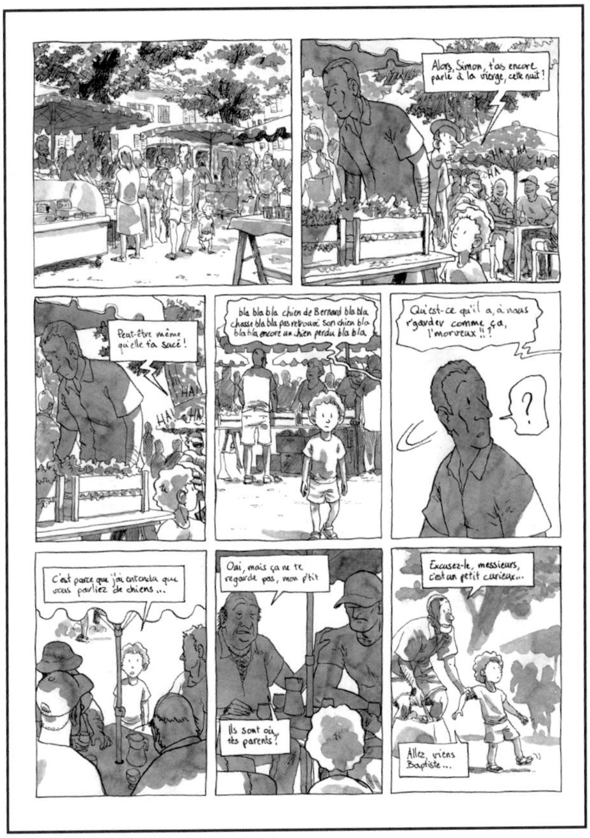

Alors, Simon, t'as encore parlé à la vierge, cette nuit !
HA HA HA HA
Peut-être même qu'elle t'a sucé !
HA!
HA! HA!
bla bla bla chien de Bernard bla bla chasse bla bla pas retrouvé son chien bla bla bla encore un chien perdu bla bla
Qu'est-ce qu'il a, à nous r'garder comme ça, l'morveux !!?
?
C'est parce que j'ai entendu que vous parliez de chiens…
Oai, mais ça ne te regarde pas, mon p'tit
Ils sont où, tes parents?
Excusez-le, messieurs, c'est un petit curieux…
Allez, viens, Baptiste…

Various stages of page 56: storyboard (top left), India ink (top right), shading with wash or black watercolor (bottom left), digital superimposition of shading and line (bottom right).

Rough sketches and character designs.

JUIN 2009 - Numéro Quatre PAGES : 24 - Prix Net : 5 €

EDITEUR RESPONSABLE
CHEVAL DE QUATRE
34, RUE DE MARVIS
7500 TOURNAI
BELGIQUE
WWW.CHEVALDEQUATRE.BE

CHEVAL DE QUATRE

EDITION
IMPRIMÉ EN JUIN 2009
SUR LES PRESSES DE L'IMPRIMERIE
CARRÉ NOIR - TOURNAI
ISBN

ÉDITION SPÉCIALE

JOURNEES ROUGES ET BOULETTES BLEUES

Les Vacances de François R.

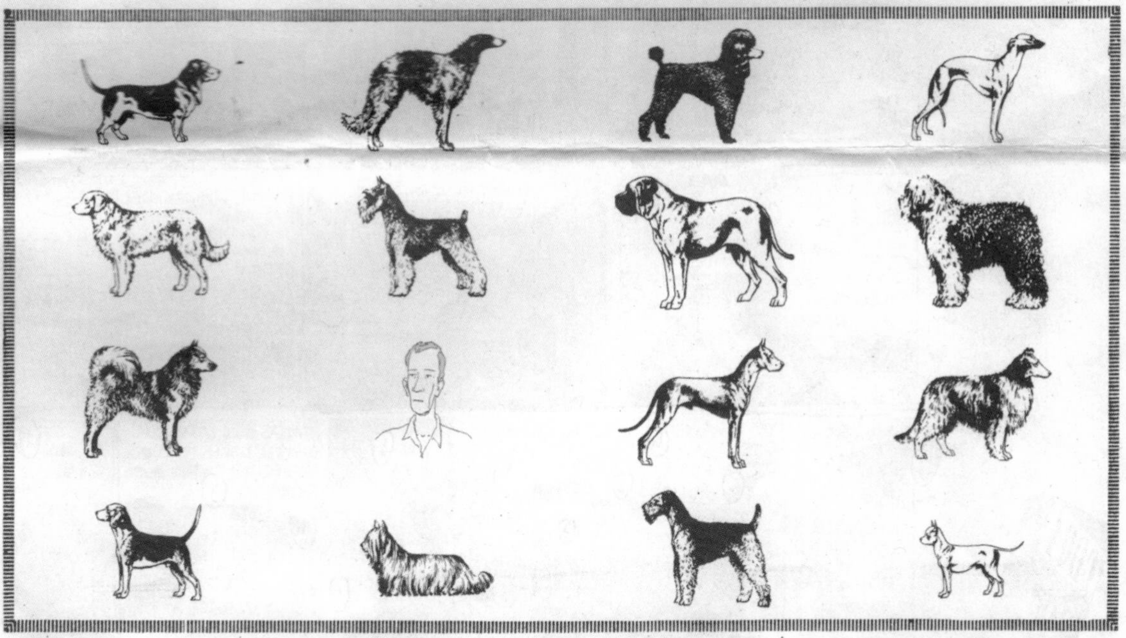

LA CANICULE N'AIDE PAS LES VACANCIERS

Cette année encore, on prévoit de gros bouchons sur l'Autoroute du Soleil. Bison futé indique une journée rouge. Mais avec la canicule qui, depuis plusieurs semaines, sévit dans notre pays la route risque d'être encore plus pénible. Si vous partez demain, prévoyez des bouteilles d'eau et faites des arrêts réguliers. Laissez l'intérieur de votre voiture « refroidir » à l'ombre des arbres. Sauf, bien sûr, si vous avez la climatisation.

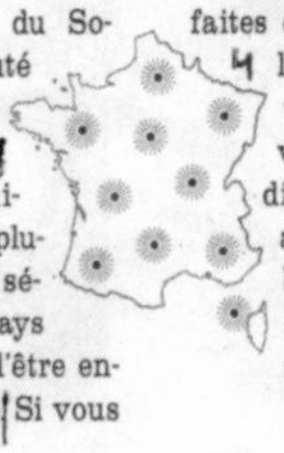

J.P.L.

Dog Days (*Journées rouges et boulettes bleues*) was originally produced in a journal format in June 2009 for the magazine *Cheval de quatre*. Alexis Tuzzolino took care of the layout and graphics while Brice Follet worked on inks. For the graphic novel edition, the creators reworked the script and redesigned all the pages to take full advantage of this new format.

P4

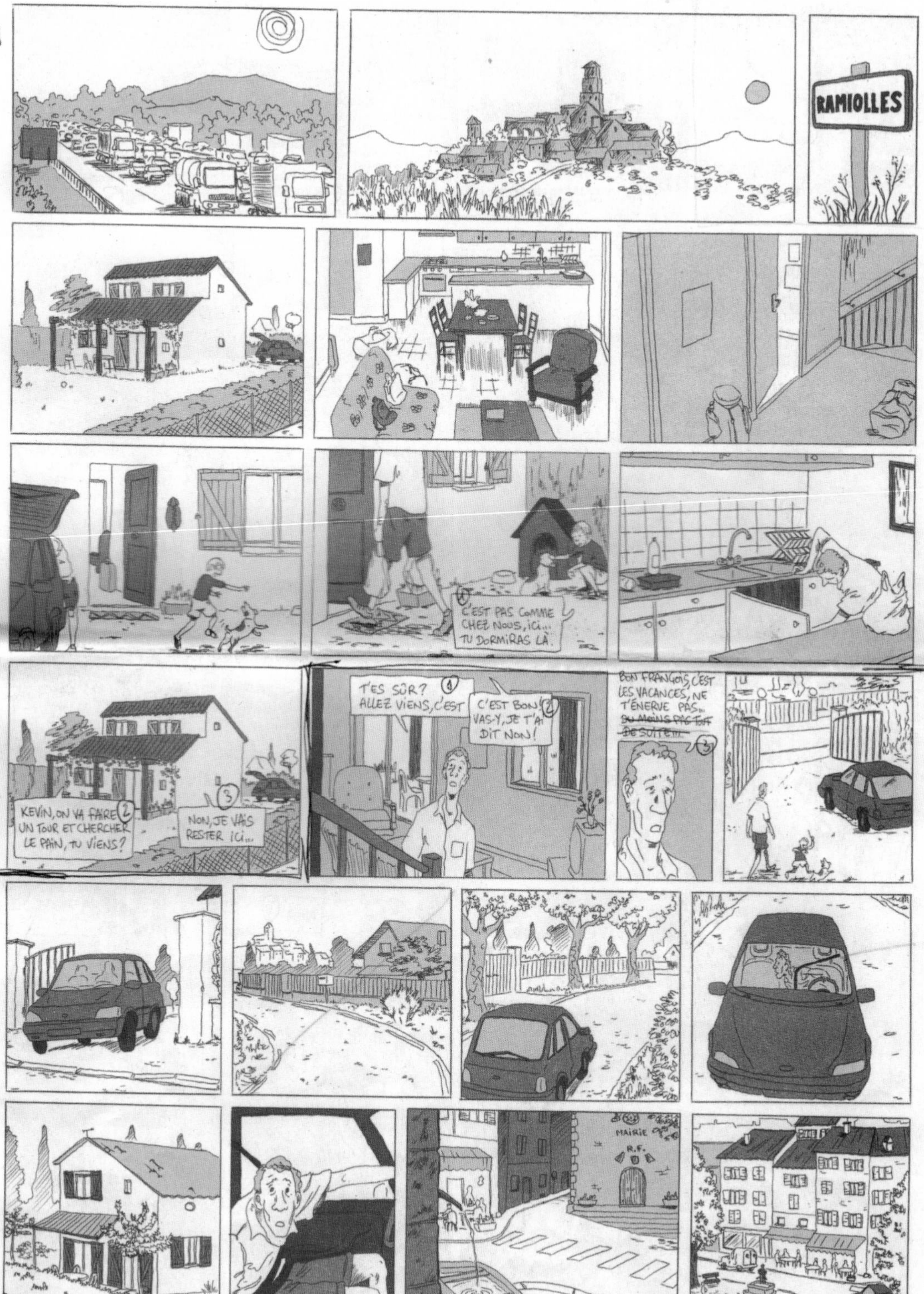
RAMIOLLES
C'EST PAS COMME CHEZ NOUS, ICI... TU DORMIRAS LÀ.
KEVIN, ON VA FAIRE UN TOUR ET CHERCHER LE PAIN, TU VIENS?
NON, JE VAIS RESTER ICI...
T'ES SÛR? ALLEZ VIENS, C'EST
C'EST BON! VAS-Y, JE T'AI DIT NON!
BON FRANÇOIS, C'EST LES VACANCES, NE T'ÉNERVE PAS...
~~DU MOINS PAS TOUT DE SUITE!!!~~
MAIRIE
R.F.

P5

voiture devant la maison

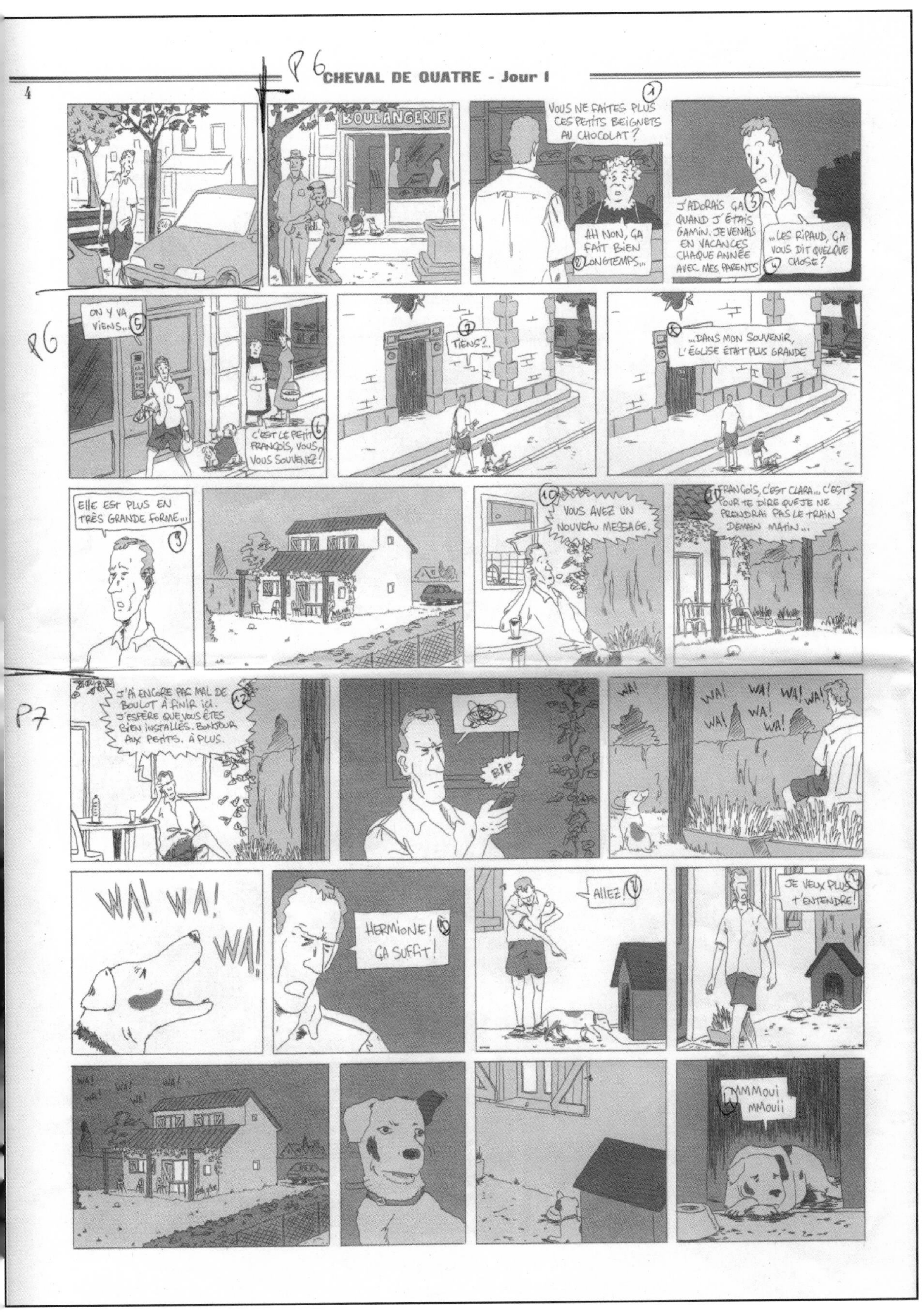
BOULANGERIE
VOUS NE FAITES PLUS CES PETITS BEIGNETS AU CHOCOLAT?
AH NON, ÇA FAIT BIEN LONGTEMPS...
J'ADORAIS ÇA QUAND J'ÉTAIS GAMIN. JE VENAIS EN VACANCES CHAQUE ANNÉE AVEC MES PARENTS
...LES RIPAUD, ÇA VOUS DIT QUELQUE CHOSE?
ON Y VA, VIENS...
C'EST LE PETIT FRANÇOIS, VOUS VOUS SOUVENEZ!
TIENS?...
...DANS MON SOUVENIR, L'ÉGLISE ÉTAIT PLUS GRANDE
ELLE EST PLUS EN TRÈS GRANDE FORME...
VOUS AVEZ UN NOUVEAU MESSAGE.
FRANÇOIS, C'EST CLARA... C'EST POUR TE DIRE QUE JE NE PRENDRAI PAS LE TRAIN DEMAIN MATIN...
J'AI ENCORE PAS MAL DE BOULOT À FINIR ICI. J'ESPÈRE QUE VOUS ÊTES BIEN INSTALLÉS. BONJOUR AUX PETITS. À PLUS.
BIP
WA!
WA! WA! WA! WA! WA! WA! WA!
WA! WA! WA!
HERMIONE! ÇA SUFFIT!
ALLEZ!
JE VEUX PLUS T'ENTENDRE!
WA! WA! WA! WA! WA!
MMMoui MMouii

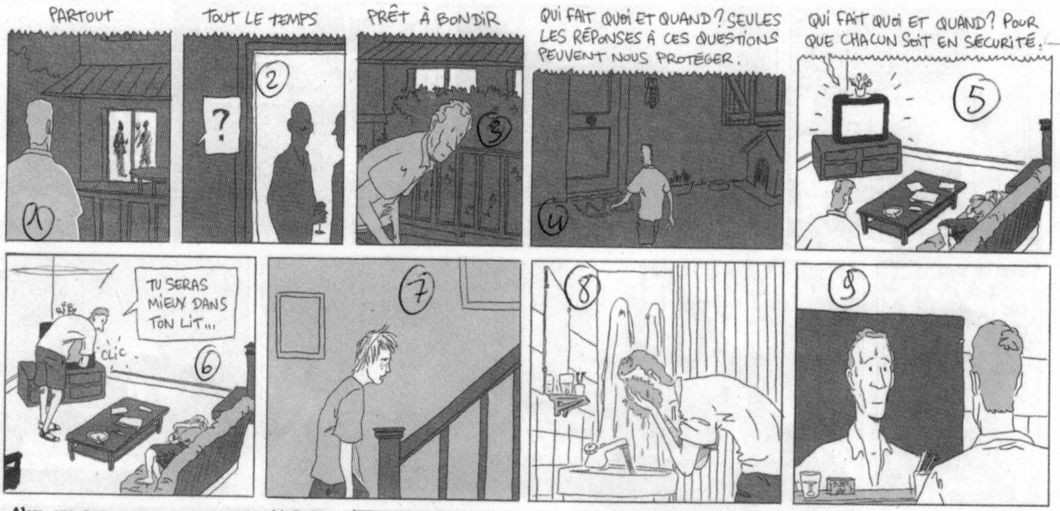
PARTOUT
TOUT LE TEMPS
?
PRÊT À BONDIR
QUI FAIT QUOI ET QUAND ? SEULES LES RÉPONSES À CES QUESTIONS PEUVENT NOUS PROTÉGER.
QUI FAIT QUOI ET QUAND ? POUR QUE CHACUN SOIT EN SÉCURITÉ.
TU SERAS MIEUX DANS TON LIT...
CLIC

LE MYSTERE PERSISTE !

Alors que nous sommes toujours sans nouvelle des deux chiens disparus mardi et mercredi, la police vient de retrouver un labrador mort sur la Nationale.

Avec quatre disparitions canines cette semaine, notre village se fait remarquer d'une bien curieuse façon. La police est sur le qui-vive et compte bien résoudre ce mystère au plus vite. « Je vous avoue qu'on s'en serait bien passés » nous confie Georges Paillac, le responsable de l'enquête. C'est au bord de la Nationale reliant Ramiolles à Villedieu, qu'a été retrouvée la dépouille d'un chien atrocement mutilé. « Nous n'excluons aucune hypothèse mais la bête a l'air drôlement amochée pour que ce soit une voiture qui lui ait fait ça, » continue M. Paillac. « De plus, en sachant que le même jour M. Laurent était venu déposer une plainte pour perte de chien, ça nous semble suspect ». M. Laurent, berger de profession a en effet constaté la disparition de son chien hier matin. Il s'est rendu sur les bords de la Nationale et a formellement dit que le chien qui y était mort n'était pas le sien.

Souhaitons que l'enquête se conclue au plus vite pour le bien de MM. Ménard et Laurent et espérons aussi que ces événements ne viendront pas gâcher les vacances de Kevin et de Baptiste, les enfants de M. Ripaud : « Hermione nous manque très fort » nous confiaient-ils hier soir.

R.B.

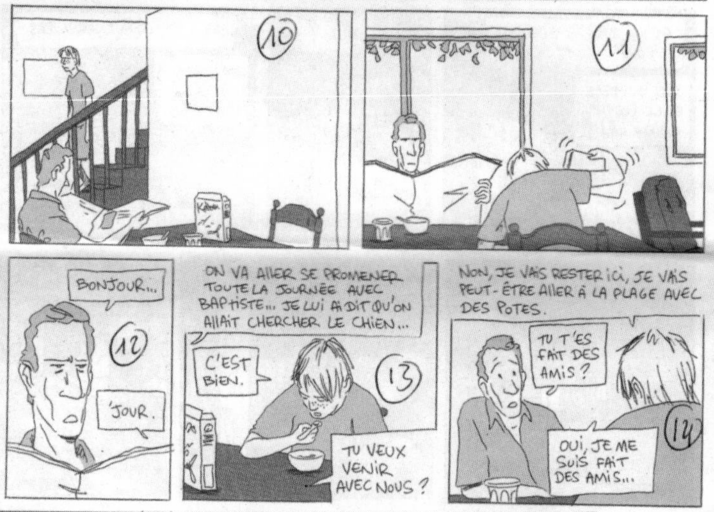
BONJOUR...
'JOUR.
ON VA ALLER SE PROMENER TOUTE LA JOURNÉE AVEC BAPTISTE... JE LUI A DIT QU'ON ALLAIT CHERCHER LE CHIEN...
C'EST BIEN.
TU VEUX VENIR AVEC NOUS ?
NON, JE VAIS RESTER ICI, JE VAIS PEUT-ÊTRE ALLER À LA PLAGE AVEC DES POTES.
TU T'ES FAIT DES AMIS ?
OUI, JE ME SUIS FAIT DES AMIS...

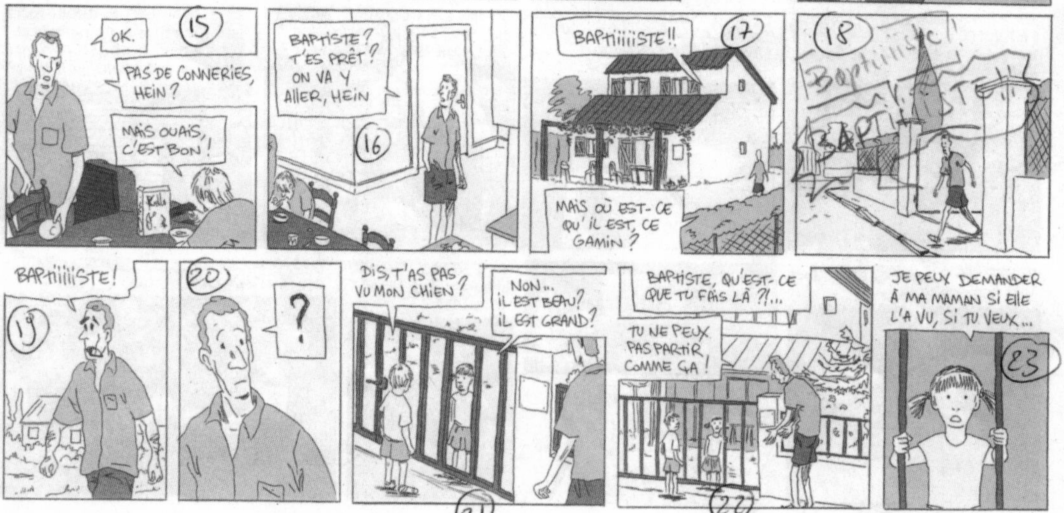
OK.
PAS DE CONNERIES, HEIN ?
MAIS OUAIS, C'EST BON !
BAPTISTE ? T'ES PRÊT ? ON VA Y ALLER, HEIN
BAPTiiiiSTE !!
MAIS OÙ EST-CE QU'IL EST, CE GAMIN ?
BAPTiiiiSTE !
?
DIS, T'AS PAS VU MON CHIEN ?
NON... IL EST BEAU ? IL EST GRAND ?
BAPTISTE, QU'EST-CE QUE TU FAIS LÀ ?!...
TU NE PEUX PAS PARTIR COMME ÇA !
JE PEUX DEMANDER À MA MAMAN SI ELLE L'A VU, SI TU VEUX...